Darf Publishers

Twilight in Jakarta

Mochtar Lubis (1922-2004) was an Indonesian journalist and novelist. His novel *Senja di Jakarta* (Twilight in Jakarta) was the first Indonesian novel to be translated into English. In 1949, Lubis cofounded *Indonesia Raya*, later serving as the daily's chief editor. His work with *Indonesia Raya* led to him being imprisoned numerous times for his critical writing. Lubis was outspoken about the need for freedom of the press in Indonesia and gained a reputation as an honest, no-nonsense reporter. In 2000, he was named as one of the International Press Institute's 50 World Press Freedom Heroes of the past 50 years. He is the author of six novels and two short stories collections.

Published by Darf Publishers 2017
Darf Publishers Ltd, 277 West End Lane,
London, NW6 1QS

Twilight in Jakarta
By Mochtar Lubis

First published in Malaysia under the title *Senja di Jakarta*
by Pustaka Antara, Kuala Lumpur, in 1964; first published in
Indonesia by Penerbit Indonesia Raya, Jakarta, in 1970; second
Indonesian edition published by Pustaka Jaya, Jakarta in 1982.

English language translation first published Hutchinson & Co.
(Publishers) Ltd. 1963; first issued in Oxford in Asia Paperbacks,
1983; revised English language edition copyright © 2014 The
Lontar Foundation; copyright to revised English language text ©
2014 Claire Holt and John H. McGlynn.

The moral right of the author has been asserted

Printed in UK by Clays

ISBN: 978-1-85077-307-8
eBook ISBN: 978-1-85077-308-5

MOCHTAR LUBIS

Twilight in Jakarta

Translated by

Claire Holt and John H. McGlynn

DARF PUBLISHERS,
LONDON

Introduction

Twilight in Jakarta: Fifty Years New

Half a century ago in London when Mochtar Lubis's *Twilight in Jakarta* originally appeared, it was the first Indonesian novel ever to be published in English translation. Its passage to print in 1963 remains one of the most fascinating in modern Indonesian literary history. That English edition, together with subsequent translations into Dutch, Spanish, Korean, and Italian, propelled its author—and Indonesian literature—onto the world stage.

The Indonesian manuscript, with the original title, *Yang Terinjak dan Melawan* (Down-Trodden and Resisting), was written during the 1950s while Mochtar Lubis was being held under house arrest. Lubis was not only a highly regarded author, but also editor of one of the country's most outspoken daily newspapers, *Indonesia Raya*, which had been highly critical of key government policies and political practices. The typescript of his novel was secreted out of the country during a visit by one of Denmark's leading WWII resistance figures, Frode Jacobson, in November 1960.

Jacobson was a prominent member of the Congress for Cultural Freedom, an international coalition of writers, artists, and cultural figures which projected itself as broadly anti-authoritarian, supporting oppressed intellectuals around the globe. Lubis had joined the CCF in 1954, and the organization enthusiastically sponsored the translation and publication of *Twilight in Jakarta* as the first novel in its planned "New Voices in Translation" series. (Lubis felt betrayed on discovering, through public revelations in 1967, that the CCF had been bankrolled by the United States

Central Intelligence Agency as part of America's Cold War anti-communist strategy.[1]

Despite the international circulation of *Twilight in Jakarta* it was not until 1970—seven years after the publication of the English translation—that the original Indonesian novel appeared in print in the author's homeland.[2]

Mochtar Lubis was an iconoclast and political maverick. He had established his literary reputation with a series of satirical short stories in the early years after Indonesia's independence from the Dutch. His influential 1952 novel, *Jalan Tak Ada Ujung* (A Road with No End)[3] was hailed by Indonesia's leading literary critic, HB Jassin, as one of the three best works of the "Generation of 1945", along with fiction by Idrus and Pramoedya Ananta Toer.

Lubis also attracted attention as a crusading journalist and editor of *Indonesia Raya,* founded in 1949. The paper had quickly become known for its frequent criticism of President Sukarno and the Indonesian Communist Party. Lubis himself, though close to the secular modernizing intellectuals around Indonesian Socialist Party leader Sutan Sjahrir, was never a member of any political party. Rather, he shared many of the critical views of civilian politicians held by army leaders in the early years after national independence, and maintained a lifelong opposition to communism.

Lubis believed in the power and responsibility of the media to hold politicians to account for their actions. *Indonesia Raya* established a reputation for investigating corruption and abuse of power. After several cases ended up in the courts, Lubis was eventually detained without trial from December 21, 1956, and held under house arrest until released without explanation on April 29, 1961. Though arrested on the instruction of the Army Chief of Staff General AH Nasution, and accused of having links with regional military officers then taking up arms against Jakarta, Lubis himself maintained that communist influence upon President Sukarno lay behind his arrest.

On his release in April 1961, Lubis was invited to Tel Aviv to address the General Assembly of the International Press Institute (IPI), delivering a rousing critique of what he saw as a global clash between democracy and totalitarianism in the Third World. Traveling on to Europe, he spent several days in Paris editing Claire Holt's draft translation of *Twilight in Jakarta*.

When he returned to Indonesia he was detained again, on July 14, 1961, questioned about his IPI speech, and then held for a further five years, mainly in a military prison in Madiun, East Java. Following the rise to power of Major-General Soeharto after October 1965, Lubis was eventually released on May 17, 1966, ending virtually a decade in detention under President Sukarno.

An outspoken critic by nature, Lubis was returned to jail by President Soeharto for two and half months in 1975, under suspicion of involvement in anti-Soeharto demonstrations the previous year. Although unable to publish a newspaper after this arrest, he remained a passionate public intellectual and political critic until his death in 2004.

In the diary he kept during his house arrest in the 1950s, Mochtar Lubis was explicit about his motivation for writing *Twilight in Jakarta*. He wrote in December 1958:

I wanted to depict in a novel the social and political conditions in our country. How the thirst for power, greed for possessions, and the power to use party positions have wrought such great damage upon our society. I have written it effortlessly and with great ease, although I realize that it may well be a long time before this book can be published in Indonesia. Yet I feel, in writing it, I have compiled a report our society needs to know about in the future.[4]

One Western reviewer regarded it as "a superb journalistic indictment" of Indonesia's leadership.[5]

Twilight in Jakarta depicts social and political events in the capital between May to January of an unspecified year.[6] The novel moves between stories of the very rich and politically powerful, Western-oriented urban intelligentsia, middle-ranking public servants, political party organizers and activists, and, beneath them on the social and economic pyramid, the urban poor. The lives of these rich and poor collide in the streets of the capital.

The novel attributes the moral decay of Indonesian society to the nature of its political leadership. The party system is depicted in universally negative terms, as essentially unworkable, endemically corrupt, and corrupting. It serves the politically powerful, and is unjust to, and unconcerned with the fate of, the destitute.

For readers familiar with Indonesian politics of the 1950s, several of the novel's characters appear as thinly disguised allusions to known figures.[7] The rapacious editor Halim is modeled on BM Diah, editor of the daily newspaper *Merdeka*, with whom Lubis had numerous editorial polemics and occasional courtroom clashes over their long careers. The idealistic intellectual Pranoto is regarded as something of a composite of the Indonesian Socialist Party figures Soedjatmoko and Sutan Takdir Alisjahbana. The poet Yasrin, who is wooed by the communists, has been likened to both Rivai Apin and Utuy Tatang Sontani. Raden Kaslan is reminiscent of former Economics Minister, Iskaq Tjokroadisurjo. Husin Limbara, head of the fictional Indonesia Party, resembles Djody Gondokusumo of the Indonesian Nationalist Party. The "Movement for People's Culture" described in the novel is a swipe at the Communist-backed Institute of People's Culture. That such parallels were so readily recognized gave the tale an immediacy and realism.

The novel depicts a society adrift, failing to live up to the aspirations of the independence struggle against the Dutch (1945–49). In a novel written during the nation's transition from liberal parliamentary democracy to Sukarno's so-called "Guided Democracy" (1959–65), it is noteworthy that Sukarno, though never named, is constantly present through allusion, in the numerous criticisms of the national political leadership.

Lubis's characters present a grim vision of society. The politicians lack redeeming qualities. The intellectuals appear impotent and out of touch with their own society. The journalists are unprincipled opportunists. Artists and trade union officials are seduced by inducements from political parties. The leftists are manipulative, and more concerned with building party power than genuinely serving the interests of the people. The Muslims are ineffectual, impetuous, and unable to counter the Communists. Interestingly, given that the author was detained for his presumed sympathies for officers launching a regional military rebellion, military figures are absent from the novel, and are thus absolved from any responsibility for Jakarta's gloomy twilight.

On the other hand, from the vignette opening the novel, Lubis depicts the lives of the poor with sympathy—at least until they lash out in collective action near the end of the novel. Lubis had previously published several of these vignettes as short stories, and stylistically they reflect his experience as a working journalist, evident in the "City Beat" sections which punctuate the novel.

The publication of *Twilight in Jakarta* was a major achievement for Lubis, establishing his reputation as an international author, and strengthening his political and moral stance against the Indonesian government. As he expressed it, he felt that in this novel he had been able to speak to the world. His pre-eminence as Indonesia's best-known novelist abroad was surpassed only by Pramoedya Ananta Toer, two decades later, whose most celebrated works were also produced during political detention.[8]

In *Twilight in Jakarta*, Lubis was condemning political practices in Indonesia in the mid-1950s. Yet international reviewers and readers recognized in it problems common across the Third World. Similarly, readers familiar with Indonesian politics today will find much in this novel that resonates still. It is re-published here at a time when, after three decades of authoritarianism and more than a decade of post-authoritarian transition, Indonesia once again has a boisterous multi-party system of competing and collaborating political parties. Parties are often personality-driven. They face a mass media which often both serves particular political interests and thrives on sensationalist stories of corruption and malfeasance.

Mochtar Lubis's surgical dissection of social conflict and political self-interest may be as evocative for today's reader as it was when originally secreted out of Sukarno's Indonesia more than half a century ago.

David T Hill [9]

References

1. Mochtar Lubis's complex association with CCF is discussed by the author of this introduction in *Journalism and Politics in Indonesia: A Critical biography of Mochtar Lubis (1922-2004) as Editor and Author* (Routledge, London, 2010).

2. There was a Malaysian edition, *Senja di Jakarta*, (Pustaka Antara, Kuala Lumpur, 1964) but the first Indonesian imprint was not until 1970 (*Sendja di Djakarta*, PT Badan Penerbit Indonesia Raya, [Jakarta], 1970).

3. An English translation of *Jalan Tak Ada Ujung* (A Road with No End)— translated and edited by Anthony H Johns—was published by Graham Brash, Singapore, 1982 (first ed. 1968).

4. Mochtar Lubis, *Catatan Subversif*, Sinar Harapan, Jakarta, 1980, p.144, entry dated December 1958. Although the 1970 Indonesian text concludes with a modern colophon "completed/jakarta, 7 march 1957" (p.280), evidence in Lubis's diary, *Catatan Subversif*, suggests the manuscript was actually completed more than three and a half years later. In the entry dated December 1958 he wrote that he had "begun my novel given the name *Yang Terinjak dan Melawan* [Down-Trodden and Resisting]" after which the published diary added the footnote, "[this] book was later published in English in London with the title *Twilight in Jakarta*" (p.144). In the entry for November 22, 1960 he wrote he had "completed writing the novel *Yang Terinjak dan Melawan* several days ago" (p.149).

5. Rohan Rivett (1963) "Corruption Denounced—from a Prison Cell", *IPI Report*, Vol. 12, No. 2, June, p.16.

6. Internal references in the text relate to various historical incidents (suggesting a setting between about May 1954 to January 1957), but there is no direct congruence between the fiction and history.

7. This is Mochtar Lubis's only novel which (in the Indonesian) includes a prefatory disclaimer stating that all characters and events are fictional—which may alert the reader to historical allusions, yet circumvent libel. Mochtar Lubis discussed some of these similarities in an interview with me at his home in Jakarta on March 11, 1981. Others are mentioned in Henri Chambert-Loir, *Mochtar Lubis: Une Vision de l'Indonésie Contemporaine*, (Paris: Publication de l'Ecole Française D'Extrême-Orient, 1974, p.154).

8. For one account of Pramoedya's impact internationally, see Chris GoGwilt, "Writing to the World: Pramoedya as an All-Round Revolutionary Writer" in *Inside Indonesia* (No. 88, Oct-Dec 2006, http://www.insideindonesia.org/feature-editions/writing-to-the-world).

9. David T Hill is professor of Southeast Asian Studies at Murdoch University in Western Australia.

Author's dedication: "For Hally, to whom I owe a debt of love"

Twilight in Jakarta

Aquí tengo una voze nardecida,
Aquí tengo un vida combatida y airada,
Aquí tengo un rumor,
Aquí tengo una vida.

Here I have an angry voice,
Here I have a combative and angry life,
Here I have a rumor,
Here I have a life.

Miguel Hernandez

May

Saimun tightened his belt, his stomach again rumbling with hunger. He'd had nothing to eat since waking and now the day was getting on. The drizzle which had started at dawn increased his hunger; Saimun blamed the rain. With his bare and grimy foot—mud, filth, and germs were stuck to that bare foot—he kicked a refuse-filled basket off the top of the rubbish heap. The basket rolled down until it was stopped by the dilapidated wall of a hut, one so very battered, so very rotten, and so sadly dripping in the drizzling rain. A woman stuck her head out and shouted hoarsely, "Hey, watch it! Where're your eyes?"

Saimun started a little, then looked down and stared at the woman. He laughed roughly, without anger or malice, because he always laughed that way; momentarily, lust stirred in him at the sight of the breasts of the woman in the hut, visible through the rents of her worn and ragged blouse. For an instant the desire flickered in him to go down and take the woman, but then he heard the rumbling of the municipal garbage truck. Turning quickly, he sprinted and jumped on as it was moving away.

Saimun crouched down at the side of his friend, Itam, who was lighting a clove-scented *kretek* cigarette. He looked at his feet on the truck's wet and dirty floor, felt the hard boards against the bones of his behind shaking loose all the tense muscles of his body, leaned against the wooden wall of the truck, and stretched out his hand towards Itam. "Please, just one," he begged.

Itam looked at him, and the reluctance behind his eyes vanished quickly. He handed his *kretek* to Saimun, watching closely how Saimun inhaled deeply, deeply, retaining the smoke in the hollow of his chest, then returned the cigarette to Itam, who immediately took a long drag. Together they blew the smoke slowly through their nostrils, for the moment forgetting the drizzling rain, the dirt, and the smell of the truck, even forgetting themselves. There was only the scent of the *kretek*, the warmth of the cigarette upon the tongue, and the relaxation of the body.

Itam inhaled the smoke once more, then he handed the cigarette to Saimun and scratched the back of his ear, while the other hand brushed off the flies, swarming in the truck, from the scabs below his knee.

"I'm hungry," said Saimun.

"One more drag, then we'll go get our wages. But first we can stop and eat at Ibu Yom's."

"Just thinking of food, my body goes limp," said Saimun, his stomach feeling emptier and emptier, as if that emptiness was draining the last bit of strength left in his blood. He leaned back against the truck wall. Suddenly he felt exhausted and very faint.

Itam offered Saimun another drag from his *kretek*. Saimun inhaled avidly; Itam watching anxiously how rapidly the glow moved towards the end of the cigarette. As soon as Saimun finished, Itam retrieved it hastily, drew on it until it burned his fingers, and then threw the tiny stub out of the truck.

Saimun pondered. How was it that when something is difficult to get or you don't have it, and you get a chance to taste it for just a moment, a small matter can become so big, doubling, trebling, growing ever larger? This morning one *kretek* cigarette dominated his whole soul—as if his life depended on one cigarette and if he could get that cigarette his life would be prolonged, as it were, forever. One cigarette could fulfill his existence. He remembered that when he was still in his village—before it was attacked by a group of bandits, and his father and mother died in the slaughter, and he fled to the city when the harvest was over—he didn't think twice before throwing away a half-smoked cigarette; or throwing away a boiled yam after only a few bites. And when there was a wedding feast, or the *lebaran* holidays, or some other celebrations in the village, no one ever gave a thought to a drag on a cigarette. Now, to smoke a *kretek* with Itam was like some kind of grand ceremony. Each drag was of enormous significance; it was done carefully and with undivided attention. All one's senses were keyed up to tasting this one drag on the cigarette. A *kretek* never tasted as good as in this dirty and stinking garbage truck.

Meanwhile, if he remembered life in the village, it all felt like a dream. Sometimes he didn't believe that he had ever lived in such a village, as though it had been another person altogether, not himself, who had worked in the rice field, who had bathed in the river with Putih, the buffalo, which had gotten its name from the white patch of hair behind its left ear. Ah... he still remembered it all so well, but now somehow did not believe that it was really he who went bathing with Putih. It was as though a person's existence was shut away in different boxes that had no connection with each other. As though he had become a stranger to himself—with no connection at all any more to that man who had been himself in that other life-box.

He remembered how, in the first weeks after his arrival in Jakarta, he had wept when evening came and he didn't know where to go; how he'd looked for a place to sleep under the awning of a shop—until he met Itam, who befriended him, and they got work as garbage coolies. Later they were able to rent lodgings in the hut of Pak Ijo, a pony-cart driver. Just one room, next to the room where old Ijo slept with his equally old wife and their three children. But the hunger which gnawed at his guts never ceased, and the weariness in his bones never really went away.

"How about driving a *becak*? Wouldn't that be better than this sort of work?" said Saimun suddenly.

"I don't think so," said Itam, thinking of the strength required to drive a pedicab for a living. "You remember Pandi, don't you, that *becak* driver who died just like that, spitting up blood? Drove a *becak* only a year before his heart gave out!"

Saimun scratched with his toes at the floor of the truck, its thick crust of dregs, and for the moment all life around him seemed to vanish, himself remaining in a dismal void, suspended alone in that void, as if all dimensions of life were lost: there was no past, no present, and there was no future, only himself alone in existence.

He woke with a start as the truck stopped, and Itam called, "Come on, time to get to work."

Saimun felt stiff all over as he forced himself to get up, jump off the truck, and lift a basketful of refuse into it.

By noon the truck was back at the dump, and as he was unloading the rubbish, Saimun remembered the woman he had seen that morning. He stepped down towards the hut. The woman was there, bathing in a small pool, a few yards from the hut, its stagnant water dirty and yellow. Saimun shouted to attract the woman's attention, and his desire revived as he saw her, naked and bathing in the shallow pool. The woman laughed at him, turning her body, challengingly. Saimun unwillingly turned away only when he heard Itam call his name and the sound of the truck's engine. But he called to the woman, "I'll be back."

Garbage carts and trucks were assembled near the office where the men were to be paid. There was a row of vendors, selling cigarettes, packets of cooked rice, and fried bananas. An Arabic-looking man with a blue notebook and an umbrella and another heavy-bodied man sat eating fried bananas under a tree. The distribution of wages had not yet begun, but Saimun caught a glimpse of the cashier, busy counting the various denominations of rupiah notes that were stacked behind the small window.

He walked with Itam to Ibu Yom's food stall. As soon as they were seated, the woman served them, knowing already what they wanted to eat.

"When you get your wages, don't run away," Ibu Yom reminded them.

Saimun and Itam were silent; they ate ravenously.

"Shit, I owe close to five rupiah," Saimun said, "so Big Boss Abdullah and his sidekick, Iron Man, over there are going to have to wait. How much do you owe him, Itam?"

"About five rupiah! That damned Arab; there's never an end to a debt with him."

"Lucky I owe only a *ringgit*, two and a half rupiah," said Saimun, "but I still have to pay him four rupiah this week."

Saimun calculated his wages. Garbage coolies were paid twice a month, every third and eighteenth day. Today was the third. From the last eighteenth he had worked only eleven days, because there were two Sundays off in between. As a new hiree, he was paid only four and a half rupiah a day, which meant that—eleven times four and a half—he would be paid just forty-nine and a half rupiah. But deducting what he owed to Pak Imam in the office, who had sold him a pair of shorts for thirty rupiah in ten-rupiah installments, he would get only thirty-nine and a half rupiah. It's lucky that this was the last installment. But the shorts, thin as they were and made from some kind of flimsy green material, looked to not last much longer either. What else? Taking off the debt to Abdullah, that left thirty-five and a half rupiah. Minus the five rupiah debt he owed Ibu Yom, plus one more rupiah for the meal he'd just eaten, that left him with only twenty-nine and a half rupiah.

Bewildered, Saimun counted and recounted. With just twenty-nine and a half rupiah in hand, he had to live fifteen days more, until the eighteenth day of the month. The price of a plate of rice with vegetable broth cost one rupiah and he had to eat at least twice a day. Coffee and a fried banana or a yam was another half a rupiah, which meant he needed fifteen *ringgit*—thirty-seven and a half rupiah!

Even before adding in anything else, he was going to be short eight and a half rupiah. What about cigarettes? Counting one pack a day, the cheap *kawung* cigarettes that were rolled in palm leaf cost one and a half rupiah. All that, and that wasn't even counting the rent, which cost him five and a half rupiah a month.

Finally, Saimun stopped counting and resumed his meal, gulping his food as he ate. His eyes caught sight of a plate of fried chicken. For an instant he was tempted to ask for a piece but then he remembered the price—the calculations ran through his head—and, with heavy regret, he suppressed his appetite and drank his coffee, to the last drop.

The other coolies had already started to line up before the cashier's window. Itam told Saimun to join the line, too.

Ibu Yom called after him as he left, "After you get paid, don't forget to pay your debts!"

"Such a nag," Itam muttered beneath his breath, "like we never paid our debts."

As they had joined the line, Itam announced, "I'm going to stop eating at Ibu Yom's and find another place. She's always harping. For me, it's forbidden not to pay a debt. Even if all you've got left is your underwear, you still have to pay your debts, especially a debt for food."

Saimun felt refreshed by the food and coffee. "Yeah, she nags, but she has a good heart. Even when we're in debt she never refuses to serve us. The ones I hate are the boss and Iron Hand. What's your life worth if you don't pay what you owe them?"

Itam suddenly coughed and spat towards the ground, accidentally hitting the foot of the man standing in front of him.

"Damn you! Where's your eyes?"

Itam said nothing and turned to Saimun. "There was a guy once who tried to run off without paying his debt to Abdullah. You know what happened to him? Iron Hand beat the shit out of him."

"Where do you want to go after we collect our pay?" Saimun asked.

"I don't know. Any ideas?"

Saimun thought of the woman in the hut near the garbage dump. "I don't know either."

After Saimun had received his wages from which the installment of ten rupiah for his shorts had been deducted, paying four rupiah to Abdullah, and six rupiah owed for food to Ibu Yom, he stood at the roadside waiting for Itam who was still calculating his debt to the food stall owner. He bought himself a *kretek* cigarette, feeling guilty and rather extravagant, but unable to resist the craving for the aroma of cloves from the cigarette. He squatted beside the road, at the edge of the ditch, smoking with deep contentment. Calm now reigned in his heart and he felt at peace with the world and his fellow man. In his pocket were twenty-nine rupiah. He felt rich. But his thoughts kept returning to the young woman in the hut near the dump. His mind was no longer on the *kretek* cigarette, or the tens of *kretek* that he could buy. All he could think of now was the woman. These thoughts did not disturb his feeling of peace, however. In fact, they were accompanied by delectable visions, burning and enchanting. He fingered the small roll of money in his pocket.

That same morning, while Saimun the garbage coolie was busy unloading baskets of refuse onto the dump in the drizzling rain, Suryono was stretching his body in his warm bed, too lazy to get up. How pleasant it was to lie in bed this way and look out at the drizzling rain blown by the wind against the windowpane. For some time Suryono lay very still, contemplating his room in the dim light and comparing it with his apartment in New York City. Three months ago he was still in New York, that giant metropolis, and now, three months later, he was back again in Jakarta. After working three years abroad, he still felt ill at ease in Jakarta. The city had too many shortcomings to count.

It had been decidedly more pleasant to live abroad. Jakarta was a frustrating place. It was annoying to work in an office that was so disorganized. He was still attached to The Ministry of Foreign Affairs but had yet to be given a clearly defined assignment. He was also dissatisfied by the way he was treated. And because he had no car of his own, even going to the office was a chore. He was sorry not to have shipped to Jakarta the car he'd owned in the United States.

He looked round his room at items he had brought from overseas: a radio and an electric record player. And over there, on the table in the corner and on the floor as well were stacks of books in French and English, on economics, international politics, and dozens of other subjects. All of them looked nice and new. On his desk and the nightstand beside his bed were more books: Westerns and foreign sex novels with covers depicting women in a variety of poses. One cover showed the image of a woman sprawled on the floor with her thighs bared, her eyes closed, and part of one breast exposed, while behind her in the shadows loomed the figure of a masked man. The title of the book: *The Sex Murders*.

The bookcase was filled with stacks of records, from the works of Mozart, Haydn, Beethoven, and Chopin to tangos, sambas, rumbas, foxtrots, and American jazz.

Suryono turned over, overtaken by laziness and memories of his life in New York, so marvelously luxurious and pleasant compared with the boredom and desolation he'd felt during these past three months at home. It seemed as if there was no place for him in his own country. He was at a loss as to what he should do. Nothing really seemed to attract him.

Suddenly, the door to his room opened and Fatma, his stepmother, entered. "Are you still in bed?" she admonished.

Suryono smiled at her, unashamed to be seen in bed with only his boxers on. "What's the use getting up in the morning? I go to the office and there's no work for me to do."

His stepmother moved past his bed to open the curtains, but as she passed, Suryono caught her by the hand and pulled her onto the bed.

"Is Father gone?" he said, kissing her neck intensely.

"Yes, but don't be naughty; the servant girl is outside, sweeping the living room."

Fatma stood and opened the curtains. Suryono studied her with his eyes. She was still young, his age-mate in fact, just twenty-nine years old. His father had married her while he, Suryono, was abroad, a year and a half ago. His father, Raden Kaslan, was fifty-six years of age; his mother had died when Suryono was fifteen. When he learned that his father had remarried, Suryono had only shaken his head in surprise. And now, lying on his bed and looking at his stepmother, Suryono was surprised again, wondering how it was possible for a relationship between himself and his stepmother to have developed as it did.

When he returned from New York his father was out of town on a business trip and so, for the first two weeks at home, Suryono was alone with her. They shared the house, went to shows, and went dancing together as well. Fatma told him not to call her "Mother"; it was enough to call her just Fatma. And then.... Suryono smiled to himself recalling what happened between him and his stepmother for the first time, and in his father's room at that. They had just returned from a dance, and his stepmother had already gone into his father's room. There was not a soul in the house. He remembered that he had wanted to look through an old family photograph album that his father kept in his bedroom. He went and knocked at the door.

"Come in," he said, hearing Fatma's voice. He opened the door, and saw that Fatma was changing her clothes behind a screen near the wardrobe.

"I'm looking for that old photograph album of Father's," he said. "Do you know where it is?"

"It's over here. Come and get it."

He hesitated at first, but then went up to the screen after all, and saw that Fatma had already taken off her clothes and wore only a very thin nightdress. Suryono could not clearly remember how it began. All he remembered was how later he was getting up from his father's bed, with Fatma still lying on it naked, and himself rushing out, back to his room. He was surprised to find that, despite his agitation, he did not feel remorse but, instead, a great satisfaction. True, for a moment his innermost conscience scolded him, but he quickly suppressed it with the thought that it was his father's own fault for having married such a young woman. But after that he fell asleep.

When his father returned home, the situation was further eased when, hearing how his son and his wife addressed each other familiarly, using personal names instead of formal terms of address (which was something they could not make themselves do), he remarked, "Well, I see you two have already become close friends. Wonderful!"

Raden Kaslan worked as director of the trading company Bumi Ayu and was a member of the governing board of the Indonesia Party. Formerly he had been a government official, but after the recognition of Indonesia's national sovereignty he had grown dissatisfied with the bureaucracy and withdrawn from public service. Because of the support he found through his party connections, his enterprise grew rapidly.

After the first incident between Fatma and Suryono, the second one occurred easily, and so it continued. After that first night, he slept every night in his father's room with Fatma for an entire week. The two of them were as if drunk. Only when the cable arrived from his father asking to be met at Kemayoran Airport did they wake up from their intoxication.

"What if your father finds out?" Fatma asked, but there was no fear in her voice or any trace of anxiety. The question had a taunting tone, as if she were convinced that she could manage to deceive her elderly husband.

They were in bed together at the time, and Suryono answered with a question of his own: "Who do you like better, my father or me?"

Fatma giggled and nibbled his cheek, then embraced him with ardor. "What, you don't know? You're crazy to even ask."

Fatma told him that his father was impotent, and had married her only for the sake of appearance. Having a young woman at his side gave him self-assurance and disguised his physical shortcoming.

"It isn't even once a month that he comes to me."

At first Suryono felt uncomfortable discussing his father with Fatma, as if his father were some stranger, but this feeling was soon drowned by the passion her body inflamed in him.

Neither of them ever raised the question of love, whether he loved his stepmother or she loved him. It seemed that their own pleasure was sufficient reason for their affair.

A week after his father's return, Suryono's feelings of tension disappeared, as if nothing had happened between him and Fatma. Frequently, in fact, his father asked him to accompany his wife to a show, to a party or some other occasion, when he himself could not accompany her.

So it was this morning that Suryono found himself in his bed kissing Fatma's neck. The drizzling rain continued to fall outside, and he felt Fatma's body becoming tense and taut under his hands. She embraced him tightly and kissed him hard on his mouth. Then suddenly, extricating herself, she ran to the door.

"You are really naughty!" she said and then left the room.

Suryono laughed to himself, feeling excited and satisfied and rejoicing in his male superiority and the feeling of triumphing over his own father.

He put on his bathrobe and went to the bathroom. As he undressed to bathe, he stopped naked before the tall mirror on the bathroom wall and contemplated his body's image. Too thin, he thought, gripping his thigh, and his chest wasn't broad enough either. I must go in more for sport, he thought further. Then he examined his face. His features were handsome, and his new moustache was beginning to fill out. His eyes were too hollow, he thought, but his hair was wavy. He rubbed the cleft in his chin. He was rather pleased with that cleft; he shared it with the film star, Cary Grant. He got out his razor, soaped his lips and chin and started shaving, looking at his face in the mirror and humming away. He was very pleased this morning. There was nothing to trouble his thoughts: no work in the office to give him a headache, not a thing to worry about at all.

On this morning he almost felt at peace with himself, and his disappointment at having to stay in his own country was now at the back of his mind. A fleeting thought arose: If I can manage the patience for another year, the ministry is sure to send me abroad again. The idea made him feel elated and he whistled a tune very popular at that time, "High Noon".

He had breakfast with Fatma, who awaited him. As the two of them sat at the table, Fatma sliced the bread for him and spread the butter on it.

"What would you like for a topping this morning: chocolate or marmalade?"

Suryono smiled at her. "What a kind mother you are! I'd like buttered bread with a slice of cheese and a coating of marmalade, and after that…" Suryono nudged Fatma's foot under the table, making her giggle with delight.

"You are a bad boy, so misbehaved, and towards your own mother," she said, and they both laughed.

Before he left for the office, Suryono kissed and caressed Fatma in her bedroom. Then he combed his disheveled hair and, as he was leaving the room, held Fatma's breast for a moment. Then he left the house whistling, hailed a *becak*, and set off to his office.

"What's in the newspaper this morning?" Suryono asked Harun, who sat at the desk next to his own.

Harun threw the newspaper he was reading onto Suryono's desk. "Read it yourself. You're late again. Only the day before yesterday the secretary general issued a circular warning all government employees to come to work on time."

Suryono laughed. "Let him arrive on time! It's easy to make rules. He has a car to bring him to the office. How about us?"

Resentment welled in Suryono—towards the secretary general; towards Harun, who faithfully appeared at the office every day but then sat at his desk with nothing to do; towards the entire ministry; towards his country, his people; even towards humanity and life itself.

He threw the paper back to Harun. "Read it yourself first." He was bored witless and didn't know what to do with himself. He sat down and picked up the telephone. He waited for a long time before the switchboard operator responded. Suryono gave the number, and soon heard ringing at the other end.

A woman's voice, caressing his ear, came floating over the wire: "Hello?"

"Is that you, Ies?" said Suryono.

"Yes, Yono, it is. So early in the morning and you're on the phone already." The voice was full of smiles and cheer.

"You know that you're in my mind day and night."

"Wherever did you learn to say such things?"

"What are you doing tonight, Ies?"

"I don't know yet."

"Really?" he said.

"I have a good idea of what you'd like to do."

"You and I…" Suryono changed his playful tone and said seriously, "Ies, I want to see you tonight."

"I won't be home."

"Don't play with me like that, Ies."

"But I won't be home, and most certainly not for a man who is bored, annoyed, and depressed. Don't think I don't know you, Yono. You only call me when you're bored and lonely. Good day!"

Ies hung up, and Suryono banged down his receiver.

Harun regarded him with lightly smiling eyes. "No luck?"

Suryono looked at him, annoyed. "You're rather eager to overhear other people's conversations, aren't you? Ies is playing hard to get."

Suryono sat in his chair, took out a pack of Lucky Strikes and lit one; but after only two puffs he threw it on the floor and crushed it with his shoe. Even the cigarette had no taste that morning.

When Sugeng returned home from his office at the ministry of Economic Affairs, he found his three-year-old daughter bawling in the front yard.

They've been fighting again, he thought, approaching the child. "Come now, Maryam, why are you crying?"

The little girl raised her head at the sound other father's voice, stood up, and jumped to hide her head at Sugeng's knee. "Iwan took my marbles," she sobbed.

Sugeng picked her up and kissed her lovingly. "There now, it's all right, don't cry. I'll buy you some new marbles."

Inwardly he sighed and cursed the necessity of living in a house shared by three families: children got into fights every other minute which, in turn, caused rows between the parents, too. It was a year now that he and Hasnah had been staying in this crowded house with two other families. In the beginning there was always hope of getting another home, as promised by the ministry. But now it looked as if they would have to live like this forever.

The house was an old-fashioned one, with a long verandah running along its front, now divided in half by a bamboo screen. He and Hasnah occupied one of the two front rooms and had one side of the verandah, which was screened in both at the front and the sides. This was the sitting room, the kitchen—with a simple oil-burning ring stove on which to cook—the dining area, and also the place for ironing the laundry. The front room, directly behind the verandah room, was their bedroom. The bath and the lavatory were in the passage at the rear of the house and were used jointly with the other tenants.

When he entered, carrying Maryam inside, he saw that his wife was not in the verandah room.

"Hasnah!' he called, "What are you doing, letting Maryam cry like that outside, alone?"

Only a moan, coming from the bedroom, answered his call.

He stopped on the threshold and saw his wife lying on the bed. She slowly opened her eyes.

"Are you sick?" Sugeng said anxiously.

"Yes, I am dizzy again and nauseous. It's already a week late!"

Sugeng quickly put down Maryam, stepped over to the bed, and held the head of his wife.

"Is Maryam getting a playmate?" he said, with joy in his voice. "I hope it's a boy."

The look on his wife's face suddenly troubled him. "Aren't you happy? We've wanted a sister or brother for Maryam for a long time. She's already three. And we do want a son, don't we?"

Hasnah nodded. "Yes, but if Maryam's brother arrives and we're still here in this place…" She looked around the room meaningfully; its appearance told the whole story of their difficulties in such overcrowded conditions.

Immediately conscious of all this, Sugeng was saddened, too; but he spoke with optimism in his voice: "Before the baby is born we are sure to get our own house. The ministry is working on the problem. I've heard they've begun to build houses for employees in Kemayoran. Don't worry!"

Hasnah blinked. "When we moved into this house you said it would be for only a few months. Now it's been over a year. I can't live here, not with two children, and especially not with a baby. Where will we put him? How about his health? If you're not sure that we'll get a house of our own before then, maybe it would be better if we don't have him. I heard of a doctor who can help, with just an injection. It's only a week now; there's still time."

Sugeng suddenly went very pale and then quickly embraced her. "Don't talk like that. I swear to you, before the baby is born we will move to a house of our own."

There was a ring of conviction in his voice, which made Hasnah open her eyes and raise her head. She embraced Sugeng and kissed him. "I do want another baby. And it will make Maryam very happy, too."

They caressed each other until Maryam came and climbed on the bed, clamoring for food.

During the meal, Hasnah mentioned that the family next door would be moving the following week.

Maryam piped in: "Iwan's mother said they're going to Kalimantan!"

"Well, at least Maryam won't be bothered any more by that wicked boy," Sugeng said in an undertone. "I only hope that whoever moves in next will have better behaved children."

CITY BEAT

The night was like any other night with a busy crowd at the Glodok bazaar. Thousands of electric bulbs gleamed like fireflies dancing in the night. The headlights of passing automobiles were yellow balls of light. The spice-laden smell of food wafting from restaurants hung heavy on the air, almost as if one could touch it, put it into one's mouth, munch it. Two men, Tony and Jok, stood outside one of the restaurants, their mouths watering, their saliva gathering in their throats. As if on cue, they coughed up the phlegm and spat on the ground.

The man named Tony was wearing a Hawaiian-style shirt with green flowers on a yellow background. His hair was smooth, oily, heavily smeared with brilliantine and brushed up high over his forehead like a woman's waved hair-do. His cheeks appeared to be lightly powdered, which gave him a distinctly feminine look. Jok, on the other hand, was a much more crude-looking man, with short thick fingers and a heavy-lipped mouth with large, strong teeth.

"Let's get something to eat," Tony suggested, nudging Jok with his elbow.

They entered the small restaurant and found a place in a corner.

The Chinese man who ran the restaurant and was also the cook approached their table. He was wiping his neck, his cheeks, his chest, and his armpits, with a dirty cloth, taking up the sweat of his body overheated by the large brazier in the other corner of the room. His smooth, oily skin glistened.

"I'll have some fried noodles," Tony said. "What about you?" he asked his friend.

"I'll have the same."

"And to drink?" the proprietor asked. "Beer?"

"Okay, beer."

"Two fried noodles and beer."

The proprietor nodded and waddled back to his kitchen. The fat under his skin below his armpits wobbled as he moved. He wiped his chest once more, then took a plate from a stack on the table, wiped it with the same rag, took a second plate, and wiped it, too. And then he started to cook the noodles.

Tony and Jok had finished their portions of greasy noodles. Three empty beer-bottles now stood on the table. Their two glasses were still about a third full.

"Where to now?" said Tony with the Aloha shirt.

"Home, I suppose," said Jok. "Not enough money to go anywhere else. I don't get it," he added, "the guy looked well off but his wallet was almost bare: only thirty-five rupiah."

"Well, you were the one who chose him," Tony reminded his friend.

"Hmm, yeah."

"If we don't go home, I wouldn't mind going back to the house of that Arab woman, but there is the slight problem of money."

Jok pinched Tony's thigh with his stubby fingers and smiled. "Then I guess you'll be sleeping with me!"

At that moment, three men entered and sat down at the table next to theirs. Jok and Tony stopped talking as the three new arrivals sat down.

The proprietor waddled over, took the new customers' orders, and returned to the kitchen.

Tony's and Jok's ears pricked up when one of the trio began to speak. He was a small middle-aged man, dressed in cheap shirt and trousers.

"Pretty good day, I had," he told the others. "Brought in more than seventy-five!"

"It must be nice to own your own taxi," one friend said.

"Yeah, but it's not like that every day," the third man added. "Yesterday I made thirty, but today only fifteen."

Tony briefly studied the trio of taxi drivers, then rested his eyes on the driver who had said he had made more than seventy-five rupiah that day.

"Another beer, Jok?" he asked his friend, who nodded in reply. "More beer!" he shouted to the owner. The two stopped paying attention to the taxi drivers, who were now eating.

Outside the restaurant, the night was much like any other, busy with people and lit up with the electric lights of vendors. There among the crowd were Tony and Jok.

"See the guy in the blue jacket?" Tony said.

Jok's eyes followed Tony's glance and fell on a man who was stooped over a peddler's table.

"The usual way," said Tony.

Jok nodded slowly, and took off. He looked about, to the left and to the right, like someone out to buy something, scanning the place for the thing he wants to buy, yet also like someone who doesn't particularly care if he finds the thing he's looking for or not.

Tony walked several paced behind.

When Jok was close to the man in the blue jacket, he pretended to trip, and his body fell hard against the man's back. Tony stepped up quickly, his hands moving with lightning speed to the pocket of the man's trousers.

While Jok was murmuring "Sorry, I beg your pardon," Tony was already lost in the crowd. He crossed the street and then walked slowly on.

Jok stepped back without haste, as he would if he indeed had tripped. After he apologized, he moved on. And that was that.

A few minutes later Jok also crossed the street at a leisurely pace, and found Tony waiting for him in front of the Orion cinema. From afar, Jok could see that Tony had not been successful.

"He was careful, that one; had his hand on his pocket all the time," said Tony.

"The fucker. Now what?"

"I'd say we go home."

They walked on, passed the police station; and under the big trees outside the darkened Lindeteves commerce building, they came upon several women who were just standing there, waiting. Tony pinched the breast of one, too hard it seems, for it caused the woman to shriek and swear. The two men laughed and went on, the cursing of the women following them through the darkness of the night.

They walked on. Crossed a bridge. Entered the shroud of darkness under old tamarind trees. Yellow balls of light from taxicabs came and went. Tittering giggles of women punctuated the air. Grasping hands invited. A hoarse voice swore obscenely, then burst into roaring laughter, like Satan's glee when startling a human being. Three *becak* raced. The winning driver yelled in triumph.

Tony and Jok continued walking.

Tony took out his pack of Lucky Strikes. "Smoke?".

Jok took a cigarette, pinched it with his lips. He got out a match and lit Tony's cigarette. The light of the match flickered up and illuminated Tony's face, revealing a sensual mouth but hard and cruel lines, like that of a sadist.

A taxi moved slowly alongside them. "Taxi?" a voice called.

Jok looked at Tony.

"Why not?"

At the intersection in front of the Thalia cinema and the Olimo general store, Tony ordered the driver to turn left, towards Prinsenpark, the city center's large and shady square. The light of street lamps at the intersection shone on the driver's face. Instantaneously both passengers recalled the tableau at the Chinese restaurant in Glodok, with the three taxi drivers chatting and eating at the table next to theirs. Their taxi driver was the one who had said, "Brought in more than seventy-five."

As the driver started to turn into Prinsenpark, Tony ordered him to keep straight on; then to turn right and follow the railroad tracks. It was dark. No lights. A deserted street. All the houses already shuttered.

"I think I'll go see that Arab woman after all," Tony said suddenly in a loud voice. He half rose from his seat, tapped the driver on his shoulder and told him to stop.

Something in Tony's voice, some hidden menace, struck the driver's consciousness. Suddenly gripped by fear, he continued driving.

Anger rose in Tony. "Stop!"

Now the danger in his passenger's voice was stronger and more startling, and the driver, in growing terror, stepped on the accelerator as the thought of robbers flashed through his mind.

Jok noticed an iron rod on the floor and picked it up. "Stop, damn you!" He raised the rod and swung it towards the driver's head.

Tony tried to stop him, but before he could say "Don't!", he heard the thud of the iron and the stifled scream of the driver as blood gushed from a wound in his head.

The taxi raced forward, as if drunken, careening left and right, and then plowed into a ditch between the road and the railway line.

Tony and Jok jumped out of the car and looked around. Seeing no one in sight, they ran a short distance to a side street, and walked down it rapidly.

Tony swore at Jok, "Why did you hit him, you idiot?"

"I didn't mean to. I just meant to scare him."

"You never wait for orders!"

"I was just going to give him a tap on the head, give him a little scare."

They slowed their pace, now walking normally as they turned onto another street, which was still busy with people and pedicabs. Servant girls were joking with the *becak* drivers.

Tony's anger began to subside, but Jok continued babbling, "I didn't mean to hit him hard."

Suddenly Tony burst into loud laughter. "'I didn't mean to hit him hard! Just to scare him'. How are you going to scare him if he's already dead?" He laughed again, pleased with the wit of his own joke.

Jok tried to laugh too, but deep inside something stirred, a premonition of something, a chill that made him shrink. And Tony, no longer amused, was now saying in a cold, sharp voice: "It was you who hit him, Jok, not me."

Jok knew this was true and that he alone would have to deal with the feeling of terror that had begun to grip his body. He glanced at Tony and suddenly felt hatred towards his friend Tony for laughing at his terror.

Tomorrow, in a few hours, the police would be looking for the taxi driver's killer. Is the driver dead? Is he or not? Yes, he's dead! You killed him! I killed him! He's dead! He's dead!

Fear and horror enveloped and strangled him. As Tony pinched his buttock and said, "I'll sleep with you anyway," Jok swung his arm and punched Tony in the face. Tony fell with no chance to parry, and Jok, whirling round, ran swiftly away, with Tony shouting after him: "Hey, Jok, where are you going? I'm not mad at you!" But Jok kept running, not slowing until Tony's voice was lost behind him.

He turned into a narrow alley and ran on, not knowing where he was going but already sensing, deep in his heart, that he wasn't going anywhere. The hunt was on and he was the hunted one now, running away but going nowhere. Jok kept on running, his rasping breath like the sound of rusty hinges. And in the night, all that was heard was the trotting of his shoes as he ran, turning this way and that, endlessly. Running yet unable to run away, forever.

June

The crowing of a rooster behind the hut, loud and clear, pierced the dawn. The sun's rays, still feeble, tried to creep through the cracks of the decrepit, darkened bamboo wall whose paint was peeled off by rain and the hot sun in turn. The wobbly and crooked window, pulled and pushed by the strong night wind, was half open, and through the opening a flowering guava tree was visible outside.

Saimun stretched himself on his sleeping-bench. From under his covering of two plaited mats, he slowly opened his eyes and then looked at the woman who slept beside him. Her small mouth was half open; her camisole undone except for the lowest button; and her wrap-around *kain*, untied around the waist, covered her limbs loosely. Saimun was very still as he regarded the woman; he was at peace and happy. When he laid his hand on the woman's belly she moved a little, and her hand held his.

"Neng," Saimun whispered as his hand moved upwards and his blood rose. The previous week he had gone back to the dump and brought the woman to his hut. Just like that. He was surprised at his own daring, but also that the woman had so readily decided to follow him.

All he'd said was, "Come with me." And she got up, tied her clothes into a small bundle, and the two of them walked over to his hut.

Neneng, the woman, was now his. She slept on his *balai* while Itam slept on his own bench, not two yards away from theirs, separated from them only by an old batik cloth which was hung up at night near the edge of the bench. Neneng slept with Itam, too, but she always returned to Saimun's sleeping-bench.

They never discussed it, but everything seemed to arrange itself on its own. That week it was Neneng who cleaned their little room. And they gave a part of their wages to her for cooking.

Suddenly Saimun embraced the woman with ardor, his body burning. Neneng, awakened, smiled at Saimun, aware of his intent, and happily gave him what he desired. Hunger, which never loosed its grip upon him, so easily fanned his passion for the woman. The passion of their embrace seemed to dispel the craving nagging at his gut and to give him a feeling of power and confidence in himself: he, too, was a man; he, too, was human. In such a moment the breath of life stormed through him, and the moans and little cries of the woman under him proved the force of his male assault.

The more the woman moaned, the stronger he felt his maleness and power. He was great and strong, and not a garbage man of no significance.

Then he lay back. Neneng tied up her *kain* and got off the bed.

"We're late," she said. She pushed back the batik hanging and looked over to the *balai* where Itam was still lying, but with open eyes.

As Neneng passed by his bench, he caught her hand to pull her down, to sit on his bed, but Neneng laughed, extricated her hand, and ran to open the door.

Saimun got up and put on his pants, "You're not quick enough, Itam! Your turn tonight!"

Behind the thin bamboo partition that divided the hut, they could hear Pak Ijo's family beginning to stir, and Pak Ijo complaining to his wife that he was sick. "I've got a fever.... Look at the boils on my back! But if I don't go out to earn a living, what are we going to do?" Then the voice of his wife telling him, "Just be careful." And then the voice of their youngest who had started to cry.

They went down to bathe in the stream, where many of the inhabitants of this squatter community had already gathered. Then, after coffee cooked by Neneng in a former butter tin, Saimun and Itam hastened to the meeting place of garbage carts. The truck was there with Miun, the driver, inspecting its engine. He was swearing to himself when they arrived. The engine wouldn't start. The battery's dead again, Miun muttered. How many times had it been in and out of the repair shop and still it didn't want to start.

Itam and Saimun stood behind Miun watching him scrape the battery cables. Saimun was always amazed when he looked at the truck's engine. He couldn't understand how a lifeless thing like that could move such a big and heavy machine, but neither could the driver explain it to him clearly. Saimun had once asked Miun to teach him to drive. This was the highest aspiration of his life: to become a driver like Miun, to get higher wages, to sit comfortably behind the steering wheel, and to control the engine and the truck. Miun had said jovially that he would teach him if Saimun would wash the truck every evening. Saimun had been washing it every evening for a whole week now, but Miun still had not started to teach him. Saimun was full of dreams of how he would one day drive that truck.

He was afraid to press Miun to start the lessons for fear that he'd become angry and refuse to teach him altogether. Suddenly Miun turned to him and said, "Saimun, get in, switch on the ignition, and press the starter. Step on the accelerator a little."

Saimun's heartbeat quickened, so unexpected was such an order from Miun. This was the beginning of his driving lessons, he thought. By now he knew where the ignition key was, where the starter was, and how to step on the gas.

Saimun climbed into the truck, sat down at the steering wheel, turned the ignition key, and pressed on the starter pedal with his foot. How proud he felt! Smiling, he looked around at Itam, who regarded him with envy. But the motor still wouldn't start. Meanwhile, the first carts of refuse had already arrived and coolies started to toss the garbage into the back of the truck.

Miun shouted for the coolies to stop filling the truck. "Come on and push; the engine is dead."

The whole crowd of them pushed the heavy truck, and at last the engine started but only after they had pushed it repeatedly and were all out of breath. Saimun and Itam felt a smarting pain in their insides, because their stomachs were still empty. But the moment the engine started, they all jumped on the truck, shouting and cheering, and in the hubbub the truck returned to the place for the loading of rubbish from the small hand-pulled carts.

Saimun was overjoyed, because Miun had told him that he could begin his driving lessons today, at break time, around noon.

"I'll ask for you to be moved, to be my assistant," Miun told him. "Ali, my regular, has been gone three weeks. Sick, probably, or gone home to the village and not coming back, I don't know. But I need someone now."

Sitting on the truck, now piled high with refuse, Saimun told Itam of his dreams once he became a driver: "When I get my license I'll look for work as an *oplet* driver, and then I'll teach you to drive. Miun drives a taxi afterhours, you know, and he says an *oplet* driver brings in a lot of money. You can take home up to twenty, or fifty, a day. Just think!"

Itam joined in daydreaming of how Saimun would be an autolette driver—a vivid, resplendent vision that filled him with gladness. Thus they daydreamed, sitting together on the garbage truck, its stench gone, all the rubbish emptied, and the dream filling them with joy.

Hasnah was busy sewing a gown for the baby she carried when Dahlia knocked at the door and immediately entered, without waiting for a response.

"Idris is off on an inspection tour again, this time to Kalimantan, for ten days."

Hasnah smiled and invited her to sit down. "You're only one year in Jakarta, and fed up already?'"

"What do you think? Staying in a house like this... who can stand it? It's almost the same as before, when we stayed in a hotel. And what with my husband constantly going off to the field.... But how can you bear it? And with a child, no less! I don't even have one but I'm already losing my mind, staying here."

Hasnah smiled. "We're going to move to another house, soon. Sugeng promised that before the baby is born we'll have a house of our own."

"Lucky you! I have no idea when we'll get our own place. My husband is much too good a man—a dedicated civil servant. He doesn't want to pester, he says, to keep on asking for a house. If there's no chance yet, that's that, he always says. What's the use of a husband like that?"

Dahlia stood up to look at her face in the mirror near the window, and stroked her forehead and around her mouth. "It's time to go to the beauty shop again. Make-up, and a permanent wave, is what I need." She turned and looked at Hasnah. "Don't you ever get a permanent for your hair? Doesn't your husband want you to?"

"No, it's not that," Hasnah replied. "It's just expensive is all."

"That's nonsense. It's just you wanting to stay home. Come on, just try and see how it'll change you. Your face will be prettier when your hair is done up."

Dahlia got out a comb, took hold of Hasnah's hair, and went to work with zest. At first Hasnah protested, but she did not interfere.

When Hasnah's hair was done, Dahlia got out a lipstick from her handbag and applied some to Hasnah's lips. Then she lifted the mirror from off the wall and held it up to Hasnah. "There. See how pretty you look?"

Hasnah looked at her face in the mirror. She was very embarrassed, but inwardly pleased. "Is it really proper for me to be made up like this?"

"Of course. You can't let yourself go. All men, your husband included, much prefer to see you pretty like this."

"But with my belly getting so big like this, what's the use of prettying up?"

"That's why it's needed all the more: so that your husband forgets your big belly and keeps looking only at your face."

They both laughed.

"I am so pleased to have you living next to us," said Hasnah. "The family before you had lots of children and it was a constant uproar. Maryam kept getting into fights with them. How long have you been married?"

"Three years!"

"Don't you want to have children?"

"In the beginning I did. But it seems it's not in the stars. And now, with housing conditions as they are, I'm not eager to have a child."

"Don't think that way! Every child brings its own luck. Our second baby here will bring us a house."

"How come you're so sure that you'll get a house?"

"Sugeng has promised it."

"And if he says so, does it mean that you're sure to get it?"

"Yes."

"You have no doubts whatsoever?"

"No. Why should I doubt it, if Sugeng has promised it?" said Hasnah, astonished.

Dahlia shrugged her shoulders. "Who knows, maybe your Sugeng is an exceptional person. But I never believe people's promises. Especially promises made by men and even more so, promises made by my husband. Idris can be such a fool. He's an inspector at The Ministry of Education. His friends are all rich by now, but he isn't worth even a half a cent."

"But you don't seem to lack anything. Your clothes are always beautiful. The material is always new. No lack of perfume, either," Hasnah observed.

"Yes, but I don't get those things from him."

Hasnah was about to ask her where she did get them, but something held her back.

"Women today must be smart and look out for themselves," Dahlia said. "You must always be pretty. That's the only thing men want from a woman."

Hasnah shook her head. "Not Sugeng. He also loves his child."

"I'm sure he does but don't you ever think he might be playing around with another woman?"

"No, Sugeng is not like that," said Hasnah.

"How can you know for sure?"

"Somehow, I just know. Besides, no one forced us to marry. We got married by our own choice."

"Then you're lucky…. Hey, do you like to go to the cinema?" Dahlia asked suddenly.

"We do. But it's been a long time because of this," Hasnah said, pointing to her swollen belly. "But the next time you want to see a show, invite me, will you?"

"Sure."

Cheered at the idea, Hasnah said, "What film stars do you like?"

"Male or female?"

"Male. I like Gregory Peck, but sometimes I feel he's not quite forceful enough."

"Do you know who I like? Gary Cooper! There's a real he-man for you!"

"But he's so old!"

Sugeng was busy reading incoming mail when he got a call to appear before the chief of his bureau. His heart was beating fast as he went to the man's office, hoping that the problem of his house was at last solved. The nearer Hasnah's due date, the more nervous he felt. He had battled so often with the people in charge of housing for the ministry's employees, but he was constantly told to be patient, that at least he had a place to live when so many other employees were living separate from their families for lack of housing.

The bureau chief told him to sit down, and then said, "I have good news for you. Based on the minister's decision"—and here he handed Sugeng a letter—"at the end of the month, that is, on the first of July, you will be promoted to head of the import section."

Sugeng shook the hand of the bureau chief and quickly left. He was very happy: his salary would be higher and, as head of a section, the chance for getting a house would be greater. How pleased and happy Hasnah will be—this was a real professional advance.

For two hours now they had been debating the same issue over and over again, and it still seemed like the end was nowhere in sight. Suryono looked around him, and was amazed. Were these friends of his really convinced of what they were saying? Were they serious in believing that what they were doing here was of benefit to the nation? He felt trapped. He was there because Ies had challenged him to come, telling him that if he was so dissatisfied with the situation the nation was in, then he should do something about it; that he should help her and the other members of her debate group come up with feasible solutions to the problems the nation faced.

Several times now, she had dragged him along to these relentlessly boring affairs.

Only six members of the debate group were there that day. Besides Ies and himself there was Pranoto, the well-known essayist, who often wrote on Indonesia's cultural problems and was the driving force behind this small club. He had an intellectual mien and always spoke in an unduly sincere tone of voice. Then there was Achmad, a labor leader; Yasrin, a poet, who as time went on felt that there was no chance for him to grow and develop in his own country; and Murhalim, a young provincial comptroller who was constantly enraged by the conditions in his office.

"Is there a crisis, or isn't there?" Pranoto was asking. "The fact that this question is being raised at all shows that a feeling of responsibility already exists in society. And..."

Suryono stopped listening to Pranoto's exposition and thought of how often he had heard such discussions—about the role that culture played in nation building, about the loneliness of the individual in Indonesian society, about where Indonesian music was going, and so on—and he recalled a particularly heated debate about Europeans having reached a dead end, and how the debate finished with a question from one of the people in the group— Who was it? He forgot—why were we worrying whether the peoples of Europe were stalemated or not? Were we Europeans?

He was conscious of Ies sitting at his side, of her fine face and the full curves of her breasts, and in his imagination he saw her naked, lying beside him in bed, and he compared her with Fatma.

Feeling his stare, Ies turned her head to glance at Suryono. What she saw in his face caused her to blush and she quickly turned away.

Suryono suddenly woke from his daydream with a start.

Yasrin was speaking: "I received an invitation to visit Peking at the expense of the ministry of education. In my conversation with the minister I explained my desire to go to China to study how they develop art among the masses over there. In my opinion, the problem of social integration in our nation is very closely connected with the development of a national culture. In fact, I think that the problem of our society is a cultural problem."

"Just what do you mean by national culture?" said Murhalim. "I know people are sick and tired of hearing this problem discussed, but why is it that we get excited about the problem of a national culture? Why do people want to synthesize regional cultures in order to produce one national culture? Why do people want to synthesize Western dancing with the *serimpi* dance, or nationalize Javanese court dance? Why must *gamelan* music be 'national-orchestrated' with the addition of a viola, piano, and cello? Why don't we view the problem from an angle in which the *gamelan* is national music, as the Sundanese *angklung* and lute are equally national music, and the *serimpi* dance of Central Java, the dances of Bali, the plate and handkerchief dances of Sumatra, the *cakalélé* of the Moluccas, the *pakaréné* of Sulawesi, and so on? All are national dances, because aren't they all the property of the Indonesian people, but only of different regional origin? I believe the problem is not a matter of national culture, but Indonesians themselves who are not yet mature enough to feel that they are one nation, and who still differentiate between the regions."

"I protest," said Achmad. "What you just said is surely nice to hear but this means being blind to history, and to reality. The problem of national culture *does* arise, because the Indonesian people indeed do not have a national consciousness. This is why a national culture must be created, to achieve our national integration."

Murhalim retorted, "Is it possible to organize a national culture when the people don't have a national consciousness? Which comes first, a national culture, or a national consciousness?"

"Your thinking is naive," Achmad said. "It's decadent bourgeois thinking. It is necessary to establish a concept of national culture at the top and then to spread it downwards. This is why I agree with Yasrin's plan to study the development of the people's culture in China. He will probably learn a lot and be inspired by their example."

"But perhaps what is possible in China cannot be applied in Indonesia," said Ies.

Achmad turned towards her. "What do you mean?'

"In China, power is in the hands of the communists and everything is run by a dictatorship. Here in Indonesia, we have respect for democracy."

"What does democracy mean today to the Indonesian people?" Achmad said. "That's the voice of the bourgeois class wanting to retain its power over the ignorant and confused masses. And how do we stand with our democracy? Is our provisional parliament democratic? Are our people already capable of realizing a democracy? Can you answer that honestly?"

"Well, it's certainly not mature, but nonetheless…" Murhalim began.

"There it is!" said Achmad. "There you have that lack of certainty, the lack of courage of Indonesians to face the true reality. That's why our country is confused. That's why moral, cultural, and other kinds of crises continue to arise." He saw that both Murhalim and Ies wanted to speak. "No, no, please let me finish. I hope you can refrain from interrupting me."

Achmad drew a deep breath and looked around him with the air of a man confident of his coming victory. "According to Marx and Engels, it is the system of production which determines the process of social, political, and intellectual life of man. This is the very root of our crisis: the system of production in our country, which is not only imperialistic but the height of capitalism. All sorts of crises are going to occur, so long as their roots are not eradicated. And is any effort being made to eradicate them, or even attempt to eradicate them? No! You here worry about a cultural crisis but the discussion is all up in the clouds, because you don't want to face reality. The bourgeois spirit causes all this."

"I protest," shouted Ies.

Pranoto rapped his knuckles on the table. "Let Achmad finish speaking."

Achmad looked around again, formulating his thoughts before he began: "It is not man's consciousness or the personal condition that determines the condition of the self. It's the social self or the social situation which determines the consciousness of the individual. And because the system of production also determines the social life of man, it is clear therefore that a certain type of production system, such as capitalism, is a chain which constricts the social self of man, which further means pushing self-consciousness towards a conception of individuality. So it's clear that capitalism directly enslaves the human soul, and that from such a system of production inevitably arise all sorts of crises, especially because of the conflicts among peoples who wish to free themselves from enslavement to this capitalism. So, if we discuss cultural crisis, we really should be discussing the basis of our economy."

Ies now interrupted. "You seem to propose that Indonesia should become a communist state. But Indonesia is based on Pancasila."

"Yes, yes, 'Panca-sila', the all important 'Five Principles'," Achmad said with mock solemnity. "I can muster arguments which will convince people with equal success that the aim of Pancasila is, in fact, the creation of an Islamic state, or a Christian state, or a socialist-welfare state, or a communist state. I'm not going to discuss Pancasila, because its not a fully-developed philosophy; so how can we debate it here? My friends, I beg you not to interrupt me. As I said before, you are not viewing the problem realistically. We cannot discuss the cultural crisis now confronting us without touching on the economic system that still prevails in our country. As Engels said, political development, law, philosophy, religion, literature, art, and so forth, are all based on economic development."

"Are you finished now?" said Murhalim.

"Yes."

"Then may I ask a question?"

"Certainly," Achmad replied.

"I want to ask only one thing and that is, Achmad, if you are a communist, or a member of the Communist Party?"

Achmad looked annoyed. "What connection is there between my being a communist or a member of the Communist Party and the problem we're discussing?"

"Well, if you are a member of the Communist Party, then it would be futile to continue this debate," Murhalim said, "because, to the end of days there will be no meeting of minds between us. I believe in democracy. Marxism, as practiced by communists, not only doesn't bring freedom and happiness to man, but ends up by bringing enslavement and loss of humanity. What you want is for a dictatorship of the proletariat to be established in Indonesia. But what you forget is that human beings are not machines who can be ordered to become parts of a production system. Next to material needs, there are also spiritual values of no less importance for ensuring the good way of life. Just as a man needs food in his stomach, he also needs food for his soul, which needs freedom for it to grow and thrive.

"You, Achmad, want an economic system wholly controlled by the state, one hundred per cent. Such a totalitarian system must, of necessity, control the lives and thoughts of people, because without such absolute control and authority it would be impossible to attain what you wish for. I can agree that some parts of an economic system can influence the cultural development of a people. But one cannot completely disregard the human factors. The peoples of Persia, India, Egypt, Rome, and Greece attained the peaks of their cultural glory under a system of absolute monarchy, which, according to communist theory, could not possibly produce anything of high value. The painter Picasso, who glorifies the communists, is himself the product of a bourgeois society and of capitalistic Western Europe. And I want to ask further, where are those cultural products that are supposedly coming out of Russia today? But, anyway, to return to my question, are you a communist?"

Achmad shook his head. "Your question implies an admission that you yourself are unable to carry on the debate. I am not a communist, but if conditions in our country should continue as they are today, with a leadership that continues to deceive the people, with corruption on the rampage, disintegration, and confusion, then I shall become one!"

Murhalim shrugged his shoulders. "It's a bit difficult to continue a debate when one is accused of being unable to continue it."

"I am not an expert on Islam," Ies intervened, "but I want to introduce a thought for all of us to consider: could not Islam be made the mainstay of our people's spiritual uplift? A modernized Islam, with a new dynamism?"

"Islam? What utter naivety!" said Achmad quickly. "I once talked to a man from a Middle East country who had visited its Islamic university, one of the highest, most widely acclaimed centers for the study of modern Islam in the world today. And do you know what he told me, Ies? He told me that he was very disappointed. What he found was incredible dirt, people sleeping on dirty floors, and nothing organized. And what did this Islam bring to these Arab countries? All we see is that one class of society exploits the masses who for hundreds of years have lived on the brink of starvation and in darkest ignorance."

"But this isn't reason enough to reject the idea of seeking a new dynamism in Islam," Ies replied. "Probably, with sufficient conscious stimulation, some Islamic thinkers capable of finding it could emerge in Indonesia, too! The conditions we see today in Islamic countries are not the fault of Islam, but of some Muslims who disregard the teachings of their religion. They make the study of Islam a completely dead thing—no different than if one made a mynah bird recite the verses of the Qu'ran, or from putting the verses of the Qu'ran on gramophone records and then letting them play day and night. Since the majority of our people adhere to the religious teachings of Islam, if some Islamic leaders would come forward bringing a new vitality into Islam, couldn't Islam then become a tremendous force in the development of our people?"

"Theory! Vain hope! Impossible!" said Achmad heatedly. "There isn't a single historical proof that religion can bring about a good human society. Christianity at the time of its greatest glory, Islam at the time of its greatest glory, and Buddhism at the time of its greatest glory…. Which one of these religions succeeded in eliminating the contrasts between the classes and bringing justice to humanity? The time of Islam's glory was, as we know, an era of royal power and enslavement is still the order of the day! So where is your just society? As Christianity flourished with its crusades, so also the Catholic Church of Spain spread death and hatred in South America."

"Our friend Achmad appears to be completely against religion," Murhalim remarked, "and, to criticize religion, he uses communist clichés. What Ies meant was to seek out and develop the valuable principles contained in Islam, just as there are valuable principles in any religion. Values which are now dead should be revived and given a new life. That is the problem suggested by Ies's question: can a new dynamic Islam be employed as a mainstay for the development of our people? This question was posed, I believe, because—with the exception of you, Achmad—all of us here reject communism with its totalitarian system as a means to build up our nation."

"I don't reject communism," said Suryono, speaking up for the first time. "Why should communism be rejected? Look at Russia, where it succeeded in freeing the people from feudal oppression and provided them with livelihood. Look also at China, and the tremendous progress initiated by Mao Tse-tung in numerous fields—plus the liberation of the people from the oppression and corruption of Chiang Kai-shek's clique. If it can be done there, why not here?"

"Stop playing games!" Ies said to Suryono, "I know you. You don't even believe your own words."

"You're right," said Suryono. "Of course I don't believe what I've just said. Hasn't it ever occurred to anyone that we live today not in an atomic age, but in an age of disbelief, one caused by the deep frustration that mankind has felt since the end of the last world war, when they realized that this war would not end all wars either? Isn't it evident that the Americans are afraid of their own atom and hydrogen bombs, do not believe in themselves, and the Russians, too, don't dare trust each other, that the Asians do not trust the West, that the West fears and doesn't trust Asia? Apartheid in South Africa, the white-skin-only policy in Australia, suspicion against foreigners in Indonesia and in other Asian countries, discrimination against Negroes in America—all this underlies this absence of faith. Because people don't trust each other, they don't believe that human beings are equal and that, in fact, they can and must be able to live together. The communist is like this, the imperialist is like this, the democrat is like this, the Indonesian nationalist, with his cry of 'Freedom!' is like this. They're all the same. What's the use of spending all our time exchanging ideas, as we do here? Isn't it best to take care of oneself, seek one's own happiness in any way one chooses, and to the devil with the world?"

"You're joking!" said Ies accusingly.

Achmad smiled lightly. "No, he's not joking. It's quite true what Suryono said about that non-belief. But he forgot to clarify the cause of this lack of faith in the world today. It is the evil outcome of capitalism and imperialism which still..."

"And therefore we should all become communists!" said Murhalim.

Achmad glanced at Murhalim with great annoyance. "It's hard to exchange ideas in an intelligent manner with people who are as prejudiced as our friend Murhalim here," he said.

"I want to intervene before the discussion strays off elsewhere," said Suryono, a smile playing on his lips. "If this discussion continues without a change of direction, we are sure to get absolutely nowhere, because, my friends, you're all taking the wrong view of the problem. Achmad, who adheres to historic materialism, is wrong, and Ies, who wants to put forward Islam, is also wrong. The root of the matter is man himself. That which is called crisis of leadership, cultural crisis, economic crisis, moral crisis, crisis in literature, is nothing but man's crisis. That's why an Indonesian must first of all realize that he exists, and that his fate is in his own hands. That his life is not determined by society, is not determined by his family, not by the economic system, but that he has enough inner strength to determine himself."

Achmad sneered. "Oh, an existentialist, are you? What pessimistic and bourgeois ideas!"

Suryono laughed and looked at him. "I admit frankly that what I've just said is lifted straight out of Sartre, but only a person who is ill-informed would call existentialism 'pessimistic'. Quite the contrary; existentialism is the most optimistic of philosophies, because it says that man, and not outside influences, can determine his own self. Sartre said it in *L'existentialisme est un humanism*. Have you read it?" he asked Achmad with a taunt.

Achmad stared at him furiously, but Suryono smiled and continued: "In fact, Sartre himself opposed Marxism, because Marxism conceals the truth that man is fully responsible for his attitudes and choices. Sartre's argument is that the individual is responsible for what he is and what he does. That's why there is no other philosophy that is more optimistic than this existentialism, optimistic in the recognition of the individual's capacity to determine himself, and to act as an individual, which is the only hope for humanity, as only by acting can man survive."

Pranoto coughed lightly, looked round, saw that Achmad was tearing to jump into the debate again, and quickly said, "Look at the time! It's almost seven o'clock. I'm really sorry to have to adjourn our meeting at a time when the discussion was becoming so very interesting, especially since Suryono, who kept quiet at the beginning, has now leapt into the arena with both feet. Although we have not arrived at any conclusion, I believe that many valuable ideas have been expressed, whether one agrees with every one of them or not. That such ideas have been raised, and the readiness of us all to discuss them and to listen, shows that we can hope this exchange of ideas will lead each of us to think more deeply about them. I think that the most fortunate among us is Achmad, because to him everything is already clear. For him the road to our people's development and human happiness is communism— while the others are still questioning and still searching for the way which seems best according to their views and convictions."

"I cannot discern the good fortune in Achmad's situation," said Murhalim. "His thoughts are no longer free."

They laughed, and Achmad joined in laughing with them.

Pranoto stood. "Before we adjourn, remember that the meeting next week is on Wednesday."

Once outside Suryono said to Ies, "Would you like me to see you home?"

"It's not necessary. I have a bicycle."

"Leave it here, I have my father's Dodge. He just bought himself a new Cadillac. You can get someone to fetch the bicycle tomorrow."

Ies looked hesitant.

"You're angry with me," said Suryono. "You suspect that I was being sarcastic and was making fun of them with this existentialism?"

Ies regarded him for a moment, then said, "All right, you can see me home."

Inside Suryono's father's car, Ies sighed. "It's embarrassing to be seen in such a luxurious car. People will suspect me of riding with a black marketeer or a corrupt government official."

"Why these allusions?" said Suryono. "If my father is wallowing in money that he made in business, there's no need to throw it into my face."

"I'm sorry. Forgive me for speaking that way." Ies lightly patted Suryono's neck and playfully wiggled the tip of his ear.

Startled by her touch, Suryono glanced at Ies, a thrill passing through him, but he quickly suppressed it. He was afraid to disturb the mood in the car. Never before had he felt so close to Ies.

"I swear I wasn't intending to mock with my talk about existentialism," he said to her. "I really do believe that man has the strength to determine what and who he is."

"I'm tired of pondering these convoluted problems," said Ies. "I just want to rest." She leaned her head on his shoulder. "Let's not go home directly. Let's first take a little ride."

Suryono, smiled happily and pressed Ies's hand with warmth.

In front of the restaurant, rows of new motorcars were parked at the curb. That evening the restaurant was crowded. A dark red Cadillac arrived, seeking a place to park, but the places at the curb were filled, and finally it stopped with its two left wheels resting on the sidewalk.

Raden Kaslan was at the wheel, and at his side sat his wife, Fatma. From the dark red Cadillac there emanated an air of luxury: from Fatma's finery, her elaborate gilt slippers, her coiffure fresh from the hairdresser's salon, and also from the glossy smile which she directed at her husband.

Thus, on that clear evening, the couple, exuding wealth and luxury, left their beautiful car, parked half on the sidewalk and half in the street, glistening in the light of the setting sun. They seated themselves in the garden in front of the restaurant, at a table somewhat isolated from the others.

From the loudspeaker behind the restaurant's bar came lively music; at the tables people ate, drank, chatted, and laughed. Raden Kaslan ordered dinner without bothering to consult the prices on the menu, and then they returned to their rather expensive and luxurious ideas, to which Fatma responded with a luxuriant smile.

It was extremely pleasant, that atmosphere of the clear evening, the deep blue sky overhead, and the fresh breeze.

An old delman carriage, drawn by an old emaciated horse, came by, empty except for its driver, Pak Ijo, dozing in his seat. For years the horse had been accustomed to pulling the delman through the big city, even if the driver fell asleep. This often happened on hot days—Pak Ijo, who hadn't had any passengers or anything to eat since morning, had indeed fallen asleep—and the horse would continue to draw the delman along his accustomed route, stopping by himself when hailed by a passenger, awakening the driver by the shock of the sudden stop. Or when a traffic policeman barred the traffic's progress, the old horse stopped too, its muzzle pressed against the side of a car or a truck.

So it was on that evening. The horse walked along the street pulling the delman cart while the driver dozed. Near the restaurant, from behind the fence of a house across the street, a big dog chasing a cat suddenly jumped out, loudly barking. The horse, badly startled, tried to dodge the dog and the cat at its feet, slipped, and fell. The left pole of the delman with its blackened copper capping hit the side of the red Cadillac parked at the roadside, damaging its chromium and paint, and the protruding iron brace of the cart roof struck the car's side window, shattering the glass.

Pak Ijo, jolted from his nap, staggered down from the cart. He helped the old horse to its feet and then just stood there, dazed, stroking the horse's head.

The noise of the collision also alarmed the people in the restaurant. Raden Kaslan jumped up and hurried to the street. The moment he saw the damaged chromium and paint on his car, and the shattered glass of the door, he flew into a rage.

"Hey, you idiot, where're your eyes? Look what you've done to my car. You've ruined it. You're going to pay for all this damage!" Raden Kaslan was beside himself.

Pak Ijo, white in the face and his whole body quivering, was like a man seized by an attack of malaria. He was sick already, anyway. His ragged and dirty clothes hung on a thin body, and his inflamed, watering eyes were sunken above his hollow cheeks.

He tried to say something, but his voice, quavering with befuddlement and despair, was lost on his trembling lips, and his hand kept stroking the head of his horse.

Raden Kaslan eyed him furiously, exchanged glances with Fatma, so finely attired, then he looked again at his damaged car, and his wrath flared even higher.

"I'll call the police and make sure that you pay for all this damage. Look at this!"—and he jumped to point to the chromium on the car door—"and this"—and he pointed at the scars along the side where the paint was scraped off—"and this"—and he kicked a piece of the broken glass. "You shall reimburse me for all this, at least one thousand, two thousand rupiah!"

Pak Ijo almost fainted at the mention of the sum. He found his voice and said, weeping, "I admit my guilt, sir. Kill me if you like, but I cannot repay. I am a poor man. It's best you just to put me to death!" He kept stroking the head of his old horse.

The horse nuzzled Pak Ijo's chest as if begging forgiveness for his misdeed.

At Pak Ijo's words, Raden Kaslan, now silently furious, walked back to the restaurant, where he telephoned the traffic police.

On the street many people stood watching. Pak Ijo continued to stroke the head of his horse; and when Raden Kaslan returned, shouting "Don't you go anywhere. I've called the police!" Pak Ijo and his horse were dying a thousand deaths and facing the fires of hell. He imagined the police arriving on motorcycles with their engines roaring. At that instant his mind flashed back to his village and the sounds of the guns wielded by the invading bandits who had forced his family to flee and seek shelter in the big city.

Meanwhile, the other customers had returned to their tables, eating, drinking, and laughing again. A collision was an ordinary matter; now that the police had been called, it was in their hands.

A policeman arrived and Raden Kaslan greeted him. He identified himself and, pointing to the trembling old delman driver, said, "It's entirely his fault. My car was parked at the curb, even half-way on the sidewalk, and he still ran into it."

The traffic police inspector was a young man who had dealt with collisions hundreds of times. This was a routine matter and, in this instance, quite an easy case. It was clear who was at fault.

"I demand damages," said Raden Kaslan.

At these words Pak Ijo suddenly cried out weeping. "Just kill me now," he said, bowing with folded hands to the police inspector. "I'm a poor man, I have no money at all."

"So you admit your guilt?" the inspector asked Pak Ijo

"I admit it, sir. Just kill me. I cannot pay for the damage. I am a poor man."

"Why did you run into my car which was parked at the side of the street?" fumed Raden Kaslan.

"I dozed off, sir," said the old driver. His voice was trembling.

"Dozed off?" Raden Kaslan shouted in fury. "What sort of a driver are you! If you want to sleep, sleep at home, not in the delman, endangering other people. Why did you fall asleep?"

Pak Ijo's voice quivered all the more. "Because I'm sick, sir,"

Raden Kaslan sneered, "You fall asleep and you're sick. If you're sick you shouldn't be working! Stay home! Take medicine! Otherwise you'll cause accidents! How would it be if you ran into a little child and killed him?"

"But I'm hungry, sir, and my wife and my children are hungry. Yesterday we had nothing to eat, sir."

For a moment Raden Kaslan was still, but then he shouted, "You're lying. What are you sick with?"

Still weeping and shaking, Pak Ijo unbuttoned his jacket and bared his back. "Here, sir, look." On his back were two boils the size of a fist, red and swollen. Then he lifted one side of his sarong and showed a big boil on his thigh. His entire thigh was red and swollen. After he had done this, the old man seemed to have come to the end of his strength: every part of his body shook, his teeth chattered, and tears streamed from his eyes.

The inspector looked at Pak Ijo and then at Raden Kaslan and Fatma.

Raden Kaslan turned to the police inspector and spoke like someone at the end of his wits. "How do we stand in this case, Inspector? Who will reimburse me for the damage? Who is responsible?" With no answer forthcoming, he asked again: "Who is responsible?"

Pak Ijo continued to shiver and kept stroking the head of his horse. As the question of responsibility hung in the air, it seemed as if the shadows of the driver and the horse grew longer and longer on the pavement under the setting sun, and that they, the old driver and the old horse, died and lived hundreds of times.

Raden Kaslan swore again at Pak Ijo, but finally realized that it would be impossible for the driver—so old and poor and ill—to pay for the damage to his car.

"That's that," he said to the police inspector. "Let's go."

He drew Fatma back to the restaurant, but his former joy was now spoiled.

"The devil!" Raden Kaslan muttered. "A brand-new car, just purchased!"

CITY BEAT

The eyes of Wang Ching-kai, also known as Tony, were red because he had cried all night in the detention room of the police station, calling for his father and mother who still had not come. His cheeks were hollow, his hair disheveled. During the night he was kicked several times by other prisoners, who were annoyed with his incessant crying.

That morning he didn't touch the coffee and other fare distributed to the people in detention. He waited for his father and mother to come to his rescue.

At ten o'clock his name was called by a police agent, the door was opened for him, and he was ushered into an office. His face lit up as he saw his father seated near the police inspector's desk. But a moment later he became apprehensive, because his father behaved like a stranger and looked at him with such anger and loathing that he was frightened. Tony's face dropped. He sat down on a chair in front of the desk as soon as he was ordered to do so.

The police inspector read the report prepared the preceding night: "The accused confesses that he stabbed with a knife a woman named Siti Danijah residing in Kaligot in a brawl about payment of money…"

His father lowered his head and looked at the police inspector with despair.

The police inspector asked the man, "Is this your son, sir?"

The older man bit his lip. The words he had wanted to utter—that the young man seated there was not his son—had almost escaped his lips. But he had restrained himself and now said in a shaky voice, "That's true, sir. But now I do not wish to acknowledge him any more as my son. I gave up trying to teach him. He was a scoundrel already at seventeen. We can't teach him and he won't learn. And… did that woman die?" he asked fearfully.

"No, but she was seriously wounded and had to be taken to a hospital. It's very lucky that she didn't die."

Greatly relieved, Tony's father gathered his courage and said, "I beg you in all earnestness, sir, to sentence this boy. We are afraid that if he goes free he will kill someone. He even once stabbed me, six months ago. At that time he stole a gold ring from his mother. He sold it in order to gamble. When I got angry at him he fought, fetched the cleaver from the kitchen, and attacked me. But his older brother arrived and so he ran away."

Tony's father rolled up the sleeve of his jacket. "This is the scar! He doesn't want to study. If you send him to school he always runs away. His mother is afraid of him. Punish him, sir. He's not our son anymore."

The old man stood up and quickly left the room. The police inspector called him back, but he old man walked on rapidly, large tears streaking his cheeks and dimming his sight.

July

Raden Kaslan, director of the Bumi Ayu Corporation and member of the Indonesia Party, closed the door of his office in his home and turned to his visitor, Husin Limbara, party chairman. "There! Now we can have some privacy. Please sit down."

Husin Limbara sat down in a dark brown leather armchair and leaned back comfortably. "Oh, my shoulder still hurts. None of the doctors seem to be able to cure it."

Raden Kaslan picked up the cigar box from his table, mumbled something in sympathy about Husin Limbara's shoulder trouble, and, as his visitor helped himself to a Triple Five cigarette, Raden Kaslan held up to his cigar a silver lighter made by the Yogya silverworks.

Husin Limbara inhaled deeply, puffed the smoke slowly, his eyes steadily fixed on the face of his host. For a moment Raden Kaslan felt uncomfortable. He thought to himself, the party needs money again. Well, this time I won't give them more than one or two thousand rupiah. Having decided so, he felt at ease again, and said to Husin Limbara, "So, what's on your mind? On the telephone it sounded like a very important and pressing matter."

With a little groan Husin sat up in his chair and said, lowering his voice, "The executive council has taken an important decision. As you know, the general elections are very near. Our party needs a lot of money. We must establish a trade organization to raise as much money as possible. Of all our members, we have selected you to prepare a plan, because of your long experience in the business world. We want you, my friend, to prepare a plan on a really large scale, to cover all economic activities. You needn't worry about your own money. It's not our intention to trade, really. But if some of the arrangements could remain permanent, all the better. Our members who are in positions of authority have already received instructions to support the party's efforts. What do you think?"

Raden Kaslan looked at Husin Limbara. He had heard already of the party's intentions to raise this money, and for some time he had been hoping that he would be invited to participate. Even though his name was being mentioned among the council's members, he had solicited on his own the help of friends among the council members. And he had already spent several thousand rupiah in connection with these efforts.

"If the members of our party in positions of authority will give their support, it will not be too great a problem," said Raden Kaslan. "Of all the economic sectors, the easiest to get money from is certainly the import sector. Whereas other sectors—for instance, transportation, export, and industry—require a great deal of time, organization, and personnel, the import sector requires next to nothing.

"All we'll need is the name of a corporation. The only thing we'd really do is to sell the import licenses that we obtain. I suggest that we make two plans: one for quick results—that is, via the import business—and the other, a long-term plan, including the establishment of banks, industries, and so on."

Husin Limbara laughed. "Aha! Not in vain do people say that Raden Kaslan is an expert in economics."

"No, it's really not so difficult," said Raden Kaslan. "Importers are willing to pay good money for licenses, particularly for public necessities, up to two hundred percent or more from their official value. So if, for instance, the combined price of the licenses we obtain is one hundred thousand rupiah, they could be sold for up to three hundred thousand rupiah and we would get two hundred thousand rupiah clean without investing a single cent!"

"Good!" said Husin Limbara and clapped his hand on the table with delight. "According to our calculations, in order to win the coming general elections, the Indonesia Party is going to need somewhere in the order of thirty million. Do you think we can raise this amount within six months?"

Raden Kaslan was silent a while, calculating. "No trouble at all," he said confidently.

"Good! Then I leave it to you to prepare the plans."

"However, there is one more principle which ought to be settled," said Raden Kaslan. "What percentage does the party get, and how much for the people who implement the plan? This work involves a certain amount of risk."

"Risk? No need to be afraid. Our ministers will provide protection."

"That's not what I meant," said Raden Kaslan suavely. "Even though the corporations we establish will be fronts, there will arise financial consequences such as taxes, certification fees, and many other things."

"So, what do you think would be proper?"

"I think fifty-fifty would be fair. Fifty for the party and fifty for the people whose names we use."

Husin Limbara frowned. "Isn't that a bit steep?"

"Steep? Not really, if the party is sure to have the money it needs in six months," said Raden Kaslan.

"You realize, of course, the importance of maintaining complete secrecy in this matter?" Husin Limbara said softly.

"Of course! I will exercise the greatest caution. Isn't my own reputation on the line?"

Husin Limbara rose from his chair, and, stooping slightly to favor his hurting shoulder, stepped to the door. There he turned to Raden Kaslan. "When do you think you can bring the plans?"

"Give me a week."

"All right, a week. Just let me know."

As the men stepped out of Raden Kaslan's office and into the front room they saw Fatma, seated on the divan reading, and Suryono, lackadaisically playing some tunes on the upright piano in the corner.

Fatma put her book down and looked up at her guest, "Do you have go right away? Won't you stay and have something to drink?"

"I'm sorry," Husin Limbara said to Fatma. "Another time, perhaps. Today I have too much work."

Raden Kaslan motioned to his son. "Suryono, come here for a moment. Meet Mr Husin Limbara, chairman of the Indonesia Party." He said to his guest, "This is my son, Suryono, who has just returned from abroad; he works in The Ministry of Foreign Affairs."

Husin Limbara shook Suryono's hand. "Good, that's very good. And have you joined the party too?"

"It's quite enough with just Father in it!" said Suryono pleasantly.

The three men laughed heartily, and Raden Kaslan accompanied Husin Limbara to his car waiting outside.

When he came back into the house, Raden Kaslan closed the door and rubbed his hands. He then looked in turn at Suryono and Fatma and he laughed broadly. "*Wij zijn binnen!*" he exclaimed in Dutch. "We're in it! We've got it made now!"

Raden Kaslan sat down next to Fatma and then called Suryono to join them. He spoke to them in a confiding tone. "This is very secret and you must not tell anybody, but it's a great catch for us!"

He quickly described to his wife and son the scheme he had developed to raise money for the party. In conclusion, he said: "So, to sum it up, it is my intention to establish a number of kinds of corporations, with you, Fatma, becoming the director of one; Suryono, the director of another; and so on and so forth with the other corporations, so that we have a part interest in each of them. That way we get the largest possible share at the division of profits."

"But I can't do that," Suryono said, "not if I'm working as a government official."

"Well, quit, then, or ask for a prolonged leave of absence. I'll talk about it with the party. I'm sure it can be arranged."

The three of them talked for a long time after that, making all kinds of plans. Something he had never suspected in himself gripped Suryono, a joy at the thought of the money he would have at his disposal. And why not, he asked himself. I have decided for myself that I want it. If I get tired of it, I'll do something else.

By the time they had finished talking, Suryono had convinced himself that what he was doing was perfectly normal. Other political parties were doing the same thing, he thought. Why shouldn't I?

Pak Ijo lay sprawled in the semi-darkness of the room in his hut. Since the accident between his delman and that car, he had been seriously ill, his body consumed by fever. The boils on his body caused incessant pain, and Pak Ijo kept muttering, "*La ilaha illallah. la ilaha illallah.* There is no God save Allah, there is no God save Allah..." He didn't eat, and only from time to time asked to drink.

When high fever attacked him, he often had nightmares and cried: "The motorcar is attacking me! Have pity on the old horse! Help! Help!"

His wife was now half-ill herself for lack of sleep from caring for him.

That morning his fever had subsided considerably, and Pak Ijo called his wife. "How's our horse?" he asked in a heavy voice.

"Amat is taking care of him. He's looking for grass."

"Amat is ten. Tell him to get a job," Pak Ijo said.

"What a pity that he's so little," said his wife, "otherwise he could drive the delman."

"Maybe he could find some light work. Tell him to look for whatever he can. How's the money holding up?"

"Saimun and Itam have paid the rent for their room. There's still a little left."

"Be sparing," he advised. "Who knows when I'll be well again."

Ibu Ijo stepped outside and called her son to inform him that the time had come for him to look for work.

Sugeng slumped in his chair deep in thought, his face tense and pale. His wife Hasnah had shut herself up in their bedroom.

They had just had another quarrel: the usual thing, the question of moving to another house. Hasnah's shrill words still rang in his ears. "All the promises were false. From month to month you just make promises. Look how my belly is growing. It won't be long before the child is born. Why do you make children if you cannot provide a decent place to live? We might as well get rid of it!"

Their joy at Sugeng's promotion had not lasted long. His promotion had given them hopes for a new home but, once again, they had proved futile.

"Do you want me to become corrupt like other people?" Sugeng had shouted at her. The words kept reverberating in his mind.

By God, he swore inwardly, I know that until now I have fought off every temptation with all my strength. But if Hasnah must have a house, and if the only way to get a house is by corruption, then I will engage in corruption. For Hasnah, for the baby who will be born, my baby!

He rested his chin on his hands.

The world was not fair. People who want to be honest are not given a chance to remain so. A matter of a simple house, that's all, and a man wouldn't need to degrade his honor. No, not I, I will not succumb. Let Hasnah be angry, let Hasnah hate me! But even as he tried to steel his courage, he knew that in the end he would give in. It was beyond his strength to fight with Hasnah every minute about the house.

He got up and went to the bedroom, straight to the bed where Hasnah still lay sobbing. Sugeng embraced his wife and whispered, "Forgive me, Has, of course I'm wrong. But this time I truly promise that I'll get a house for us."

He spoke with such sincerity that Hasnah, discerning this new tone in his voice, turned and embraced him. And they held and caressed each other with new peace between them.

Dahlia was walking along, looking at shop windows in Pasar Baru shopping arcade. She couldn't remember the number of shops she had visited. In each one she had looked at the wares on display, but hadn't bought a thing. She was beginning to feel discouraged. In one shop, luck had seemed within grasp. While she was examining a length of cloth, a rich-looking man came and stood next to her. Dahlia had flashed him an alluring glance—and she had caught the response in his eyes—but the man had not followed up this opening, and while Dahlia was still pretending to bargain he had walked out.

He's probably dressed so well just for show, Dahlia thought to herself.

As she walked away from the shop, practically all the men who passed by turned to look at her, but there wasn't a single one she found to be attractive enough. Dahlia slowed her pace, then stopped before a shop window to tidy her appearance. She was alone. Her husband would be away another two weeks, and for two weeks she would be alone, quite free.

Suddenly she was startled, uttering a little cry at the shock of someone bumping into her.

A male voice said, "I'm sorry. I beg your pardon, ma'am, I didn't see you."

Dahlia turned around to see the man who was speaking. He was a young man, smartly dressed, with a package in his arms. Their glances locked, and they both smiled.

"May I escort you somewhere?" the young fellow asked without hesitation.

"Thank you, if it isn't too much trouble."

"No, not at all, my car is across the street."

The young man held her elbow and led her across the street to a Dodge sedan. He opened the front door for her, and then climbed in behind the wheel. He started the motor and turned to Dahlia and laughed. "Excuse me, we're not acquainted yet. My name is Suryono."

Dahlia smiled broadly. "And my name is Dahlia."

"A lovely name. And its bearer is as lovely as the flower."

"You have a glib tongue, sir!" said Dahlia. Then, cocking her head at him, she said, "How can you be out shopping in the middle of the day? Don't you have a job?"

"I actually work at The Ministry of Foreign Affairs.. But I've taken a leave of absence to work in business temporarily—imports, that kind of thing. My company is NV Timur Besar."

Leaving Pasar Baru Street, Suryono turned towards Gunung Sahari Avenue. "Are you in a hurry to go home, Dahlia?"

"Why do you ask?" she answered archly.

"If you're in no hurry, we could take a ride to Tanjung Priok. I haven't been to the harbor in a while."

"My husband is out of town and won't be back for two weeks. So, hurry or no hurry, it's all the same to me."

"Well, fine. In that case we'll go for a spin first. Is your husband a businessman, too?"

"If only he were!" said Dahlia. "Then I would be delighted; but he's a civil servant, an inspector at The Ministry of Education and Culture. It's hard to be a government official these days," she mused. "As you well know yourself, I would imagine. Government salaries are barely large enough to get you through just one week."

"How very true! It's almost silly for anyone to want to be a government official these days. But if he wanted to, he could get along nicely by doing favors."

"That's what I've been telling my husband, and how many times. But he says if all government officials were corrupt, where would our country be? It would go to pieces!"

"Your husband is an exceptional person," said Suryono. "Too good a man, it seems, refusing to see our world how it really is— that whoever is honest goes under. Other people just go ahead."

"My husband doesn't want to accept reality."

As they were passing the electric power-station at Ancol beach, Suryono took Dahlia's hand. "Your hand is exquisite. And you are too, quite in keeping with your name. How lovely you are!"

"You're just fooling," said Dahlia, and as she smiled her eyes flashed coquettishly.

"What are we doing, going to Priok?" said Suryono suddenly. "If your husband isn't home, why not go to your place instead?"

"That would be impossible. We only have two rooms; it's much too crowded there, and people would see."

"A hotel in the city?" Suryono suggested.

"I'm afraid to go to a hotel. I've never gone to a hotel."

"Are you serious?"

"Yes," said Dahlia slowly, "but I do know of one place, on Petojo, the house of a woman I know called Aunty Bep."

Suryono swung the car round and headed back towards the city proper.

"And what's this place of Aunty Bep's like," said Suryono as they approached Petojo. "Is it nice? Where is it?"

Dahlia showed him the way until at last, in front of a good-sized house, she told him to stop. "This is her place," Dahlia said. "Aunty Bep is quite old and lives here all alone. She has a son, but he lives in Bandung, so on occasion she's willing to put up people she knows well." Dahlia added, "It's quiet here."

Dahlia knocked at the door and waited a moment until she heard the sound of heavy, shuffling steps inside.

The high voice of an old woman came from behind the door and said in Dutch, "Who is it?"

"It's me, Dahlia."

A small cry of delight came from voice inside, followed by the sound of the key turning in its lock.

An old woman opened the door. "Good morning, Dahlia! Come in!"

Suryono didn't seem to exist for her. She glanced at him only fleetingly, and when he said good morning, her response was very short, almost curt. After they were seated, Aunty Bep immediately left the room.

"Stay here a second," Dahlia said to Suryono as she rose and followed Aunty Bep. Left alone, Suryono looked around the sitting room. The furniture was old but well cared for. On the wall facing him hung a family portrait. In the center sat a young man, dressed in a Royal Netherlands Indies Army uniform with a sergeant major's insignia and wearing a plaited bamboo hat with a rim that was turned up at one side. Next to him sat a young woman and two small children, a boy and a girl. Suryono, attracted by the picture, stood up to examine it closer.

Just then Dahlia returned. Seeing Suryono inspecting the picture, she came up and stood close to him. "This is Aunty Bep and her husband and their children, before the war. Her husband is dead. The daughter disappeared during the revolution. The son works in Bandung."

Suryono inhaled the scent of Dahlia's perfume and felt the warmth of her body as it flowed into his own.

Dahlia drew him by his hand into an inner room and locked the door. The bedroom was very neat. The sheets on the bed were clean and white and freshly laid. In the corner stood a dressing table. Dahlia closed the window and quickly started to undress.

Suryono soaked in the sight with pleasure. "You really are beautiful!"

Sometime later Suryono loosed his embrace on Dahlia, rolled over to the edge of the bed, and reached for a cigarette on the bedside table. "Would you like one?"

She nodded.

He lit a cigarette, gave it to her, and then lit one for himself. Dahlia, rolling over, nestled her head between Suryono's shoulder and neck, and whispered, "You're so virile."

Suryono was quiet, feeling very pleased. He had chalked up numerous encounters since he had gone into business as an importer, but this time it was exceptionally good. Usually there would be preliminary haggling—always a financial negotiation to get through, which for him always spoiled the promised pleasure. He much preferred to pay more afterwards, provided the woman did not start by discussing prices as if she were nothing but a peddler. This time, from the very beginning, there had been not a single word about money. He had decided that he would give Dahlia the nice round sum of five hundred rupiah. But not yet, a little later. He had no desire to go home now. He would wait for it to get dark first.

"How long may we stay here?" he whispered to Dahlia.

"As long as we like."

"Then we'll stay until dark." But they didn't stay until dark. An hour later Suryono decided that he had spent enough time with Dahlia and suggested they go home.

When they had dressed, Suryono asked Dahlia how much he owed Aunty Bep.

"Fifty rupiah," she said.

Suryono took out a fifty-rupiah bill and handed it to Dahlia. As she moved to leave the room he held her back and took out five one-hundred-rupiah notes. "And this is for you."

Dahlia looked at him. "I'm not asking for money."

"Yes, I know. But do accept this." Suryono pressed the money into her hands.

Dahlia smiled and kissed him on the mouth. "You really are a sweet boy."

Suryono took Dahlia to her house; but when he asked when they would meet again, she said, "Well, now you know where my house is. Come and ask!"

Dahlia stood at the gate until Suryono's car disappeared around the street corner, and then hastened to her room.

"What a chic escort that was, and his car is quite new," called Hasnah as soon as Dahlia appeared on the verandah.

Dahlia smiled at her. "A new friend, Has!"

CITY BEAT

In a room of the dormitory for juvenile delinquents, Sung Chai-Yong, sixteen years of age, was signing a confession with an intent expression on his face. Witnessing his signature were the administrator of the welfare organization that ran the dormitory and several other people who worked there.

The statement read: "I, Sung Chai-Yong, aged sixteen, residing on Halimun Street, declare herewith in the presence of the Dormitory Administrator as follows: I had not attended school for five months; thereafter I attended a mechanic's school located on Spoor Lane, in Kemayoran, paying sixty rupiah a month. Then I left that school, too. I have some friends. One is Ali, thirty years old, who watches over bicycles at night outside the Roxy cinema. He says he's a member of the veterans' organization. I've known him one week. Another is Idrus, aged thirty-five, who lives in Jembatan Merah. He told me that he's a member of the military command in the city. Then there is O Bung, who is a locally-born Chinese, who lives in Jatinegara, and who works in Pasar Baru at a money exchange place. The last is Sapi'i, who lives in Mandur Lane and works as a night watchman. The four of them often ask me for money. Sapi'i once ordered me to steal money and things from my parents, and it was Sapi'i who sold them.

"I have stolen from my parents seven thousand rupiah in cash in the course of two months. I sold my father's Philips bicycle, which cost nine hundred rupiah, for four hundred. The money I divided with my friends, and we used it for gambling and for having fun. I also stole from my father a Parker fountain pen costing one hundred and sixty rupiah and sold it for ninety-five. I have stolen from his wardrobe seven pairs of woolen trousers and sold them at thirty-five rupiah each. A wristwatch I stole from home, I sold for only fifty rupiah. A pair of my father's sharkskin trousers I gave to Sapi'i to keep.

"I further state that at the age of ten I began to sleep with the street girls at Gambir Square and that I paid them ten rupiah a time. It was a friend who first invited me there. After the first time, I kept coming back with money stolen from my parents. The last time was when I slept with a woman O Bung introduced me to. That was on Sadar Lane, which used to be Hauber Lane, and I paid her twenty-five rupiah for a quarter of an hour. As the result I contracted a venereal disease and bubonic syphilis.

"Finally, I hereby state that I spent three months in the Pra Juwana Training Center for Boys in Tangerang because I stole a key to the warehouse of the Nyan Chan coffee-shop and then gave it to two *becak* drivers so that they could rob the place."

An administrator of the dormitory now spoke to Sung Chai-Yong. "Your father is applying to the government and the immigration authorities to obtain the permits necessary to send you to China. Until that time, you will reside here. I hope that you will not make trouble and will behave properly."

The young man looked at the administrator and burst into loud laughter.

August

Husin Limbara banged his fist on the table, his face purple, his voice choked with rage. "How did this happen? Here, read this!" He pushed a sheaf of newspapers on the table towards Raden Kaslan.

Raden Kaslan remained calm. He glanced meaningfully at Halim, chief editor of the daily, *Suluh Merdeka*.

"You might think this is humorous," Husin Limbara continued, "but what about our party's reputation?" He picked up one of the newspapers, obviously reluctant to read it again, but forcing himself to do so. "Look at this headline: 'Leaders of the Indonesia Party Enrich Themselves'." Then he read the body of the text:

> "According to a statement made by the Ministry of Economic Affairs, it has been acknowledged that the director of Cinta Hati import corporation is Mr Kusuma, a member of the Indonesia Party; the director of Barat Laut Corporation is Raden Sudibyo, and its vice-director Chong Eng Kouw. Raden Sudibyo is also a member of the Indonesia Party. The director of Timur Besar Corporation is Suryono Kaslan, the son of Raden Kaslan. Bahagia Corporation is headed by Madame Fatma who is the wife of Raden Kaslan, a member of the Indonesia Party. The director of Sumber Kita Corporation is Husin Limbara, general chairman of the Indonesia Party. As is already known, some time ago some members of the Indonesia Party established a bank with a board composed

of members of the party's executive council. This is how they enrich themselves."

Husin Limbara seethed. "This ruins our party's reputation. Your plan was all wrong."

"Calm down," Raden Kaslan urged. "It isn't the plan that's wrong. How many millions of rupiah have come into the party treasury during this time? Count them for yourself. Of course, it was going to be hard to keep this matter a secret for long, but we must counter this attack with one of our own. That's the reason I invited my friend Halim from our newspaper to discuss it. Turns out, he has an excellent suggestion."

Husin Limbara looked at Halim, who took a breath before speaking. "I have a great deal of experience in newspaper work and in how to influence public opinion. It's obvious that if we let the opposition newspapers get away with the disclosure of secrets in such a manner, our reputation will certainly suffer. But fire must be fought with fire. That's why we must counter-attack. I suggest that you, Husin, release information, at a general meeting and in interviews, that there are certain groups in our country who are stooges of foreign powers, and that these foreign powers have stored secret funds. Just name a sum—ten million dollars, fifty million dollars—anything will do. You should say 'certain groups'. That will be safest. People will automatically suspect the opposition groups. But we're not going to make any direct accusations naming the opposition groups we mean. Thus we'll be quite safe, and we'll be able to counter the accusations made against us."

Husin Limbara scrutinized Halim in silence at first, then, slowly, his face lit up as if the sun had broken through a cover of dark clouds. He stood up, swaying a little, grasped Halim's hand and pumped it as he clapped him on the shoulder. "You're a genius! That's a brilliant idea!"

Releasing Halim's hand, he rubbed his own and looked at Raden Kaslan. "Forgive me, but it's understandable that, as general chairman of the party, I think of the interests of the party first." He looked at one man and then the other. "From now on I shall trust you entirely."

He then sat down again.

Raden Kaslan coughed lightly, and Husin Limbara glanced at him. From previous meetings with the man, he knew only too well what that little cough portended: usually a demand for a higher percentage of profit from a special license because of greater risk or some other pretext.

"Yes?" Husin Limbara smiled at Raden Kaslan, knowing full well what was coming.

Raden Kaslan again coughed lightly. "This matter I speak of is actually one of minor consequence for the party, but of considerable importance for our friend Halim. And I'm speaking not on my own behalf, but for him. As you know, Halim here is, for all practical purposes, a member of our party, except that he doesn't hold a party card."

"Well, that's easily taken care of," Husin Limbara enthused, pleased that what was being talked about was merely a matter of a membership card, not a demand for a greater share in profits. "We can issue a membership card to Halim tomorrow!"

Raden Kaslan coughed again. "Excuse me, but you didn't permit me to finish. You got the wrong impression. What Halim proposes is that, in the best interests of our party's struggle, it may be advisable for him to stay out, to appear neutral. Isn't it right?"

"Ah, yes. Brilliant!" Husin Limbara agreed.

"As you know, a parliamentary seat recently opened up, that of Mr Hadiwibrata, who decided to retire. So, what we are thinking now is, how would it be if we proposed that Halim fill this seat?"

Husin Limbara clapped his hand on the table. "Brilliant! A stroke of genius! We can arrange this with the other government parties. Will you please excuse me now? I have an appointment with the minister." Husin Limbara rose to go, but when he heard another cough he sat down again.

"There's just one more thing," Raden Kaslan said, "and quite an easy matter. As you know, Halim's paper owns a printing plant and this plant took out a two-million-rupiah loan from Nusa Bank. But what newspaper is able to operate with a profit these days?" Raden Kaslan paused for effect. "This is no small loan we're talking about, and now the bank wants to foreclose. If the bank seizes the plant, we're going to lose the support of an important newspaper. Therefore I suggest that it would be desirable that the bank be persuaded to desist from pressing so hard."

"That can be arranged," Husin Limbara said summarily. "Don't worry, Halim. That matter can be taken care of."

Husin Limbara stood up again, shook hands with the overjoyed Halim, and then left, escorted outside by Raden Kaslan.

With the two men no longer in sight, Halim chuckled to himself. They think they can use me as their tool, he said to himself. Well, I will use them for my own ends.

Hearing footsteps in the hall outside, Halim immediately picked up a magazine from the table and pretended to be engrossed in it.

The door opened and Raden Kaslan came back inside. "The party owes you no little thanks," he said to Halim as he closed the door.

Halim looked up. "There's just one more small matter. The newspaper needs a little money, a bridging loan, only one hundred thousand rupiah for two or three weeks. Do you think you could help me with that?"

"Didn't we already help you secure a bank loan?" said Raden Kaslan.

"That was used for the purchase of machines and to pay off old debts. Now I need some money to buy newsprint and pay the workers. Just a personal loan. Of course, if it cannot be done, well, it doesn't matter, but…"

For a moment Halim looked fixedly and with significance at Raden Kaslan.

Raden Kaslan wanted to say something, wanted to refuse outright, but he stopped short, and after a moment's thought made an attempt to bargain: "It might be difficult to get hold of one hundred thousand rupiah now. If it were fifty thousand I might be able to swing it."

"Why must we haggle about this?" Halim said, irritated. "Wasn't it just last week that…" He stopped and looked at Raden Kaslan.

Raden Kaslan understood at once what Halim meant. The preceding week Halim had acted as go-between in the sale of a special license to a foreign company, a transaction that had netted Raden Kaslan not less than seven hundred and fifty thousand rupiah.

Raden Kaslan went to his desk, took out a checkbook from the drawer, and wrote out a check for one hundred thousand rupiah.

As he handed it to Halim, he made a strong effort to laugh, and to make it appear a hearty, open laugh, not a forced one.

"Here you are," he said. "With someone like you, Halim, it's hard to bargain."

"Thank you. And remember, it's only a loan."

Halim stood up, shook hands with Raden Kaslan, and stepped to the door. Then he turned round and, looking hard at Raden Kaslan, said, "Remember. With me there is no bargaining."

As Halim closed the door slowly behind him, an unpleasant feeling crept over Raden Kaslan. There was a great deal he didn't like about this Halim.

Halim smiled to himself as he read again the editorial he had just written for his newspaper:

> "The opposition party's tactic appears to be to never give the government a chance to resolve any of the problems the people face. Its only aim, it seems, is to cause the cabinet's downfall in order to fill the ministerial posts with its own people. Why are they so eager to undermine this cabinet, which has proven to be progressive, patriotic, and concerned with the people's wellbeing? In this regard, we would like to remind the readers of the speech made by Husin Limbara of the Indonesia Party, which indicated that certain leaders of the opposition are being bought by funds from a foreign country. We leave it to our readers to draw their own conclusions."

He called in one of the editors. "Here is the editorial for tomorrow. It must appear on the front page alongside the text of Limbara's speech. Give it a three-column headline: 'Certain Leaders Receive Bribes from a Foreign Country!'"

Halim wrote down the headline on a slip of paper and handed it to the editor.

The telephone on the table rang. Halim picked up the receiver: "Hello, *Suluh Merdeka*!.... Yes, this is Halim. Is that you, Limbara?.... How are you doing?.... So, what's the news?.... Really? That's incredible! I can hardly believe it! Really?! I've been appointed to be a member of parliament? You're not joking, are you?.... So, it's true? Well, many thanks!.... Yes, yes, we've started the offense. I've just written an editorial linking them with probable subversion from a foreign country.... No, no, it doesn't matter. We don't mention any names, but the public will know whom we mean.... Yes, quite an easy matter.... Thanks again!"

Halim replaced the receiver and rubbed his hands. Hmm. Member of parliament, he said to himself, satisfaction and pleasure written all over his face.

Suryono gazed at Dahlia, fast asleep at his side. He lit a cigarette and slowly inhaled the smoke. He was very pleased. They were resting in the bedroom at Aunty Bep's house. Since Dahlia had brought him there the first time, they had come back repeatedly, sometimes during the day, but occasionally at night as well. During the daytime, as at this moment, it was a particularly pleasant experience, he thought. Outside, the rain came down in streams, and Suryono let his thoughts drift. All kinds of memories came to his mind. He fleetingly recalled the women he had met while he was working at the Indonesian consulate's office in New York. Decidedly, Indonesian women win out, he thought, remembering his experiences with different American women. His thoughts then drifted to his stepmother.... But there was no comparison between her and Dahlia. Then for some reason he remembered his schooldays during the Japanese occupation and how furious he and his classmates had been when the Japanese ordered their heads shaved. He thought of the time when he joined PETA, the "Defenders of the Homeland" paramilitary organization that the Japanese had established, and how he had trained to be a section commander: a *shodancho*, as they were called. Then came the proclamation of independence on August 17, 1945, and his division had been assimilated into the Indonesian National Army. But his division had remained based in Yogyakarta and he had never really fought. When the Dutch occupied Yogya he had discarded his military uniform and remained in town, where he helped friends who were constantly sneaking into and out of the city. But he hadn't done much, really, always haunted by fear of arrest. And later Yogya was surrendered by the Dutch to the Republic. President Sukarno and Vice-President Hatta returned to Yogya. In the confusion of the first week, he managed to secure work with the ministry of foreign affairs. He had managed to create the impression that he was a much-deserving ex-guerilla. Later, in Jakarta, he was given the chance to attend the foreign service academy, and at the first opportunity he was sent out to work abroad.

Suryono extinguished the stub of his cigarette in the small plate on the adjoining table. He reached out for his trousers hanging on a chair near the bed and got out his wallet. The weight of the wallet in his hand filled him with pleasure. What a good life this is, he thought: plenty of money, plenty of women, and no worries. What else could one wish for?

He suddenly thought of Ies, or "Iesye" as he more often called her, with the affectionate Dutch diminutive attached to her name. Should I ever want to marry, I'll marry Iesye, he said to himself. Then an uneasy feeling crept in: Iesye will never agree to let me play around with Dahlia and other women. Well, forget that idea! But, but.... Suryono stopped short in his musings. There was something in Ies that challenged him. Was it because she was not easy to get, or was it because she put him on the defensive? There was something about Ies that made him want to overcome her. But soon the disturbing thoughts about Ies were pushed away. He took out two five-hundred-rupiah notes from his wallet, placed them under the little plate which had served as ashtray, and returned the wallet to the hip-pocket of his trousers.

Outside, the rain poured harder, and Suryono turned over towards Dahlia, who was still asleep. He awakened her.

"Come on, it's time to go home. It's already dark out."

Dahlia stretched and opened her eyes. She threw her arms around Suryono's neck and pulled him down towards her.

Suryono's protested faintly. "But after this, we have to go home. I have a meeting to attend."

"I'm so hungry I could faint!" said Saimun to Itam as they got off the garbage truck.

Itam joined in complaint: "I'm broke and we don't get paid until the day after tomorrow!"

"Go home, you two. It's raining," shouted the driver Miun.

"How about we try Ibu Yom," said Itam.

Saimun shook his head. "She's not going let us eat on credit. We haven't paid for last week."

"We can at least try."

Saimun was doubtful. "We'll get nothing from her but abuse."

"So what's the harm of abuse?"

Because of the rain, Ibu Yom had moved her portable food stall across the railway line, to wait out the weather under the tent-like awning of a semi-permanent *warung* stall. Right now it was empty of customers. No one was seated on the small benches that Ibu Yom owned either.

Her eyes were sharp and cold as she saw Itam and Saimun approaching. "Here to pay what you owe me?"

Itam and Saimun looked around before Saimun spoke: "We haven't got paid yet."

"So, you want another handout? Is that it?"

"Come on, we're hungry!"

Staring coldly at the two men, the old woman told them to sit down and then filled two plates with rice, adding to each a ladle of vegetable broth.

"All you two know is credit," Ibu Yom muttered.

Neither of the men replied; they ate voraciously. After eating a few spoonfuls, Itam began to praise Ibu Yom—for the goodness of her heart, for her attractive appearance, and her excellent cooking.

Gradually the old woman's resentment mellowed, and from a tin she poured them each a cup of coffee.

"No other place would do this for you," she grumbled. "No one else would give you the time of day."

"But not if her name is Ibu Yom!" Saimun called out. "Is there another Ibu Yom in Jakarta?"

"She's the one and only!" said Itam.

"You boys, why don't you look for some other kind of work?" said Ibu Yom.

"I am," Saimun declared. "I'm learning how to drive and when I can, I'm going to be a taxi or *oplet* driver."

"And I'm going to work with Saimun," Itam added.

"Why don't you look for indoor work?" asked Ibu Yom.

"What, like in an office?" said Itam. "What office people are going to want a garbage man, ma'am?"

"That's right," said Saimun. "Office people don't want to know our kind, not even the office boys who work for them. Even if we made the same money as them, they still wouldn't want to know us."

Itam prodded Saimun. "This rain isn't going to stop. Let's just go home."

The two young men rose and hurried out into the rain.

"Look at me," said Saimun. "My body is getting weaker. The hunger makes my stomach burn. That wasn't enough rice, but I was afraid to ask for more."

"Same here," Itam agreed. Then he said, "I wish Neneng were still around,"

"Me, too. I wish she hadn't gone."

"Yeah, and living with Uwak Salim in Kaligot! I saw her once. She was all dressed up, with new clothes on her back, powder on her cheeks, and lipstick, too, but it was like she didn't want to see me."

Saimun said nothing. Ever since Neneng left their hut to go to Kaligot and turn professional, he felt as if he were lost. It wasn't clear to him just what it was that he missed, but it was as if Neneng had left a great emptiness in him. There was nothing to go home to—as if now it didn't matter where he slept. He felt grieved to have been abandoned just like that, without even a farewell. Yet, had

Neneng spoken to him, asked his permission to go, he didn't know what he would have done. All he knew was that he now felt joyless.

Vaguely, somewhere in him, causing confusion in his mind, there floated visions of a future life with Neneng, and somewhere too, the crying of a little baby. A small house, a small plot of ground, he and Neneng. But all that was over now.

Suddenly Saimun was rattled into wakefulness by the frantic honking of a car horn behind him. Brakes screeched on the wet asphalt. He felt Itam's strong push, which threw him to the side of the street. He felt the impact of his ribs hitting the pavement, knocking the breath out of him. Tears spurted from his eyes and he heard a loud voice cursing him: "Hey, you fool! Want to be killed? Watch where you're going, you idiot!"

Then there was the sound of the accelerating motor, and a beautiful car swiftly receded into the rain. He was drenched with water spattered by the wheels.

Itam quickly helped him to his feet. "What were you dreaming about? It's lucky I pushed you out of the way."

Saimun stood there, not knowing what to think as his eyes followed the diminishing form of the car in the distance.

In the car Suryono drew Dahlia's body closer to himself and said, "What a yokel! He could of have been killed, doesn't even know how to walk. How's this country ever going to make progress with people like that?"

Dahlia giggled and laced her arm around Suryono's waist.

"So, it's twenty-five thousand rupiah?" Sugeng asked Said Abdul Gafur after inspecting a small house on Probolinggo Street. "And the housing permit has been cleared?"

"The housing permit will be in order. Don't worry."

"I'll pay when I have it in hand," said Sugeng.

"That's fine. Once the permit is assured and the key is in your hands, then you can make payment," said the old Arab. "Why shouldn't I trust a ministry official?"

A Dutchman came out from the house and walked towards the pair.

"When may I move in?" Sugeng immediately asked the man.

"I leave on the *MS Oranje* on August tenth," he replied. "I will make the arrangements. I'll come and bring you the key. Meanwhile, I'll have some people occupy the place so nobody can seize it."

Sugeng thanked the Dutchman and climbed into a waiting car.

In the car the Arab said to Sugeng, "So, now that I'm helping you, I hope that you will help me. For helping to arrange for that import license at your office, you'll get a cut of forty thousand rupiah. Of that amount, we have to set aside twenty-five a finder's fee for my friend who owns the house. We also have to give a kickback to the Dutchman who was renting the house and, on top of that, something for the official at the Jakarta housing bureau who cleared the housing permit for you. You understand all that, I assume."

"Yes, I understand," Sugeng said, beginning to understand the complexity of making shady operations look legitimate. "What I need is to get the house now."

"Don't worry. The permit is in order. You may come to the office tomorrow and get it."

When the car stopped in front of Sugeng's house, the old Arab took Sugeng's hand and shook it repeatedly. "Please excuse me, sir. I'll not get out. It's raining and it's about time for evening prayers."

"All right. Many thanks. Just see to it that nothing goes wrong."

"Good heavens, don't worry. Rest assured, I guarantee that everything is clear."

Sugeng ran lightly across the grounds in front of his home. As he approached the verandah he noticed Dahlia standing outside the door to her room.

"Get caught in the rain?" she called.

"Looks like you did, too. You're wet!" Sugeng countered.

"Yes, I just came in."

Sugeng stepped onto his side of the verandah and hastened inside. There, Hasnah was sitting in a chair sewing baby clothes.

Sugeng went to her quickly, embraced her, and whispered, "We're moving on the tenth! I found a house for you."

Hasnah faced filled with joy. "Really?"

"Yes, really."

"How did you manage to find one?"

"From the housing bureau! The permit is cleared. I got it from the office."

"You see? If only one persists, and does everything necessary the right way, one cannot fail to get it."

Hasnah drew Sugeng close to herself and whispered, "I love you."

Sugeng felt as though he were choking and as if his body were suddenly drained of strength. This was the first time he had lied to Hasnah; there had been no secrets between them before.

Hasnah sensed something was wrong. "What is it?"

Sugeng forced a smile and put his arm around Hasnah's shoulders. "Nothing. I'm just relieved that we've finally got a house at last." To himself he swore that this would be the one and only time that he would engage in corruption. Never again.

He embraced and kissed Hasnah with such passion that she was startled and cried out: "Ow! Careful of my belly! You're naughty, that's what you are."

"Sorry for being late," Suryono said to the group as he entered Pranoto's house, interrupting the meeting that was already in progress. He took a seat next to Ies and murmured, "Hello."

Murhalim, who had been talking, waved to Suryono and said to the others: "And now, after this brief interruption caused by the arrival of our highly esteemed friend Suryono, may I continue with what I have to say?"

"It might be good to recapitulate what you've said so far, so that Suryono can follow the discussion fully," Pranoto suggested.

"No need for that," said Suryono with a smile. "Pick up where you left off."

Murhalim continued immediately. "The problem confronting us in our relationship with Europe is this: which of Europe's basic values we should accept, and which to reject? This question is obviously not new, and one that our people have been facing a long time. Also, it is not exclusively an Indonesian problem, but one that confronts all Asian peoples. We may take as an example the case of the Japanese. As we know, the Japanese learned the secrets of Western technology, and used them to build up their own nation.

"Pranoto once wrote that before we will ever be able to utilize Western technology our people must first undergo a psychological change. For example, take our Indonesian fishing community: you can't give them modern equipment, such as motorized boats and so forth, before there takes place an entire change in their belief systems. Only then will they be able to make full use of it. So, for instance, there is one fishing village where, I understand, there are strict taboos connected with their fishing gear, which is still very primitive. But the advent of engines and all sorts of modern appliances, which will overcome the problems of a tropical climate, will change all this. Their whole way of life must be changed to conform to the acceptance and utilization of this European technology.

"Similarly, the expansion of industry, with the use of machines in factories, in mines, in transportation equipment, on land, at sea and in the air, in the offices of the government and in private enterprise, all this brings new values into the life of Indonesian society. The question of the spiritual values that underlie this technology is complicated. To state it again: should Indonesian life be made to conform to this new technological sphere, or should the technology from Europe be made to harmonize with the Indonesian spirit? These are the questions which arise, and it is my hope that we can discuss them tonight."

Pranoto gestured to Murhalim. "May I be permitted to say a few words first? Since you just referred to something I once wrote, I would like to explain that when I wrote that the spiritual life of the people must change in order to receive European technology, I didn't mean it as an absolute condition. More precisely, I meant to indicate that if we wish to preserve harmony in our society, the acceptance of technology makes a change in the people's mentality inevitable."

"I'm baffled," Suryono interjected. "Why do we worry about whether or not to accept European values? Considering the developments in the world today, it makes little sense to toss around the problem of ourselves and Europe. It would be more to the point, in my opinion, to discuss the problem of ourselves and the United States, or our problems vis-à-vis communism as represented by the Soviet Union and the People's Republic of China. As a matter of fact, the perpetuation of Europe's civilization depends on American help. Therefore this discussion is just meandering and is quite useless. I suggest that we undertake a study of ourselves in relation to the US, and ourselves in relation to communism."

Murhalim now spoke up: "Seeing that Suryono and I disagree so greatly, there would be little use of my trying to convince him of the importance of discussing our relationship with Europe."

Achmad now cut in: "I agree with Suryono. The situation in the world today makes it impossible for us to consider problems of our relationships with only one part of the world. Moreover, what do we really mean by Europe? Today Europe is no longer the Europe of before the Second World War, the Europe that left such a strong influence in Asia. If we want to look at our problems, the problems of ourselves in relation to the world—and I think that only in this context are they worth considering: our country, and ourselves, and the world—then all this confusion, all the complications will be cleared up if only we apply the principles of Marxism. If we are willing to adhere to historical materialism our problems can be quickly solved. Marx has demonstrated the historical initiative of the masses. Read Lenin's book about Marx, Engels, and Marxism."

"And that is where we go wrong!" Pranoto was quick to say. "If you continue to expound ideas based on communist practices in Russia, our debate will never end. As I see it, all of us here have assembled as supporters of the concept of democracy, and we reject a totalitarian system, whether it be fascism or communism, as a method for building up our nation and assuring its progress."

Achmad's face was distorted with anger as he stared at Pranoto. He stood and looked at each of his friends in turn. His voice trembled as he spoke. "I greatly regret what you just said, Pranoto, because to me it means closing the door to my further participation in this study club. If every time I want to express my opinions you all immediately brand communism as evil and unacceptable, then what's the use of my attending these discussions? I've seen it for some time. These meetings make no sense. You keep talking here one night after another, but what are you doing? This is the difference between you and people of my mindset. I am indeed a follower of Marx and Lenin. But, in addition to theorizing, we also work. We go to the worker and the farmer, the very people you say you want to protect but whom you do not even know. We are convinced that we must win. We are convinced that we are right. Even now, you don't know where you stand or what you should be doing. So, with that, I bid you all farewell."

Pranoto quickly rose and grasped Achmad's hand. "Forgive me if anything I've said has hurt your feelings. I never meant to offend you. If we must part, let's part in friendship. You have your convictions, but I have my convictions, too. In my view every advance of man should be attained only by means of, and on the principles of, democracy. This is, of course, a difficult and probably a slow way, yet we are convinced that it's the only way to ensure freedom and human happiness."

Achmad looked at Pranoto, and in the end their longstanding friendship triumphed as he shook Pranoto's hand. Then he shook hands with his other friends and quickly departed.

After Achmad left the other members of the group sat staring, until Pranoto finally broke the silence: "Do you think Achmad was angry?"

"Not really angry," Murhalim posed. "He is now active in a workers' organization, and actually was only waiting for an excuse to get out of our discussion group. It's not likely that he would be angered merely by what you said. We've had much more bitter debates before, and nothing happened then. I think he's received orders to leave our club."

CITY BEAT

Abu jumped slightly when Mandur Kasir, who was busy lighting an oil lamp on the wall, said to him, "Please, sit down. My wife is busy with the child in the bath." And he felt even more disconcerted when he was then left sitting alone in the room with its windows open and doors ajar. Outside twilight was descending, but the blue of the sky was still visible. His eyes roved wildly around the room: a room with plaited bamboo walls pasted over with old newspapers; an old mat on the brick floor; a bamboo sleeping-bench with a thin mattress on it; the worn rattan chair in which he sat; a table to eat on with four dilapidated chairs. There was a cupboard with one of its doors open, and inside only a few tin plates, the other shelves empty.

From the back of the house he heard Mandur Kasir talking to his wife, and the voice of a woman answering, and then the cheerful cries of a child splashing in water. And he felt increasingly uneasy in this room with its windows and doors wide open, not locked.

He stepped over to the window and looked outside, feeling very odd. At that moment he heard his host's footsteps and, once again, was startled by the sound of the man's voice: "Please, Abu, sit down. We'll have some tea. My wife will come in a few minutes." For some reason, he felt guilty to be standing there at the open window.

Abu sat down at the table with Mandur Kasir, who poured hot tea into cups, carefully spooning out some sugar from an old butter tin. The two of them sipped their tea in silence. Abu didn't know how to open the conversation, so he remained sitting there quietly, holding his cup of hot tea with both hands.

Finally, it was Mandur Kasir who spoke. "You may sleep here tonight. Tomorrow morning I'll take you to the station. There's no need to be afraid any more. What's past is past."

Mandur Kasir's wife appeared carrying a baby about a year old, and Mandur Kasir introduced her to Abu. He rose to his feet awkwardly, facing the woman who stretched out her hand to him. He didn't know what to say when she excused their poor home. What could he say? The place where he had stayed for the last twenty years could not be compared at all with this room at Mandur Kasir's.

Saying nothing more, Mandur Kasir's wife went to the kitchen to prepare food. Then, a few moments later, Mandur Kasir went out to join his wife in the kitchen and he was again left alone in the room. He sat quietly, holding his warm and now almost empty cup of tea.

In the kitchen Mandur Kasir chastised his wife: "Maybe you didn't mean to, but you humiliated the man. Apologizing to him about the state of the room. Don't you know that he spent the last twenty years of his life in prison?"

Mandur Kasir's wife sighed.

"He just got out of prison this morning. He'll be going back to his village in Kediri, but because of a delay with his papers, he can't leave until tomorrow. I felt sorry for him and have invited him to stay overnight with us. Tomorrow morning I'll see him to the station."

Mandur Kasir's wife looked at her husband in fright.

"Don't be afraid. I've known him for the last eight years," her husband said. "He never made any trouble in prison. Just worked quietly. He was sentenced for having killed a man twenty years ago. Why he killed him I don't know. But if it will make you feel less afraid, I'll sleep in the outside room with him, and you may lock the door of the bedroom from inside."

When Mandur Kasir came back to the front room, he saw Abu tilting one of the rickety dining chairs.

"That chair really does need to be repaired," said Mandur Kasir. "I'll get a hammer and some nails." He then went to the cupboard and took out a hammer and a box of nails.

"I'll do that for you," Abu quietly offered.

Mandur Kasir glanced at him, then handed him the hammer and nails. Abu quickly went to work repairing the wobbly chair. When that was done, he tackled in turn the three other chairs, so that by the time he had finished repairing the fourth one Mandur Kasir's wife had finished heating the vegetable broth in the kitchen and had come in to set the food on the table.

Abu put away the hammer and nails, setting them against the wall near the cupboard.

After the meal he sat on the *balai* watching Mandur Kasir perform the prescribed *magrib* prayers. Later still, he watched his host perform *Isa* prayers, the fifth and final prayers of the day. After that Mandur Kasir went into the bedroom and he could hear the sound of whispering.

When Mandur Kasir returned to the room, he was carrying a rolled-up mat and sarong. "If you want to go to sleep, Abu, these are for you."

Abu took the mat and the sarong and spread the mat on the floor near the cupboard. Mandur Kasir stretched out on the *balai*. Abu rolled himself a palm-leaf cigarette, and Mandur Kasir lit his pipe. They both smoked in silence, while in the adjoining room Mandur Kasir's baby cried from time to time, was soothed by his mother, and finally fell asleep. Gradually the noises around them in the other houses subsided. From afar came the sound of a radio playing the melancholy tunes of Sundanese lute music.

"What will you do when you are back in your village?" Mandur Kasir suddenly asked.

The question startled Abu. How could he answer it? It was impossible for him to think up an answer to such a question. He didn't know what he would do when he was back in his village. For twenty years he had never had to think about what to do next, now, or tomorrow, so that he'd long lost the ability to think for himself. Since his release that morning, he had been completely bewildered. He had killed a man when he was thirty, although he didn't clearly remember his age when he killed the man, and even the reason he had killed him was now dimmed in his memory. All he knew was that he had spent a very long time in prison, until his hair had turned grey and his body had become lean, the body of an old man who had always done hard work, with the leanness of body which hides strength.

Because he could not find an answer, and because he felt upset by Mandur Kasir's question, his voice was abrupt and sounded indifferent when he answered: "Who knows? I don't!"

The curt sound of Abu's voice caused Mandur Kasir to turn and look at him, but Abu had lowered his face, his eyes fixed on the hammer and the box of nails near the wall.

After a few minutes Mandur Kasir spoke again: "Whatever you do, don't kill anyone again. You don't want to go back to prison." Then he turned down the flame of the lamp and lay back to sleep, pulling his sarong over his head to protect himself from mosquitoes.

The former prisoner stared at the wall. His open, unblinking eyes followed the images that floated past them. Mandur Kasir's question had increased his anxiety in his new freedom, and the darkness around him felt full of danger. In prison he had felt calm and secure. Behind the iron bars everything was decided for him. But a window one could open oneself, a door that was not locked for him, the freedom given to him after twenty years of regulated life...? Now, tossed out into the world outside the prison walls, he felt as if he had lost firm ground, as if he were naked. His hand moved towards the hammer; grasping it, he turned around to look at Mandur Kasir who was already asleep, snoring. If I kill him, I'll be back in prison. It buzzed in his brain, and he got up cautiously, approached Mandur Kasir and raised the hammer. Then something seemed to explode in his brain. He lowered his hand. He felt dizzy and confused.

When the door to the bedroom suddenly opened, Abu stepped back towards his mat.

Mandur Kasir's wife came out of the room with her baby in her arms. "Everybody is already asleep, and here he soils himself again..." Suddenly she saw in the dimness of the half-dark room that she was not addressing her husband, and she stopped. She caught sight of the hammer in Abu's hand, and she cried out. The sound filled Abu with terror.

He leapt towards her, clamping his hand over the woman's mouth. She pushed him away. As they struggled, the baby began to cry. The ex-convict brought down the hammer on the skull of Mandur Kasir's wife. Stunned, she fell to the floor. The baby, loosed from her arm, fell on the floor, screaming. Abu jumped on the baby. Again he swung the hammer. The baby was still, its head crushed.

Mandur Kasir, shocked out of sleep, yelled, and in one leap the ex-convict was near him, swinging the hammer again.

"You're mad!" Mandur Kasir screamed.

The hammer smashed into his head and Mandur Kasir collapsed near the wall and slid down, blood streaming from his broken skull.

Again, all was still again in the house, the only audible sound being the heavy breathing of the ex-convict in the dimness of the room.

Abu looked around: at Mandur Kasir, whose head was crushed; at the baby whose head was crushed; at the woman whose head was crushed; and at the blood-smeared hammer in his hand. Suddenly he hurled the hammer against the wall and ran to the door. He pushed it and it opened wide. Startled, he fell back a step and howled with terror, then burst into laughter.

September

Halim whistled softly in the bathroom. He was in high spirits. Standing before the mirror, he shaved his moustache, glancing from time to time at some neatly typed sheets laid out on the little table near the mirror. Then, turning back to the mirror, he rehearsed the speech he was going to deliver that night in parliament.

At certain passages of his address, he laughed aloud into the mirror. "There are a number of people these days who make special efforts to show that they are genuine nationalists," he declaimed, assuming a lofty pose. "And so it was, quite recently, that our fellow parliamentarian, de Vries, arrived in parliament wearing a sarong and announced that he had donned this sarong as proof of his true nationalism. Could anything be funnier? If a monkey puts on a sarong and claims to be human, are we to believe him?"

Halim paused and looked into the mirror. Here they'll certainly burst into laughter and applaud, he thought. And again he chuckled. His high spirits were occasioned not only by the prospect of addressing parliament that evening. Just before he went into the bathroom, a telephone call from the bank had informed him that his application for a two-million-rupiah loan, to expand the printing plant of his newspaper, had been approved.

He spoke to his image in the mirror. "And they think that they will be able to use you. But you're going to use them for your own ends."

His radiant mood was clouded over for a moment as he recalled the argument he had had the previous night with his wife on the same subject. She had told him that a lot of people were beginning to talk, saying that he had sold himself. Naturally, he had denied this charge, quite heatedly, and asserted that it was he who was using the politicians. Those people who talk are just envious; don't pay any attention to them, he had advised his wife.

Thinking of his wife, Halim smiled. He remembered how a few weeks ago, before he was appointed to parliament, his wife had told him about a *jalangkung*—a kind of Chinese puppet which, when manipulated by children, can be used to conjure up ancestral spirits for the purpose of seeking their advice. Hearing of such a puppet that was owned by a Chinese family in Jatinegara, she and four of her friends had gone to the family's home to witness the sight for themselves.

According to his wife, the ancestral spirit of the little girls who manipulated the *jalangkung* had indeed manifested itself. And when his wife had asked the spirit whether her husband would become a member of parliament, the *jalangkung* had immediately nodded in affirmation. And now, here he was: a member of parliament! Halim wasn't usually superstitious, but in this instance he wavered. After all, hadn't the prediction come true?

His wife believed strongly in the *jalangkung* and in shaman in general. According to his wife, her friend Mrs Suroto had gone to the *jalangkung* in Jatinegara six months previously to ask whether her husband would be made British ambassador. The venerable *jalangkung* had nodded and, true enough, three months later, Mr Suroto was appointed ambassador and sent by the government to London.

Halim cautiously guided the razor, especially near the scar on his left cheek. He had got it when he was only eighteen months old; he had fallen off a ladder and his cheek had been cut open by a sharp stone on the ground. After the revolution, however, this scar had come to stand for a wound he had sustained while fighting for national independence.

The story of how he had been wounded got its start when a foreign correspondent had interviewed him. "Did you get that scar during the revolution?" the journalist had asked. And even though Halim had told him straight out that such was not the case, when the correspondent published his article he described meeting an important and influential Indonesian newspaper man who had been wounded during the revolution.

Sometime later, after the article's publication, one of his friends who had read the article asked about the wound.

"It's nothing," Halim had said, dismissively. But that didn't stop the talk, and now there were many people who believed that he had received the wound while fighting in the revolution, even though no one knew precisely in which of the battles Halim had been wounded.

Halim laughed again at his face in the mirror while his fingers stroked the scar. A little lie has its uses, too, he remarked to himself. It can make people respectful and a bit different towards you.

He washed his face and took a quick bath. As he rubbed his body with the towel he read his speech, and then rehearsed it again, watching himself in the mirror.

Udin, Hermanto, and Bambang had been waiting for fifteen minutes in the office of the All-Indonesia Dockworkers Union at Tanjung Priok. Three days earlier they had sent in a complaint to the central committee demanding that the union take action to alleviate the workers' conditions. For many months now their wages had been insufficient to cover the ever-rising costs of living. In the beginning the union leadership told them to be patient, that the government was busy launching programs to improve the people's welfare, and that demands for pay increases at this time would in no way improve the workers' living conditions. Even worse, if the wages were raised the prices for goods would also go up, and the workers themselves would be the first to suffer. Therefore the correct thing to do would be to urge the government to force the prices down.

Six months had gone by since the leadership had issued this communiqué to the workers. Yet during this period the prices, far from going down, had actually shot up higher than ever. And now in the last week the workers again had started to press for action.

"How can they keep ordering us to pacify our people," said Bambang, "especially when the other unions continue to press for better wages? Many of our members have already joined other unions. If we continue our present policies we're sure to lose."

"Let's hear what the leadership has to say first," Udin advised. "They're going to send Achmad down to talk things over with us."

"Speaking for myself, I'm with the majority on this," said Hermanto. "If they feel dissatisfied with the present leaders who support the cabinet, while the government pays no attention to the people's welfare, then I'll go along. We should get out of this union and take our members to some other union that really fights for the workers' interests."

Udin cut in: "You mustn't speak that way. The leadership would be very angry to hear you talk like that. Aren't we supposed to trust and obey the leaders?"

"Obey them?" said Hermanto. "How can we tell a hungry and suffering worker to keep on obeying?"

They heard the sound of approaching steps; then the door opened and Achmad came in. The three men rose to greet him.

Achmad greeted them each in turn. "Forgive me for being late. The train I was on was shunted about for ages in front of the station near the harbor entrance, which delayed me by half an hour."

The four of them settled round the table. Bambang, who acted as secretary of the Tanjung Priok Harbor branch of the All-Indonesia Dockworkers Union, opened his briefcase and handed

Achmad a sheaf of papers. "This is a copy of the report that I sent to the central committee."

"Yes, we received it and examined it," said Achmad. "The important question now is how to retain the trust and loyalty of the workers. It looks as if some of you have already lost faith in the party." Achmad looked sharply at Hermanto. "This spirit of defeatism is not permissible. We are in the middle of a struggle to crush capitalism and colonialism, and the reactionaries still have many stooges among our own people, plotting with the foreign capitalists."

"The question is not one of disloyalty to the party," Hermanto said at once. He was a quick-tempered man. He could work tirelessly if he believed in the job to be done, but his anger could be aroused with equal intensity if he felt he was being cheated. "How can we keep telling the workers to be patient? How can we tell them that to go on strike at this time would harm the government now in power, and that this government is really progressive and genuinely concerned about the people's welfare? How can the workers believe us, when they cope every day with wages that aren't enough to cover their daily needs? And the prices for food, clothing, and cooking fuel keep going up?"

Achmad now spoke with exaggerated patience. "We understand the difficulties of the leaders on your level, who are in direct contact with the workers. Nevertheless, the question is one of conviction—whether you can convince the workers to remain loyal and to support our struggle. It has been stressed by the party, time and again, that the present government is more progressive than any other government Indonesia has ever had. We are not blind, of course, to some aspects of the government's policies that are not beneficial for the people. But, for the sake of our party's growth, we must continue to support this cabinet. Although we do not agree with their economic and financial policies, we intend to try to correct this soon."

"In other words," said Hermanto pointedly, "for the sake of expanding the party's power, you order us to sacrifice the workers' welfare?"

Achmad gave Hermanto a long, sharp look. It flashed through his mind that Hermanto had been tainted. He would have to very careful with the man. Hermanto could very well betray the party. He would have to be reported.

"You take the wrong view of the problem," Achmad told him. He immediately decided to change his tactics in talking with Hermanto. Pushing him won't work, he thought. "We have no intention at all to sacrifice the welfare of the working people. To the contrary: the party is working day and night trying to improve the workers' lot. We do not want to strike now, or support those strikes which are promoted by unions dominated by the reactionaries, because we know that there are other ways to improve the workers' condition."

"What ways?" pressed Hermanto.

Hermanto's blood was beginning to boil. This party man has it easy, he thought. All he does is talk. He never has to meet the workers face to face. People like him can't do anything but dish up theories. But can you feed a worker, or clothe him, with theories?

Achmad looked at Hermanto, then at Bambang, and then at Udin. Hermanto was indeed a stubborn fellow, he said to himself. His voice betrayed his impatience with Hermanto's question: "We must have complete and absolute faith in the leadership of the party. Only the party understands and can lead the struggle of the proletariat correctly."

Hermanto could no longer contain his pent-up resentment. "From the time I entered the party I have given all my strength, working day and night, to fight for the workers' interests. Time and again, I have been arrested and accused of agitating when we engaged in large-scale strikes under previous cabinets. And it was always the party that gave us orders to do so, because it was for defending the workers' cause. At present the plight of the workers is even worse than it was during previous cabinets. The workers ask us for leadership in taking action, to demand improvement of their plight. And the party says this is not permitted; that the workers must continue to be patient and must not make demands through strikes. This I do not understand. Are the workers here for the party, or is the party here for the workers?"

Hermanto glanced round him, and then looked intently at Bambang and Udin. "You have heard the workers' bitter complaints yourselves. The three of us have often discussed them and agreed that we should urge the party to take swift action to improve these conditions. Isn't that so?"

For a moment Udin and Bambang just gazed at Hermanto in silence. Then they glanced at Achmad and turned their faces away from Hermanto without saying a word.

Hermanto looked at them in astonishment. He had never seen his two friends act so strangely before. "Why are you both silent? Why don't you say anything?"

Achmad said nothing, continuing to stare silently at Hermanto. Into the room where the four of them sat, something mysterious and uncanny seemed to have crept, permeating the room with a chilly darkness. For an instant Hermanto felt as though he were in a remote and eerie world, that he was sitting there with strange creatures, scarcely human beings at all.

Hermanto was still for a moment, trying to disentangle his bewilderment. Then, in a rush, he was swept by anger. "Why don't you speak up? So you're afraid to talk? Isn't it true what I said?"

Udin and Bambang still said nothing, and then Achmad cleared his throat. "Hermanto! It seems to me that Bambang and Udin feel that our party's policy is the correct one and that they don't want to say anything so as not to embarrass you any further. I advise you to re-examine both your ideas and your attitude. If you persist in thinking as you do now, you are certain to become the victim of the reactionaries."

Hermanto looked at Achmad in amazement, and then at Udin and Bambang. His mind raced. Why have they become like this? Why are they afraid? Are they right, perhaps, and I am wrong? But his anger got the better of him. He rose to his feet and pounded the table, his eyes glowing.

"Now I see what the party's game has been all this time. In order to advance the party, the workers' wellbeing is sacrificed. This means that the working class exists for the party, and not the party for the working class!"

Achmad spoke with a sigh: "Comrade, you've got it all wrong again." Achmad had decided to recommend that Hermanto be ousted from the union leadership as soon as possible. He was too dangerous. He had all these ideas of his own; he was undisciplined and he did not trust the party. "The party exists for the workers, the peasants, the whole people. But the party can help the people only if the party is in power. In order to attain power, the party must be big and strong. That's why this phase is one of building up the party. And shouldn't we expect everyone to join forces to build up the party, the working class included?"

"All very nice words," Hermanto spat. "But is it true? When the party gets into power, won't the workers just become its tools?'

Achmad banged the table. "Those are treasonable words! How can you talk this way? I propose that we stop this argument and discuss the report on the workers' demands sent to the party."

Hermanto stood defiantly. "I'm not participating. I will not go on misleading the workers!" He stamped out of the room, slamming the door behind him.

Udin half rose to call him back, but Achmad gave him a sign to let Hermanto go. Through the window they could see him walking hurriedly towards the highway.

Achmad took a handkerchief out of his trouser pocket and wiped his face. "Hermanto has gone astray. He has no loyalty."

"You ought to be careful with him," Bambang advised. "He has a very strong influence among the dockworkers."

"Then I am asking the two of you to watch his activities carefully," said Achmad. "If necessary we will take special steps to break Hermanto. But now, let's return to the workers' complaints. Here you have to emphasize—and these are party orders—that a strike is the very thing that the reactionaries, the capitalists, and the imperialists want to happen at this point in time. We can't let ourselves be trapped or misled by these forces. The workers must be persuaded that if they go on strike, or support striking before the party has given its assent, it will mean that they themselves are lending support to the enemies of the Indonesian people, that clique of reactionaries, capitalists and imperialists. These are your orders, comrades!"

Achmad stood and took two envelopes from his pocket and gave them to Udin and Bambang.

"As deserving activists of the party, you both are again entitled to the party's support. You will find inside two hundred rupiah for each of you."

Udin and Bambang expressed their thanks and promised to execute the party's orders to the best of their ability.

When he was at the door, ready to leave the room, Achmad turned and said, "And watch that Hermanto."

Raden Kaslan, Husin Limbara, and Suryono sat at a table in the corner of the Capitol restaurant. A waiter came to their table with beer. Raden Kaslan glanced at his wristwatch and then turned to Suryono.

"Does Halim know we're all meeting here at twelve noon?"

"He knows. I telephoned him myself."

Husin Limbara raised his head and smiled at a figure walking towards them. "Here comes one of them now."

Sugeng appeared and approached their table. Husin Limbara, remaining seated, introduced him to Raden Kaslan and Suryono. "This is Sugeng, from the ministry of economic affairs. He recently joined our party and is now actively participating in our program."

When Sugeng was seated, Raden Kaslan turned to him. "Would you like a drink? Beer? Whisky and soda?"

Sugeng responded with cheer: "A whisky and soda will be fine, thank you!" For some time he had been growing accustomed to strong drink and had even come to like it. At home he now had a refrigerator, a present from one of the importers, and he always had a supply of whisky, cognac, and other spirits. At first Hasnah objected—"Why indulge in such a habit?" she'd asked—but Sugeng had only laughed and said it was necessary for entertaining visitors. By now he was used to it, and he enjoyed a whisky and soda.

A few minutes later Halim arrived. He greeted them and immediately sat down. Raden Kaslan introduced Sugeng to Halim, and the two men shook hands.

Sugeng could not stifle a feeling of contempt when he shook Halim's hand. So this was the man who daily denounced in his newspaper corruption and actions detrimental to the people and the state—and yet here he was playing the same game! Sugeng felt very little guilt about his own actions, or thought that he might be harming the country. What he was doing was only to fulfill Hasnah's wishes, and in his view her wishes were just. Especially for his baby. For a baby, every man has the right to do whatever is necessary, he thought. But here was Halim, a newspaper man. He couldn't grasp it. Husin Limbara was another matter; after all, he was a politician, and didn't people always say that politics was a dirty game? What they were doing here was only a part of that dirty politics. The party needed ample funds for the general elections. But Halim, the newspaper editor, who day in, day out called on the people to uphold honesty in their work…. He couldn't fathom it.

As for Raden Kaslan and his son, Suryono, it was clear to Sugeng that they were in it only for the money. You can't blame people for chasing wealth so they can do what they like, he thought. And he himself? He wasn't after money or power. All he wanted was to safeguard the wellbeing of his family.

Husin Limbara cleared his throat and coughed slightly before beginning to speak. "My friends, we're here to discuss the implementation of our program. As you know, we have been busy for some time raising funds for the general elections. Thanks to the assistance of Raden Kaslan, his son Suryono, and Halim as well, much has been achieved already. But now the party has decided to work even more efficiently. Sugeng, who works in The Ministry of Foreign Affairs., has been promoted by our man, the minister, to head the division which issues import licenses. Sugeng is also now a member of our party."

But I joined only for the protection, Sugeng protested silently.

"Our main problem at the moment is that we must work fast. The opposition groups have already launched attacks against the issuance of special licenses. Several of the government parties are beginning to feel that they're not getting their fair share. That's why we must move before it is too late. Halim's job is to counter all attacks directed against us. We need closer coordination. Some time ago one of our applications was delayed for over a month because they didn't realize that the application had come from us. Such things must not happen again. The minister himself will protect Sugeng should anything come up. Yet everything we do must follow the legal procedures and remain strictly within the law."

"We have no difficulties at our end," Raden Kaslan interjected. "Our organizations are all established and running smoothly. I'd only like to know whether perhaps there aren't some people in Sugeng's division who might possibly obstruct our program. Also I would like us to be notified immediately if there are any government orders, so we're not late in submitting our bids."

"As for the government orders, I can arrange that easily," Husin Limbara told him, "but as for the first question, I'd like to hear what Sugeng has to say."

Sugeng smiled inwardly. His regard for political leaders such as Husin Limbara had now collapsed completely. So they're thieves, too, he thought. In what way are they better than me, then? I'm not really doing anything wrong.

He looked at Husin Limbara and smiled. "No one will make any trouble—provided we grease the wheels."

"Great! That's fine then. That's a small matter. We'll leave the greasing to you," said the party leader. "Money will soon be easy! Now, let's get back to our program. There's a big order coming up…"

Dahlia's husband Idris had been waiting for his wife at home for over two hours now. He had just returned from his inspection tour in Sumatra, and when he got home he did not find her there. There was only the servant girl watching the house. The place felt desolate. The children of the family next door—the family that had replaced Sugeng and Hasnah, and who usually filled the place with commotion in the afternoon—were away. The servant told him that his wife had gone to Pasar Baru. Idris looked at his watch. It was already two o'clock. She takes a long time to shop, he thought, and where does she get the money? For a moment the thought of this money produced a gnawing feeling in his heart. He had long wanted to ask Dahlia how she got the money to buy such nice wrap-around *kain* and lovely new dresses. He no longer believed that she could save enough money from his salary to buy these things. But he quailed before asking her. He was afraid that Dahlia would get angry and accuse him of distrusting her. During their six years of marriage he had never been angry with Dahlia. And when she was angry he just kept quiet.

Idris rubbed his forehead. For some time he had been feeling not himself; he felt weak and he tired easily. Just sitting upright in his seat on the plane during the less than two-hour flight from Palembang to Jakarta had already strained his back. He got up to get cigarettes from Dahlia's dressing table. A portrait of Dahlia stood on the table. Idris contemplated the portrait and it made him feel proud to see how very beautiful his wife was. Then, as if something were pulling him, he looked into the mirror. Idris saw the face of a middle-aged man, with hollow cheeks and eyes bleary with weariness. He kneaded his cheeks and thought, I am old already. Much older than Dahlia.

He thought of their wedding three years ago. It was just after the Dutch had recognized Indonesia's independence. He had come to Jakarta from Yogya as a partisan of the Republic. He had met Dahlia in her office. She worked with NICA, the Netherlands Indies Civil Administration, which the Dutch had established to run the country as they tried to wrest it back from the Republican forces. Her father worked there, too. He was immediately attracted to Dahlia, and when he proposed marriage to her she had accepted at once. So had her parents, who were pleased to have him as son-in-law.

During the first years he was happy with Dahlia. It was only in these last months that a distance and a sort of emptiness seemed to have come between them. He had known for a long time that his salary could not cover their living expenses. At first he thought that Dahlia was often cool because of her dissatisfaction with their lack of money. And there were his frequent absences because of his work. He hadn't really ever stopped to think about all this clearly, but now he felt depressed. He had sent Dahlia a telegram from Palembang informing her of his arrival. Usually, if Dahlia wasn't able to meet him at the airport, she would wait for him at home. But now, for the first time, she was not there to greet him. And this caused his anxiety to grow. He became more and more agitated; but then he began to blame himself. It's hard on Dahlia, he thought, not to have any children. And it's my fault. Some time ago they had gone to be examined by a doctor, and according to the doctor it was he who was infertile. Their initial disappointment later dissipated as Dahlia seemed to have accepted this state of affairs. For a while Dahlia was even more tender to him, until he, too, was reconciled to the idea of never having children. But now he felt perturbed and dejected, and an intense desire came over him to share in the happiness of having a child.

Idris kept kneading his cheek, gazing into the mirror and saying to himself, I'm older than my real age. I'm only forty-two, but my face is that of a man of fifty. Dahlia is only thirty-two, but she looks like a young woman of twenty-five. He drew in a deep, long breath and sighed, accepting a situation that could be neither rejected nor changed. He kept asking himself, what more could he offer Dahlia? And at the same time the answer persistently recurred: he had nothing to offer which could give delight to a young woman like Dahlia.

Stop thinking about it, he told himself. If she just stays with me and we're together always, that would be enough. But then he was utterly overcome with a longing for her to be home. He longed to see her body, her face, and to hear her voice.

Tired of looking at himself in the mirror, Idris picked up Dahlia's photograph, and lay down on the bed. From the pillow emanated a perfume, a perfume unknown to him, intensifying his desire for Dahlia to return. Without knowing it, Idris then dozed off, his right hand still clutching Dahlia's photograph.

When Dahlia returned later she found Idris in the same position, asleep. She smiled to herself, tiptoed to the bed, and kissed him on the temple.

Idris woke up, smiled, and embraced her.

Dahlia kissed him again and whispered: "Forgive me, will you? I had already made an engagement with a friend. That's why I couldn't wait for you at home. You're not angry with me, are you?"

Idris could say nothing since his mouth was covered by Dahlia's mouth. Great happiness now filled his heart and spread through his whole body, and he embraced her fervently. Dahlia's handbag slipped from her hand and fell open as it hit the floor. Protruding from it was a five-hundred-rupiah note. Glancing at her handbag, Dahlia quickly abandoned Idris's mouth and sat up on the bed.

"You stay there," she told him. "I'll change my clothes."

As she got up she swiftly picked up her handbag, pushed the note back into the bag, and began to remove her *kain* and *kebaya* blouse.

Idris watching her with growing desire.

"You're beginning to get the hang of it," Miun said to Saimun, "but now the problem will be getting a driving license. To get one, you have to know how to read. You should learn to do that first. There's a course for that kind of thing."

Saimun had been learning to drive the truck for several weeks now. Overjoyed by Miun's words, he turned to Itam, who was busy washing a wheel of the truck.

"Hear that? When I get my license, the first thing I'm going to do is to teach you how to drive."

"Then we better learn to read and write," said Itam. "I want to learn, too."

Miun laughed at the two young men. "But before you do that, you're going to finish washing the truck!"

Saimun and Itam joined Miun in laughter and began to carry out his orders. The two of them felt happy; the future was full of promise.

As he wiped a tire, Saimun told Itam, "When I get my license I'm going to be an *oplet* driver. I hear they can get up to fifty rupiah a day." Saimun scratched his head, marveling at how much money he would get every day as an autolette driver.

They gazed into the distance, full of wonder at the possibilities the days to come held for them, when they could work as autolette drivers.

CITY BEAT

A whirling wind chased and scattered the flying bits of dry rubbish along the tracks of the electric train between the stops at Nusantara Street and Pintu Air II. The day was blazing hot. The wind lifted the flies, too lazy to move from the tops of rubbish heaps along the road. Car horns blared, punctuated from time to time by the screech of a car suddenly braking, followed by the shouting and swearing of a driver.

Suddenly the air was rent by a woman's piercing scream, the sound of someone being beaten, the repeated screams of the woman, and then a stream of cursing.

Along the wall near the railway, in the ruins of a half-demolished train-stop shelter, the city's vagrants had built shanties. Old charcoal baskets had been piled up to serve as walls; frayed pandanus mats were laid on the earth for floors. The roofs of these shanties were made of blackened and rusty pieces of old cans, patched together with bits of cardboard. Larger cans which once had held butter were set on cooking-stoves made of a few piled-up stones, and these served as kitchens.

A tiny, slender woman was trying to extricate her hair from the grip of a young man, also small and thin, and no older than sixteen or seventeen; he should have been at school at this time of day, not brawling with a woman by the railway line.

The woman beat the chest and the face of the man-boy. His hands were clenched into small tight fists, and he, too, screamed. Suddenly he released his grip, and she fell hard to the ground. He stepped towards her, kicked her in the head with his thin and dirty bare foot. Furious, the young woman leaped to her feet and, shrieking like someone who had gone berserk, she picked up a piece of wood and swung it at the head of the young man.

"Damn you, you stupid woman!" He shoved her to the ground, then advanced to kick her again, but the woman jumped up and retreated until her back was against the wall. She was not afraid, and she shouted a stream of abuse at him. Three or four vagrants lounged about their shanties, but paid no attention to the raging fight.

The small woman screamed at him: "Oh, so you've got the guts to fight a woman! Well, you try! Go ahead, try to kill me! Come on!" she taunted as she bared her chest that was half covered by her torn *kebaya*. Her breasts, still round and firm, were bathed by the light of the hot sun.

The man-boy stepped closer, wanting to hit her again.

"What good is a man like you!" the woman screamed again. "All you can do is brag. You promised to marry me and now I'm three months along. Why won't you marry me? You say you don't have any money. But for gambling there's money! Where's the house you promised? You told me you had money! You said you had a house!

Said you have work! Look at me! I've become a whore. Aren't you ashamed? You're eating whoring money!"

The woman wailed and threw herself on the ground and lay there sobbing. The man stood there, not knowing what to do.

"I've looked for work but there isn't any," he said vaguely.

"If only I'd stayed where I was, I wouldn't be ruined like this. Why did I follow you?" the woman cried again. "Now I'm a whore, selling myself every night without shame. I did it for you. Oh my God, forgive me!"

The woman sat up on her knees, her dirty face streaked with tears. "Forgive me, God, forgive me!" she said over and over in long-drawn wails, screaming to the scorching hot heaven, hurling her despair to the sky, begging for help, for consolation, for protection, for mercy, begging for human love and solace.

The young man looked at her. He made a step towards her, then shoved her with his foot half-heartedly. "Slut!" he said, then walked away.

October

"Just listen to their talk for a while," Suryono was saying to Sugeng. "Sometimes their discussions are quite good, though frequently they get off the track, and then they're way up in the clouds. It's really amusing when what's-his-name begins to discuss the Oedipus complex by—Who was that writer? I can't remember his name—but, even so, they're friends of mine. They're good people, just a bit mixed up. They think they're helping their country by spending their time on discussing all sorts of questions. They say these discussions are necessary to find out the kind of problems we face; that when we know what the problems are, it will be easier to solve them. The pity of it, as I see it, is that these discussions, with their high-flown theorizing, have become an end in themselves, and are no longer addressing the problem. But they mean well!"

Sugeng said nothing. He didn't care much about what Suryono was telling him. When Suryono had invited him to attend a meeting of the discussion club run by Suryono's friends, he wasn't very eager to go. But Suryono insisted that he join him. Besides, Suryono's father was very influential in the party—which had done such wonders for him since he'd joined it—and so he went along.

Suddenly, Suryono was blowing his horn hard and clamping down the brakes. He swore. "You fool!"

An old woman carrying a baby ran in fright to the side of the street.

"Lucky the brakes are good—if not, she'd be dead. Crossing the street without even looking," Suryono said in disgust. "How will Indonesia ever get ahead if people can't even cross a street?"

"Don't be angry," said Sugeng. He remembered the time before he joined the party, and how difficult it was then to live as a civil servant. "People like that have hard lives. Maybe she didn't hear the horn because she was hungry, and was worrying about how to get food for tonight."

"That's not true. When people are hungry their senses are sharpened; that's what I read in an article some doctor had written."

Inwardly, though, Suryono recognized the justice of Sugeng's remark, and this annoyed and angered him even more. I don't like this man, he thought, glancing at Sugeng sitting beside him.

As Suryono stepped on the accelerator again, he was seized by a feeling of depression, one that had been creeping up on him frequently and at the most unexpected moments: while he was enjoying himself with Dahlia; in the middle of a good meal at a restaurant; when he was on the point of signing a check or when he climbed into his fine car. He found impossible to say precisely what it was that disturbed him so, but it made him feel like something was wrong. And behind it all loomed a kind of fear. Just what he was afraid of he couldn't make out exactly either. So he ended up feeling irritable, and often found himself being annoyed by the people who happened to be around him.

It was thus that he had had his first quarrel with Dahlia.

Dahlia had sensed a change in him, and had asked him whether he was tired of her. Her question made him angry, and he had asked her rudely, did she want his money or not. But on that occasion he'd soon asked her to forgive him, and amity between them had been restored.

Once he had taken Ies out to a restaurant, and as they were sitting happily over their meal, this odd feeling had emerged again as he saw a little beggar girl approaching their table. Because this strange fear was mingled with his annoyance at the sight of her, he'd flown into a rage and snapped at the little beggar so harshly that the child fled in fright. Ies then got very angry, refused to go on with the meal, and asked him to take her home right away. In the car on the way to her home, he had begged her to forgive him, but Ies had remained silent and would not speak to him. He tried hard during the following two weeks to rehabilitate himself in Ies's eyes, but she remained unmoved. The harder he tried, the more distant she became. All this convinced Suryono, however, that he really loved Ies, and must marry her if he were to attain happiness in life. He became very jealous if he saw or heard that Ies was going out with another man, especially if the man was Pranoto.

He kept going to the evening discussions mainly to catch a glimpse of Ies and to watch how Pranoto behaved towards her. He also felt that it was easier to get to talk with Ies at these meetings. All this unpleasantness came to his mind because of Sugeng's remark about hungry people, and he felt upset and angry. But he restrained himself. He reminded himself how much they needed Sugeng. Even so, he couldn't calm down.

It's easy for him to talk, but isn't he out for what he can get, like the rest? Suryono said to himself. The moment this thought crossed his mind, it was as if a sudden shaft of light pierced him to the heart. It became clear to him at that moment what it was that he was doing, what his father was doing, what Husin Limbara was doing for his party and what they were asking Sugeng to do. He was appalled, and a terrible feeling of shame and fear gripped his heart. But a moment later the feeling was gone again, deliberately suppressed. He recalled Husin Limbara's words: "We are doing all this to further our people's struggle for social justice; to defend the Pancasila principles as the foundation of our state. Ours is the only political party that firmly upholds Pancasila as the basis of the state. The Islamic parties want to create a state based on Islamic principles; the communist party wants to create a communist state, and so on. That's why our party has to win the general elections. In order to win, the party needs money, and plenty of it. Therefore, we are simply doing our part in the struggle to save Pancasila. That's the reason we are doing all this, and we've got the full approval of the party's council."

Suryono thus reassured himself with Husin Limbara's words, and was again able to enjoy driving his Dodge sedan. His annoyance with Sugeng also disappeared and he turned to him. "Have you bought a car?"

"No, I'm still a bit hesitant. If I buy a car, the people at the office will suspect there's something fishy."

"What are you afraid of? The minister will protect you. If people start asking questions, couldn't you say that it was a present from your family? Put it in your wife's name. How much did you get this month, a hundred thousand?"

"A little less," Sugeng replied.

"If you apply for priority to get a car, as head of a division you're sure to get it. With priority status, you could get something like a Zephyr—which costs only sixty-two thousand, but you could resell it for one hundred and twenty-five. Then you could buy yourself a decent second-hand car for about fifty thousand, and you're left with a clear seventy-five thousand profit."

"Maybe I'm just not sure what to do with so much money got with so little effort," Sugeng told Suryono. "I never dreamed of such a thing. I used to feel envious seeing other people with fine houses, cars, lots of money, going in and out of restaurants as they pleased. But now, with that much money, I'm a bit scared."

"Scared? Why?" said Suryono. His resentment of Sugeng returned at once. Sugeng had reawakened his anxiety. Yet he wanted to hear Sugeng describe his apprehensions.

"Perhaps because I still think like a civil servant," Sugeng replied. "I feel somehow that even though all the licenses we issue are legal and are approved by the minister himself, what we're doing is wrong. Why, for example, do we give preference to the Hati Suci corporation—which was chartered only a month ago; has a staff of only one director; and has no office, no experience, and no business connections abroad—while other import firms, also run by Indonesians, which have been in business for years and operate on a completely bona fide basis, aren't supposed to get anything? And there's much more. For instance, there's that business run by a group of veterans who are claiming to represent tens of thousands of other veterans.... I happen to know they aren't veterans at all, and they haven't done a thing for a single veteran. When I think of all this I get scared. I'm afraid that what we're doing is improper and that we've overstepped the limits somewhere."

Doubts assailed Suryono once more; but for his own peace of mind, he had to dispel Sugeng's fears and to convince Sugeng that what they were doing was right.

"You're too much of a bureaucrat, that's all. Don't you remember what Husin Limbara said? It's all for the sake of our people's welfare. We must look at these things in a wider perspective."

"I could feel at peace if it were really just for that one purpose," Sugeng said. "But why should I be getting hundreds of thousands of rupiah? Why are so many people making fortunes out of it? They certainly don't pass on everything to the party."

Suryono was silent; he recognized the truth of Sugeng's words. Doubt and anxiety rose in him again.

"Well, just tell me, why?" Sugeng was pressing.

Suryono did not answer. He tried to cover up his own anxiety by laughing. "Because we're just not used to having tens of thousands of rupiah in our pockets. But what does it amount to, anyway? Think how much the Dutch and the Chinese have scraped up here over the centuries!"

Sugeng wanted to respond, but the car had reached Pranoto's house and Suryono was greeting Murhalim, who was leaning his bicycle against the wall.

As they got out of the car Murhalim gave a hoot. "Well, hello, Mr Millionaire. When did you exchange your car for a bigger one?"

Suryono, undisturbed by Murhalim's insinuation, laughed and introduced Sugeng. "Here's a new friend I brought along. He wants to participate in our discussions."

The hell I do, Sugeng said to himself.

Sugeng and Murhalim shook hands.

"What's tonight's discussion about?" Suryono asked Murhalim.

"Pranoto will speak on the problems Western technology poses for our intellectuals."

Oh, God, Suryono moaned silently.

They went inside and Sugeng was introduced to Pranoto, Ies, Yasrin, and six other people. The room, not too large, was already full.

Pranoto opened the discussion. "What I have to say are just a few basic ideas; what I hope to get are your reactions. As I stated last month, Western technology presents a problem to our intellectuals because of its impact on our people who, by and large, are still traditionally oriented…"

Suryono covered up a yawn and looked stealthily at Ies.

Ies, feeling that she was being looked at, turned towards Suryono and smiled. Suryono smiled back. He felt happy now and was prepared to pay attention to Pranoto's discourse.

"The particular problem our people have in confronting Western technology," Pranoto continued, "is that we've been given no time; there has been no transitional period. We either have to accept and use it or we'll go on being a backward nation. We must accept and use this Western technology, not just for the people's physical wellbeing, but also to ensure their spiritual freedom. In essence the problem can be reduced to a 'to-be-or-not-to-be' for our people. If we want to see our nation strong and independent, we must accept Western technology. To reject it is to pass a death sentence on our own people.

"In facing this choice, many Indonesian intellectuals are hesitant. Their attitudes vary. Some reject it completely, because they consider Western values to be incompatible with the spirit of the East. They see Western values as shallow and materialistic—which, of course, is true in part. Others want to adopt only what seems valuable and useful to them and to reject what they don't like; but such people never specify just which Western values they prize and which they consider harmful, or how one could make the distinction and put it into practice. I believe that we must accept them as a whole—both the good and the bad—and let our people make up their own minds, in the creative process of adaptation."

At this point, Murhalim spoke up. "If you have finished presenting your basic ideas, Pranoto, may I say something?"

"There are still a few aspects of the problem I haven't touched on, but I'll be able to bring them up in the discussion later. It's all right by me if you speak now."

Murhalim looked at the group. "First, I'd like to observe that although the problem of Western technology certainly exists for our intellectuals, we stress this problem far too much. It's as though we've been bewitched by the West. It's almost as if we're radios tuned in to a single wave length, receiving broadcasts from only one station—the West. For me the question is, why the West? And, as I see it, this continued orientation to the West won't lead us anywhere. Don't you realize that eighty or ninety per cent of our people are Muslims? The majority is deeply religious even though ninety-nine per cent of them have no real conception of the spirit of Islam. Even among Islamic leaders there are very few who understand it or its dynamic power to guide not only the spiritual life of the individual but also the total reorganization of society.

"I remember Ies once raising the question whether a revitalized and creative Islam couldn't give us an answer to the problems challenging us today. Since then I've been thinking the question over, and I've tried to find an answer in some contemporary books on Islam. After reading these books—and I'd be the first to admit that my studies are far from complete—I've become convinced that continually focusing on the West means approaching the problem on the wrong foot.

"Islam does possess standards and a spiritual dynamism to organize and run a modern state. However, the present leaders of Islam are unable to reveal its treasures. We must admit that this fault, or deficiency, is not peculiar to the Indonesian Islamic leaders alone. On the contrary, in countries which pride themselves on being Muslim, we see how, behind the façade of Islam, the people have been exploited from century to century. The condition of the *fellahin* in feudal Arab countries is even more pitiful than that of the working class in capitalist countries. The Islamic leaders of Indonesia must have the courage to open their minds to modern technology. It would be well to avoid using the term 'Western' here, as it could easily arouse irrational prejudices. It would perhaps be better to refer instead to 'modern' technology, to avoid the reactions usually aroused in many of us at the mention of the word West.

"I don't believe there is a single person in Indonesia who would want to reject modern technology: modern industrial techniques for producing the goods needed by our people, beginning with nails, wheels, screws, medicines, cars, railway equipment, ships, planes, radio, television, radar, rifles, bombs, tanks, guns, and even atomic energy."

Ies now spoke up. "I agree, of course, with the substitution of 'modern technology' for the term Western technology, but, in spite of the change of label, the actual influence of modern technology on society and on the spirit of our people will still be the same as if we used the term Western technology. This will certainly revolutionize our people's mind and spirit and will shake the very foundations of their traditional values."

"And what is the harm in that?" said Suryono. "Why should we be afraid if the traditional foundations of our society are shattered?"

"I didn't mean to say that I'm afraid," Ies replied quickly. "On the contrary, our society is so backward and lacking in initiative that I'd be only too glad to see a drastic change. Then perhaps, because of modern technology, Indonesians will become a people who are able to stand on their own feet, master nature, and assume their responsibilities to the nation and to humanity at large."

"That's a very nice statement," Yasrin remarked, "but it's not likely to lead to any definite conclusion. We reject the method the Japanese used in their adoption of modern technology: that is, using dictatorial means under the aegis of the emperor as they did before the Second World War. Nor can we accept the dictatorship of the proletariat, as practiced in Soviet Russia or in the Chinese People's Republic, to introduce modern technology to build up the country. The Indonesian nation has chosen the way of democracy. And we must have the courage to bear the consequences of this choice. Once modern technology has been introduced, let social development in our country take its own course, whether Islam possesses enough dynamism to guide the penetration of modern technology, or socialist ideology paves the way, or the Oriental soul is strong enough to support it—although I must admit that I don't know what is really meant by the 'Oriental soul'. Personally, I have no objections to the drastic changes which the introduction of modern technology may bring about in the basic values of our society or the spirit of our people, provided, however, that we do not destroy the principles of democracy. These changes are actually essential if our nation is to develop rapidly."

Murhalim cut in. "I don't agree with your view that modern technology should be allowed to come in just like that, and that we should sit back and see how subsequent developments shape the future of our homeland. I am convinced that Islam, with its dynamism rediscovered, will provide a solid base for receiving modern technology."

"May I make a comment?" said Suryono. "While listening to your talk, it occurred to me that the real problem for our nation is not modern technology, whether from West or East. Since Kipling wrote 'East is East and West is West' the world has changed a good deal. Modern technology is not the exclusive monopoly of the West. As we have seen, an Eastern nation has been able to master it, too. The problem we face is on what basic principles our country's development should be directed. On the present democratic basis, which does not satisfy us? On Islamic principles as proposed by Murhalim? On a dictatorial basis as the admirers of the people's democracies want? Even the Islamic basis that Murhalim wants carries the seeds of dictatorship in its exclusiveness and rejection of all alternatives. As we can see today, the attempt to develop our country and people along democratic lines has failed. Isn't it possible that this has happened not because of the failings of the democratic system, but because too many of our people are still unprepared for democracy?

"One of the basic assumptions in a democracy is that every person living in it must have enough intelligence to make conscious choices. How many of our people really understand what it is that they must choose? In our country a skillful demagogue can easily mislead the masses. In my opinion the problem is one of leadership. If the leadership of our country, which used to be so united, were to re-establish its unity, and on the strength of this unity govern the country, following the gradually developing ability of the people to build democratic institutions, that would be the best answer to the problem of our country's leadership."

"So you agree to dictatorial methods?" Ies asked blankly.

Suryono looked gratefully at Ies for this sign of her attention. "Yes, but only for the initial phase. What are ten years, twenty years, in the history of a nation? Let people like Sukarno, Hatta, Syahrir, Natsir, and others like them, stay in power to guide the development of our state and nation."

"You mean a sort of collective leadership?" Pranoto queried.

"Yes, and I think that a collective leadership corresponds to the instincts of our people. In the villages, where life is based on a *gotong royong* system where everyone helps one another, one can find the predisposition for such collective leadership."

"The question is," Pranoto immediately interjected, "whether personal and party antagonisms have not now become so sharp as to make it impossible for the leaders to re-establish their unity."

Suryono nodded. "That certainly is an important factor and, frankly, I think it is unlikely that our leaders will unite again."

"In that case the alternative is that some group will emerge and take over the leadership of the state," said Pranoto.

"The communists?" asked Murhalim.

"Or possibly Islamic fundamentalists," Pranoto answered.

"But it would be difficult for Muslim groups," Murhalim pointed out. "Not only are they badly divided, they don't have a militant organization ready to act like the Communist Party."

Sugeng, who had been sitting and listening all this time, now offered an opinion: "Yet another possibility is complete anarchy."

"Indeed," Pranoto agreed. "That also is a possibility—which implies disintegration of the state for which the lives of so many of our young people have been sacrificed."

Pranoto looked at his watch. "It's really a pity, but our time has run out just as our discussion was getting to the most interesting and thought-provoking basic problems. I suggest that each of us make a deeper study of the problems we have touched upon. We could ask Murhalim, for instance, or another friend with enough interest and time, to formulate the conception of a state based on Islamic principles.

"It's true, of course, that too many of Islam's foremost representatives only cling to Islam's ancient glory without trying to make use of Islamic principles to solve our contemporary problems. Perhaps we could ask Suryono to elaborate further the principle of collective leadership for our country. The consequences of the introduction of modern technology into Indonesian society could be examined more closely by comparisons with what happened in Japan, for example."

After taking Sugeng home, Suryono took Ies for a drive in his car, and on a quiet street in Kemayoran Baru he stopped the car, took Ies's hand, and drew her close to him. "Iesye..." he whispered.

He kissed her ear, his lips moved to her cheek, then with his hand he slowly turned Ies's face until his lips met the girl's lips and then their mouths were locked in a strong, deep kiss.

Suddenly, as his hand tried to clasp her breast, she withdrew and moved away from him.

"Don't," she told him.

"Why?"

"I'm not sure about you yet."

"Not sure how?" Suryono retorted. Dahlia flitted through his mind. Disconcerted, he thought: does Ies know?

"As I listened to your talk before, I believed I could trust you. And I felt as though I cared for you," she said, "but then I began to wonder if you weren't just playing with words. And then, here you are still young but suddenly wallowing in money. It seems abominable that young people should spend their time just trying to get rich while our people are in such a desperate condition. I don't know what to think of you."

Suryono stared through the windshield into the night, silently admitting to himself that Ies did know him. It was he who didn't know himself—who he was or what he wanted. He had lost hold and was full of anxiety and fear.

Suryono turned the ignition key, started the engine, and pulled into the street.

"Come, I'll take you home," he said abruptly.

"You're not angry?" said Ies.

Suryono turned to her. Again he felt their closeness and, leaning over, he caressed Ies's cheek with his lips.

"How could I be angry with you?" he said.

Ies held his hand, and the car rolled back into the center of the city.

CITY BEAT

When Tony and Jok noticed Suryono's car alone in the deserted street, they ordered the *becak* driver to stop at the corner. They short-changed the driver, who drove off swearing at them, and then hid themselves behind a dark tree.

Tony grinned and his teeth glistened in the darkness. "This is good pickings!" he said as he adjusted the pistol tucked under his shirt.

Jok clutched the handle of his knife.

"Let them get into it first," said Tony. "It's easier to rob them when they're in the middle of it. They'll be scared stiff and give up their wallets fast, and then scoot when we tell them to get out."

They saw Suryono draw Ies close to himself and then the two kissing. Tony whispered, "There now, almost…"

Tony and Jok cautiously moved closer to the car, Tony's hand ready to pull out his pistol.

Then Ies withdrew, Suryono started the motor, and before Tony could decide on a new plan of action, the car had rolled away and was out of sight.

"Ah, shit! Maybe they saw us coming,' said Tony.

"Looks like they didn't get into it."

November

A drizzling rain had been falling incessantly since dawn and the morning wind was blowing in hard from the sea. The wind whirled up dry leaves, darkening the mist that billowed in the streets. The wind sneaked into the houses, making Raden Kaslan press Fatma's warm young body closer to his own; making Suryono sink into deeper slumber in his room as he dreamed of Ies. The wind blew into editor Halim's room, who was sleeping apart from his wife, because the night before they'd had another quarrel; disturbed Sugeng's sleep, filled with nightmares; made Husin Limbara's afflicted shoulder ache more painfully in the morning chill; and caused the sago palm leaves on the thatched roof of Pak Ijo's hut to rustle. Then, having penetrated inside and hovered around Ibu Ijo and Amat, who sat chilled near the *balai*, the morning wind swept by.

Ibu Ijo sat very still near the sleeping bench; Amat, too. They had shed all their tears since Pak Ijo had drawn his last breath at ten o'clock the preceding night. The oil lamp had long since gone out.

Ibu Ijo's sorrow at the loss of her husband was mixed with relief. At last he was liberated from the torture of an illness they had been unable to cure because they never had enough money to go to a doctor and buy the necessary medicines.

Now only she and Amat were left. Ibu Ijo was confident that they would somehow manage to carry on. There was still the horse and the delman cart. Amat was working already, as a garbage coolie. All that remained to be done now was to bury Pak Ijo.

The atmosphere in Raden Kaslan's study had been tense for some time. Raden Kaslan had been silent for a long while, unwilling to participate further in the discussion. Halim sat looking at Husin Limbara with a cruel smile playing on his mouth. Then, with studied slowness, he took a cigarette out from a pack on the table, put it between his lips, replaced the cigarettes on the table, took a match from the table, lit his cigarette, then inhaled deeply and puffed the smoke upwards. Raden Kaslan watched Halim's gestures with terror in his heart. Husin Limbara said to himself that the man was dangerous but could be bought, and he decided to pay Halim's price.

Halim spoke in a cold voice, "The government, which we are supporting at the moment, is not popular in the eyes of the people. If I wanted to, I could write even more sharply and violently about this government than the opposition does. The opposition newspapers don't know half of what I know and I have seen with my own eyes as to the doings of this government." He looked sharply at Husin Limbara and Raden Kaslan.

Raden Kaslan lowered his eyes. Husin Limbara, with great calm, looked fixedly at Halim, and in the end it was Halim who averted his glance.

"My newspaper has suffered great losses as the result of supporting the government. But every time I ask for support I'm put off as if I were a beggar. I'm tired of begging from you, gentlemen. Why should I beg from you? It's you, gentlemen, who are indebted to me."

"But how about the bank loan for the printing plant, and the several hundred thousand…?" said Raden Kaslan suddenly.

Halim turned to Raden Kaslan and smiled. "What does this loan of six million for the printing plant amount to? And the few hundred thousand rupiah? They're chicken-feed, especially if we compare it to the hundreds of millions you've been making on all these deals."

"So what you really want is…?" said Husin Limbara coolly.

"I refuse to be merely your tool," said Halim. "If we are to work together I must be treated as an equal."

"But you've already got a seat in the parliament!" Husin Limbara said.

Halim laughed through a sneer. "How generous your gracious gift! A seat in a provisional parliament which will soon to be dissolved after the general elections only a few months hence. Of what significance is that?"

"But you asked for it yourself," Husin Limbara retorted.

"Of course! But surely you realize that the sums are insufficient," Halim shot back. "And the seat in parliament is only temporary anyway."

"If you wish, we can include you in the slate of party candidates for the elections," Husin Limbara said. He felt relieved; so that's what is worrying the man. "Really. That I can guarantee. Don't worry."

Halim scoffed: "That's of no use to me. You know as well as I do that it's better for our plans if I'm known in public as a non-party man."

"Halim wants a greater share of the money," Raden Kaslan said, looking at the party leader.

A light smile appeared on Husin Limbara's lips. As chairman of the party, he'd had considerable experience in dealing with people like Halim. Here he felt on firm ground once more. If the problem was one of money he, Husin Limbara, could settle it.

"Is that all?" he said to Halim. "But you know yourself that we have to be very cautious in such matters just now. Every day the opposition's newspapers persist in tearing into the various special licenses. The party itself doesn't know how much longer it can shield the minister concerned without getting embroiled in difficulties with the other government parties."

Halim leaned forward. "OK, but listen to my proposition first. Through my connections I have reliable reports that the opposition parties have worked out a plan for attacking the government through the media outlets they own. If you examine carefully the content of the opposition papers of the last few weeks, you will see that their campaign against the government is quite systematic. One of the opposition papers exposes something; it is then picked up and exaggerated in the headlines of the other newspapers, and, being centrally directed, all this makes a strong impression on the public. In contrast, the pro-government media isn't being coordinated at all. Each newspaper goes its own sweet way, expressing its own reactions; in short, the voice of pro-government media is neither united nor strong, but disjointed and ineffective in combating the opposition's campaign."

"Alas, that is true," Husin Limbara agreed. He had become interested in Halim's argument and forgot about the money problem still to be settled.

Inwardly Raden Kaslan, too, had to admit the merit of Halim's analysis of the media situation.

"I have worked out a plan of how pro-government newspapers should cooperate in fighting the opposition," Halim continued, "and I would like to suggest that as soon as possible a meeting be arranged between the editors-in-chief and directors of the pro-government papers here in Jakarta, the leaders of pro-government parties, and the more important cabinet ministers. At this meeting the basic policies for our campaign to fight the opposition should be outlined. As the famous military saying goes, 'attack is the best form of defense'. Similarly, pro-government newspapers should take the initiative and attack—and not react defensively every time the opposition takes the offensive.

"So far the majority of the pro-government newspapers, with the exception of mine, have merely reacted to attacks by the opposition press. This is a mistake. We can't win over public opinion this way. Look what's happening now: while the average circulation of pro-government newspapers is going down, that of the opposition press is rising steadily. The government papers cannot survive without organized support. My idea is to establish a press service in order to systematically collect, prepare, and distribute materials for our press campaign. These materials will then be published in all the newspapers which support the government, as news reports, editorials, interviews, and so forth."

"Very good, a very good idea," said Husin Limbara.

"But we must launch it under the guise of an independent press organization and not one tied to the party," Halim continued. "And that is why this organization will need a budget, an office, and a staff of its own. According to my estimates, about five hundred thousand will do for a start, including the purchase of typewriters and other equipment, desks and so on, and salaries for the employees."

"The financial part we can discuss with our colleagues," Husin Limbara told him and rubbed his hands. "But as for the plan, it's very good. Excellent."

Once again Raden Kaslan mentally had to applaud Halim's skill in making so persuasive a presentation.

Halim wasn't finished: "Apart from this feature service, I again want to stress the need for a new press organization. Once all pro-government media outlets are on board, we can emerge as the leading press organization. Then we can set the tone of debate. Our voice simply doesn't count in the one which exists now."

Husin Limbara again agreed. "Good, very good. That can easily be arranged."

"So, if you agree," Halim told the two men, "I can start laying the groundwork as soon as the necessary funds are available. But, all this aside," he paused for a moment, "as I've already indicated, my own newspaper continues to suffer losses because it supports the government's cause. I'm fed up with begging for support. To avoid any further quibbling about money, I'm asking for a loan of at least eight million to finance my newly established import firm—it's already been approved."

Halim picked up his briefcase from the floor by his chair and took out an issue of the *State News*. Husin Limbara took the sheet from Halim and read the item on the chartering of the import firm Ikan Mas.

"Leave this with me," Husin Limbara said. "I'll discuss the loan with the ministers concerned."

"I'm confident that you'll succeed," Halim said, but then added straightaway, "because, if not, I'll no longer be in a position to continue my support for you."

Husin Limbara laughed at the disguised threat. "Wouldn't it be better not to invest the whole eight million in this one import corporation? You must realize that the import field is now the main target for opposition attacks. Why don't you start up some other enterprise, a mine or a factory, for instance, and divide the loan, drawing it under two names?"

Halim too chuckled. "You're quite right there, provided that I'm sure of getting the loan, there'll be no trouble dividing it up later."

Raden Kaslan had been silent throughout this interchange. "So where do we stand now? Does it mean that from now on I no longer have to be involved in financing Halim's ventures?"

Husin Limbara was quiet for a moment, turning things over in his mind. "Yes, I'll see to it that your request is met. As for coordinating the pro-government press, I can take care of that, too; you can go ahead with the preparations immediately." He now stood and looked at Halim: "I hope we've finished our discussion and that our cooperation will be even stronger than it was before."

Halim rose as well and picked up his briefcase. "My car may not have come yet. If not, could you give me a lift to my office?"

"Certainly," said Husin Limbara.

Halim's car had in fact not arrived, and they left Raden Kaslan behind to marvel at Halim's slickness. Just imagine, the fellow had talked for only a half an hour, and had managed to wheedle out over eight and a half million!

In the car Halim was saying to Husin Limbara, "Raden Kaslan didn't seem very happy during our discussion."

"He's getting old, and given to changeable moods. He put in an application to have a Dutch car-importing firm transferred to him, and it hasn't been approved yet."

"He's got so much already and still isn't satisfied," said Halim. "Import firms by the dozen, in his own name, the name of his wife, his son, and whoever else. It's really amazing how greedy people can be. Who knows how much more goes into his pockets than goes into the party treasury!"

To himself Husin Limbara was saying, yes, but you, my friend, are you any less greedy than that scoundrel Kaslan? You had a bank loan for the printing works, hundreds of thousands for your newspaper, a seat in parliament, and are now due to get over eight million. Tell me if that isn't greed!

Nonetheless, he smiled at Halim. "Well, there're all sorts of people in the world. No one's satisfied. The powerful want more power; the rich want more wealth. Just look at the opposition parties. What are they shouting for? They've got no responsibility whatever for the welfare of our country and the people," he sighed. "Their continual harassment of the government means that the important work of building the nation gets held up, because we're forced to deal with an opposition that's gone off the track. How can the government do its work in such a situation?"

Halim stifled a grin as he thought: Just keep talking to your heart's content! Do you really imagine you can fool me? What you're perpetrating in the name of the people is large-scale looting. You think you're using me, but it's me that's using you.

Chuckling softly, Halim said out loud, "You're right, of course, my friend; the leaders of the opposition are all stooges of the capitalists and colonialists. They should all be wiped out."

Suddenly the car, its brakes squealing and tires screeching, came to an abrupt stop as the driver just managed to avoid colliding with a *becak*.

Husin Limbara and Halim were thrown forward. Husin Limbara's glasses fell on the floor.

Halim, being younger, quickly regained his balance. "Lucky we didn't hit him," he said.

"Hell!" swore Husin Limbara, and, as the car passed the *becak*, whose driver stood waiting in fear, Husin Limbara stuck his head out of his newly polished Cadillac. "Look before you cross! Follow the traffic rules!"

Muttering, he said to Halim, "And *becak* drivers should be wiped out, too. All they do is cause traffic accidents."

"Moreover, they're a blot on the dignity of man!" Halim mocked.

Husin Limbara looked at him, caught the joke in Halim's remark and laughed. His annoyance with the *becak* driver disappeared. "You talk just like a member of the opposition!"

The two men laughed.

Pranoto was writing an article in his room. The walls around him were lined with books; otherwise the room was very simple. A small bed filled one corner. Near his desk on a low table stood an electric record player, and at its side a hi-fi radio set. According to Pranoto, the records, especially of classical Western music, did not sound good without the high fidelity hook-up.

When he had first sat down to write, everything he meant to say seemed very clear in his mind. But as he went along he had to stop more and more often, dissatisfied with what he'd set down; he felt the sentences he'd formed didn't convey clearly what he really intended to say.

Pranoto got up and put on a record, Schubert's "Quartet No. 14 in D minor". He stretched out on his bed, listening to the beginning—"Death and the Maiden"— which merged with his own artistic sensibilities to produce within himself a feeling of great loneliness.

Pranoto began to contemplate his own situation. Here I am, he said to himself, thirty-four years old, still unmarried. He'd spent six years in the foreign service and then given it up. Now he was publishing a cultural and political journal. He remembered the time when he had worked for the Indonesian delegation in New York. Two years in New York—with Liz, Martha, Connie, and many more. Connie stood out vividly in his mind. They were still corresponding. Pranoto smiled to himself sadly. His relationship with Connie was a kind of dream, like living in another world, something that couldn't be realized under present circumstances without destroying its essence. He knew with certainty that although he loved Connie he would never be able to marry her. Pranoto had always prided himself on his practical sense, and in his letters to Connie he had repeatedly pointed out that it was impossible for him to marry her, no matter how strongly his heart, filled with love for her, urged him to do so.

I love you too much, Connie, to marry you and to bring you here into the life of my own people. You wouldn't be able to live on my earnings, as an Indonesian woman and wife could. Your standard of living is so much higher than ours. And I wouldn't want my wife to live any differently than my own people. I wouldn't want to see my family become an island to itself, far above other Indonesian families. Even though you say that you can make the sacrifice, I cannot accept it. Therefore you are free to live as you please; my love imposes no ties on you. And I say to you, I love you, love you ever so much, will always love you whatever you do, even if you marry someone else, my love for you will never change and I'll always be with you in spirit. I have a duty to fulfill towards my own people here, to vindicate the struggle of my friends who have laid down their lives in the revolution for the liberation of my people. These friends of mine have not died to free my country and then have it bled white by immoral and unscrupulous politicians. Our young people therefore have a duty to work here in our homeland, to open the eyes of the people, to raise their standard of living, until the whole of our people is capable of consciously taking the reins of their destiny in their own hands.

Connie had written back, saying that reading his letter had made her love him all the more and had made her even more determined to be at his side during his struggle.

I love you and you know how strong my feelings for you are. You say that if you married me you would feel obliged for my sake to create a separate island, alien to your society. How incredibly little you think of my love for you. Do you imagine that we American women are incapable of loving a man strongly enough to be happy to sacrifice everything for him? What does it matter having to bear the hardships you describe in your letter, having to live in one room, having to share a house with two or three other families and me having to give up the comforts of American life? As if you didn't know there are plenty of Americans who live in badly crowded apartment houses. And, speaking of comforts, I'm sick and tired of hearing about America's prosperity. This expression has been a curse for our people, and I now experience it myself——it has become a curse upon the love that binds us together. Do you really think that we can't live without an elevator, without a pressure-cooker, without a fruit-squeezer, without a washing machine, without lipsticks, permanent waves, and various other products of our giant industries? Don't you know that there are many Americans who long for a life such as in your country, without the complexities of the machine age and all its consequences for human beings? You must realize that I love you, that I want to live by your side, to help you in your struggle to elevate your people. Am I asking too much, my dearest?

Pranoto had written that he felt deeply how very fortunate he was to be blessed by a love as great as Connie's, but that evidently she hadn't fully understood what he had meant. He found it very hard, in fact, to tell her this but she needed to better understand the condition his country was in. She had to realize that while physical hardships could be overcome by the power of love, there were other things which could never be overcome, regardless how great their love might be. He tried to be more explicit:

Here in my country there's a plague of mistrust and suspicion of all foreigners, especially white people. Whether they are Americans, British, Dutch, or French, they're all lumped together; all are wicked imperialists and capitalists. And an Indonesian with a Dutch, English, American, or French wife is automatically suspect and is distrusted by his own people, particularly if he happens to be opposed to the communists or fanatic nationalists. He is finished then; and far from being any help to him, his wife only impedes his efforts to fight on. That's why, no matter how much I love you, and though I know how selfless your love for me is, we must both have the courage to renounce our love to my struggle in my people's cause. I will always be longing for you, Connie, my love!

He never sent this letter to Connie. After re-reading it he had felt that it was too hard, even cruel, and that it didn't really reflect what was in his heart—which was crying out for Connie. Also, he was still torn by doubts that he found impossible to resolve. He smiled bitterly, recalling how ardently he had always insisted that the Indonesians of his generation were heirs of all humanity, that no national barriers stood in their way and that human values were the same all over the world. And now he could not make a decision for himself.

Instead of the unsent letter, he answered Connie with a love letter in which he spoke mainly of his longing for her.

How incredibly happy I was, my darling, to receive your wonderfully noble letter. I want to assure you of one thing, so you never doubt it—my everlasting love for you. I have almost succumbed to your reasoning. But I am not yet convinced for myself that marrying you and bringing you among my people will bring you happiness, the happiness I want you to have. So please be patient, my beloved, and wait a little longer.

Pranoto woke up with a start from his musings as he heard the humming sound of the phonograph as the record came to the end. He sat up on his bed, rubbed the bridge of his nose, pinched his eyebrows. He felt even more desolate and lonely than usual. He stood up, went back to his desk, and examined the piece of paper in the typewriter, his unfinished article. He forced himself to re-read what he had written. It was a great effort to continue the work, he felt.

"That's his story. Do you think it can be done?" Sugeng asked Suryono. They were alone in Sugeng's study. Suryono was thinking it over. "Should it come off, it would mean a clear half a million for us," he said.

Sugeng had just finished telling him how three days ago Said Abdul Gafur, the land agent he knew, had come to him with a proposal. A friend of his, a big land owner, was eager to sell some property located strategically in the center of the city. Unfortunately, several of the buildings on the property were occupied by government offices, so no one was willing to buy it. If one could arrange for these government offices to be moved elsewhere, the property would become available for new housing construction and could be sold for as much as five million. The agent had told Sugeng that if he could arrange for that to happen, there would be a cut of half a million waiting for those who got it done.

"You should realize," Suryono advised, "the property is worth far more than five million. I'm sure Said Abdul Gafur will want a big cut for himself. I'll talk it over with my father and see what the party can do. But we'll have to make sure to get a bigger share. Half a million for the party, and half a million for the two of us. Just tell your Arab friend that if he's prepared to pay one million we'll see it gets done."

"If this comes off I am going to resign from my position," Sugeng said. "I want to start my own business."

"That would be much better. What's the use of being a civil servant!" Suryono scoffed.

Idris sat very still by the window of his bedroom. He had been sitting like this for the last quarter-hour. He'd just had a quarrel with Dahlia. He had been suppressing his feelings about his wife too long. Vile thoughts and suspicions kept haunting him. He saw her constantly acquiring more and more things she couldn't possibly afford on his earnings as an inspector of education: expensive batik cloths, beautiful jackets, not to mention gold jewelry with precious stones, perfumes, and other luxurious items.

That afternoon when he got back from the office he could contain himself no longer. It was not finding her home that triggered everything off. It was only after he had finished his meal that Dahlia had appeared, carrying a bundle of batik *kain*.

He could not keep the agitation from his voice when he addressed her: "I've said nothing all this time, Dahlia, but by God you had better tell the truth now and tell me where you got the money to buy these things. It's impossible on my salary!"

Dahlia looked at her husband with great surprise; she had never expected such an outburst. For months now she had been going and coming as she pleased, bringing things home, without him asking any questions.

Her shock didn't last long. She knew her power over Idris and counter-attacked at once. "What? You've gone so far as to suspect your own wife? Perhaps you think that I've stolen them all?"

Idris groped for an answer, hesitating whether or not to utter the crucial accusation.

Dahlia, sensing his hesitation, quickly pursued her advantage. She stepped closer. "Or do you think I'm selling myself to buy all these things?"

Her voice rose to the angry pitch of an injured wife, unjustly suspected and suddenly accused of the worst thing possible by her own husband.

Idris felt that he had lost the initiative and saw no way to regain it.

Dahlia pushed on with her attack. "You should be grateful and appreciate my efforts to supplement your salary and bolster our income a bit. But you're doing just the opposite. If you really want to know how I manage to buy all these things, all right, I'll tell you—by trading in a small way, buying and selling *kain* and jewels among my friends. These cloths I've just bought will be resold later."

Dahlia picked up the bundle of batik which she had brought on credit. She still didn't know how she was going to pay for them, whether to ask Suryono to settle the debt, or the young Indian manager of a shop she patronized on Pasar Baru, who kept trying to approach her whenever she came in to do some shopping.

"Apart from trading, I run some raffles among friends. That radio over there in the dining room, do you think I bought it out of your salary? And our new bed—from your salary, too?'

By this time Idris was completely crushed and now, when Dahlia began to cry and sob bitterly—"If you don't love me anymore, why don't you just divorce me?"—he felt faint all over.

As though he were laying his heart on the floor for Dahlia to trample on, he reproached himself in a hundred ways for having entertained such evil thoughts about the wife he loved. He sat very still by the window, not knowing how to win her back.

"I got work driving a *becak*," Itam announced to Saimun in their hut. "Here I was sick just one week and the foreman wouldn't take me back! He said we get paid by the day so when I was sick he used my pay to hire another guy to do my work. That's what he said, anyway. Lucky I found a job driving a *becak!*"

"But don't you need a license to drive a *becak*?" Saimun asked.

"The Chinese guy who owns the *becak* doesn't care. Only difference is, if you don't have a license you have to pay a bigger deposit. With a license, it's twenty rupiah for a full day; without one it's twenty-five."

"But that's way too much!"

"What else am I going to so?" Itam asked. "There's no other work. I've got no schooling. I can't read or write. I don't have any special skills. All I've got is my two hands and two feet. You're better off. All you have to do is to apply for a license and you can be a driver. You can already read and write."

"Didn't I tell you to come with me to those reading and writing lessons? You're just too lazy."

"It's my fate, is all," said Itam. "Every man has one, Saimun. And all we can do is trust in God. If fate is on my side, I'll earn a living; if not, I'll just have to die."

"You shouldn't talk that way, Tam. You've got to be patient."

"Well, you know, sometimes I don't know what to do," Itam sighed. "Here we are, living like this; it feels like we're being trampled on. Supposing I'd wanted to stay in the village, I couldn't work the fields for fear the bandits would kill me. And here in the city, there's nothing but misery. What happens when you get sick? You lose your job! How are we supposed to live? But out there, you see other people, the big shots, who are doing just fine. You don't see them standing in line for salt, for kerosene, for rice—not like us here. Hell, most of them line up in cars."

Saimun nodded. "I know what you're saying. I think about those things, too, and I don't see that there's been any change in our lives—not under the Dutch, not under our own people either. Things aren't any different.

"I might not know anything about politics but I can feel things for myself and I listen to people talk. I know there's no joy in our lives. For us, nothing is certain and nobody cares about our lot. If you're going to be hungry, you'll be hungry by yourself. If you get sick, you're going to be sick by yourself. And if you die, you're going to die all alone."

"You know, Mun, sometimes, when I'm feeling desperate, I get to thinking I might as well steal, become a robber, and to hell with the consequences."

"I know what you mean," said Saimun. "I feel that way, too, sometimes. Once, when I was still learning to drive the truck, the motor went dead in the middle of the street. You should have heard all those people in their big shiny cars swearing at me. 'Hey, blockhead, if you don't know how to drive, get off the street!' Our own people and full of themselves like that. Hey, if it was the president wanting to pass, that would be ok. He's the president, after all. It would only be proper to get out of the way. But when it's someone else, one of our own people, carrying on like that, I won't accept it. Aren't we all human? The only difference is that those kind of people have money and our kind of people don't."

"You can make a pretty good living driving a *becak*," Itam said. "At least that's what I heard—especially if you get to know addresses of certain kinds of women. That's where the tips are. Hey, speaking of women, yesterday I saw Neneng at the market on Sawah Besar. But it was like she didn't know me anymore."

Saimun held his breath at the mention of Neneng's name. Since Neneng had left their hut last August, Saimun had tried four times to approach her and persuade her to return.

"She puts on a fine show," Itam added. "with her fancy clothing and her lips painted red. But I say hello and she looks right through me, doesn't even answer."

Itam stretched himself out on the *balai* and lit a *kretek* cigarette.

Saimun recalled the moment when he had tried for the first time to approach Neneng. It was almost a month after she had left them to go to Kaligot. At first he had been reluctant to approach the house where she lived and worked, because there were so many other women there, on the verandah, looking at him as he stood, hesitating, on the sidewalk below. He didn't know how to behave towards them. But then, when he saw Neneng come outside and sit down among the group, he steeled his courage and made his way up the steps. When Neneng saw him she immediately jumped up and ran back inside the house. Saimun didn't dare to follow her inside the house, so he had quickly retreated and slunk away, not daring to stand and wait for her outside.

The second time he went there, he went as far as the front door; but there he caught a glimpse of a man inside the house drawing Neneng with him into the inner room. He was so upset that he ran away as fast as he could.

The third time, two weeks later, he came across Neneng at the Sawah Besar market. He greeted her, but she kept on walking as if she'd never known him.

Neneng's behavior had greatly depressed Saimun, but he didn't give up hope; and when a week later he accidentally met Neneng on the street, he greeted her again. Once again Neneng did not return the greeting, but Saimun mustered the courage to follow her.

"Neneng, why are you acting this way? I mean no harm. I just want to see you and to know that you're OK."

Only then did Neneng reply. "What's the use of looking for me?" she said in a flat, sad voice. "I'm dirty."

At these words Saimun felt as though his heart was being cut to pieces, and without a moment's thought he said, "Then leave that place, Neneng, and come back with me to our hut."

"So that it can be just like it was before, with you and Itam?" she asked. "What's the difference between that life and the one I have now? Go away. Let me be what I am."

"We'll get married if you want," Saimun suddenly announced, the words springing from his mouth before he had time to think of their implication. How was he going to support a wife when his present earnings were insufficient to cover even his own expenses and he himself was constantly hungry?

"You're a good man," Neneng said to him, "but I'm ashamed."

Neneng walked faster, trying to distance herself from Saimun, and not listening to what he was trying to tell her, how much he wanted her back.

Then, feeling embarrassed as people began to stare at him— chasing and calling after a woman in the middle of the street in broad daylight—Saimun finally stopped and let Neneng go on by herself.

From behind a cloud of cigarette smoke, Itam remarked, "I don't know any more why we were born human. God only knows what's going to happen to us."

Saimun said nothing, just sat there, musing.

Through Jakarta's scorching heat, Yasrin proceeded towards Achmad's office. He had received a letter from Achmad, the contents of which excited him. Achmad had written that cultural activities in Indonesia had been left in the hands of bourgeois intellectuals like Pranoto and his friends far too long. The result was a total lack of progress in developing a genuine cultural movement "among the people, by the people, and for the people". According to Achmad, these bourgeois intellectuals who profess to be supporters of Indonesian culture and claim to be heirs to universal human values are stuck in theorizing, analyzing, and writing pseudo-intellectual essays full of pretentious words and terms borrowed from Western books. They're so absorbed in this kind of masturbation that they're satisfied with just publishing manifestos, producing analyses, dreaming of a fine arts academy, a popular theater, a museum of modern art, etc, etc. It all starts with a barrage of propaganda but then disappears without a trace, like the old Malay saying, "Hot, like a chicken's droppings."

Yasrin recalled the letter's conclusion: "…and so, my friends and I, who have long appreciated you as a poet, are convinced that you, too, are fed up with the meaningless activities of these bourgeois parasites. We are sure that you are eager to plunge into the arena by contributing your great creative power to struggle for our nation's cultural development. We therefore very much hope, that you will come to a meeting at my office to discuss the subject."

Yasrin did, indeed, feel flattered by Achmad's letter. The fact was, he had been feeling dissatisfied with himself for some time.

This dissatisfaction had been vague and general, but after receiving the letter three days ago, the reasons for his discontent had become clear to him. It was evident now that Pranoto and his group had been exploiting his name as a front to show their concern for the people, because his poems always dealt with the life and suffering of the masses. He remembered one of his poems being praised by Pranoto in the journal *Culture*. Pranoto had written that Yasrin was Indonesia's most important poet since Chairil Anwar. Yasrin ranked perhaps even higher than that revolutionary poet, Pranoto had written, since evidence that some of Anwar's poems had been plagiarized had detracted from his reputation as a poet.

So far, all he'd received from his friends was praise. Meanwhile, several members of their group had been offered invitations to visit the United States or some other Western country, like England or France, but his own turn had never come. He once asked to be given a chance, but his request had not been given the proper attention. It was even conveyed to him indirectly that it was difficult for his colleagues to get him an invitation to the United States or England since he couldn't speak the language. He had been very hurt to hear this. He had retorted by asking why the Chinese or the Russians, for instance, invited Indonesian artists, even though these artists didn't know a word of Russian or Chinese. But he got no satisfactory reply to this question—only an intimation: did he want to be a propaganda tool for the communists?

Since receiving Achmad's letter, Yasrin had become convinced that his proper place was not with Pranoto's group, even though he and Pranoto were publishing a journal together. I've been lost all this time, Yasrin thought to himself. Why didn't I see how completely bourgeois someone like Suryono is? He goes on talking about the misery of the masses and the disintegration of the state, but all he's really interested in is money. Look how fast he's made his fortune! And for such a young man to have a car of his own and

live it up the way he does! They say that Suryono's wealth comes
from his father's connections with the party. It's clear that Pranoto's
group is just indulging in talk, without any real desire to serve the
people.

And now that he remembered how often he had written
in defense of democracy, criticizing the communists and their
totalitarian system, he felt ashamed of himself. I've certainly been
blind all this time, he thought.

He also reminded himself that although Pranoto, the unofficial
leader of their study club, was good enough at theorizing, he had
never had any contact with the common people, had never really
known the people. He always used an autolette or the tram to
go anywhere; he probably never went anywhere on foot. Yasrin
recalled how he had once invited Pranoto to eat with him at a
roadside stall.

"How can you eat there?" said Pranoto. "Look how they rinse
the spoons and plates in that dirty water."

Yasrin felt resentful as he remembered these words, although
at the time he had answered by merely laughing. But now, since
receiving Achmad's letter, he suddenly felt that he had been badly
humiliated by Pranoto. I eat every day squatting by the roadside,
Yasrin said to himself, and Pranoto says it's dirty. By Allah!

By the time Yasrin had reached Achmad's office he was almost
ninety-nine per cent determined to join Achmad and stop working
with Pranoto on the journal. He had even formulated his reasons
for leaving Pranoto; it was all so clear in his mind: he had decided
to abandon their kind of cultural activity in order to devote himself
to the people's culture, among the people.

In Achmad's office there were three others already waiting.
Achmad stood up quickly, delighted to see Yasrin arrive.

"We've been waiting for you. We were afraid you wouldn't
be able to come at all. Let me introduce you first. This is Syafei,

people's poet; Murtoho, people's painter; and Hambali, people's short-story writer."

They sat down, and Achmad opened the meeting by telling them that the time had come when all artists—poets, writers, and painters—must get together to generate a real people's culture. He surveyed the cultural scene in Indonesia, pointing out that it was still dominated by a feudal atmosphere. It was self-evident that their now-independent country could not tolerate the continuation of feudalistic influences on culture, and that these would have to be consciously replaced by a people's culture.

"That's why we've been building up a fund large enough for this struggle. To start, we will establish a people's cultural organization called Movement for People's Culture. We intend to publish a militant cultural magazine. I've invited the four of you here today to invite you to work as full-time activists for this publication. For the time being, it'll come out once a month. But, besides the magazine, our task will also be to establish branches of the organization throughout the country, organize exhibitions of books, of paintings, organize literary competitions and a popular theater, and to create new people's dances and music. We've got a lot to do, and I hope we'll get through with all these preparations without losing too much time."

Achmad's statements excited Yasrin, causing his blood to race. He couldn't wait to start.

Achmad went on to explain that each activist would receive a monthly stipend of a thousand rupiah, and that they would be sent in turn to survey the various regions of their country. Later on, arrangements would be made for them to be invited to study methods of cultural organization in the People's Republic of China, in Russia, in Czechoslovakia, and other people's democracies.

Then they decided on the division of labor, and Yasrin was given the job of heading the people's cultural magazine, which was to appear at the beginning of the new year. He was to get an office in a house in the Tanah Tinggi area, where the Proletarian Library Foundation, which was publishing Indonesian translations of books by Russian and Chinese authors, had its headquarters.

They took leave of each other with mutual assurances of cooperation in the cause of the people's cultural uplift and the destruction of the residue of feudalistic cultural influences.

As Yasrin was walking home, an extraordinary joy seemed to flow through his veins, warming his whole body, making him feel as if he were bobbing along on a street of balloons, bouncing him upwards into the sky. He wanted to fill the air with cries of joy. I will now be working for the people, he thought. Now I know where I am and where I'm going. Achmad's words came into his mind again, how they would bring justice and prosperity to all the people, how social classes would be abolished and all men would live in happiness. To attain this, Achmad had said, we must be united, uncompromising, and merciless towards our enemies, the stooges of the imperialists and capitalists, the remnants of the feudal and bourgeois cliques.

He was just about to go into his house when he remembered that he still owed his landlady, Mrs Warmana, a month's rent for his room and board. But now he had no need to come home feeling uncomfortable. His total debt was only three hundred rupiah, and next month he would have a salary of one thousand. He'd have no trouble paying off his arrears for two months immediately. And he was suddenly struck with amazement at the idea of receiving one thousand rupiah each month. He had never earned such a large income before. His earnings had always been irregular. If he happened to publish some poems in Pranoto's journal, he would receive a honorarium of fifty to one hundred rupiah at the most. Once had he been given two thousand rupiah by a publisher for a collection of his poems but that money was soon gone, as he had

had many debts to settle. To supplement his income, he took on all sorts of writing assignments—book reviews and even stories for children—but all this never brought in more than three or four hundred rupiah a month. Now, suddenly, he was to get a salary of one thousand rupiah every month. Just before they had parted, Achmad had even mentioned that should he need some money before the end of the month he could ask for an advance.

Yasrin entered the house, whistling, and as he opened the door to his room and stepped inside, he was greeted by Mrs Warmana's son, Wiria, a senior high school student whose bedroom Yasrin slept in. "What's with the whistling? You must be happy about something."

Yasrin laughed, and sat down on his bed. "Guess what! Next month I'm going to buy you the books you haven't been able to afford. And my first present for you is going to be the collected works of Shakespeare."

Because Wiria was sharing the room with Yasrin, he had become enamored with the idea of becoming a poet and writer himself. He loved Shakespeare and his dream was to possess a complete set of Shakespeare's works in English.

Wiria sat up and looked at Yasrin. "But where will you get the money from?"

"Today I became chief editor of a magazine for people's culture with a salary of one thousand rupiah per month!"

Wiria uttered a cry of joy. "Will you include some of my writings, too?" he asked straightaway.

Yasrin consented easily. There were no difficulties left in his life or in the world, as far as he could see. He was back in the true line of battle. Everything had become simple and clear: the enemy to be annihilated; the aim to be pursued; and the way to attain it—that, too, was clear. There was to be no mercy for, or compromise with, the enemies of the proletariat!

Yasrin stretched out on his bed. Its mattress was worn thin and the shabby sheet, once white, was now grey. At the head of his bed, near the window, stood a shaky table covered with old newspapers. On it were piled some books he had been able to pick up second-hand, or had borrowed from friends without ever returning them. All these books must be replaced, too, Yasrin thought, turning over on his belly and looking at the books. *Darkness at Noon* by Arthur Koestler, which he had once liked: that will have to go! *For Whom the Bell Tolls* by Ernest Hemingway—a bourgeois writer—blasé, as he'd said himself—though earlier Yasrin had dreamed of being able to write as lucidly as Hemingway. The books by Maxim Gorky will remain, of course, he said to himself. And Yasrin was already thinking of the moment he'd buy himself a new pair of trousers and a new shirt. It was so pleasant to imagine what one longed to have and to know that it was within one's power to get it.

Evening. A heavy rain had been soaking Jakarta since the late afternoon. The air was grey, and half of the sky was overcast with black clouds, which threatened much heavier rain still to come. On the street, people on bicycles who were braving the rain pushed on at top speed, but many were seeking shelter under the trees along the road. *Becak* drivers had lowered the awnings over the passenger seat in front, and lovers seated inside could embrace cozily while being driven through the evening rain. The wheels of automobiles swished along the wet asphalt, and their yellow lamps were like the eyes of wild beasts in the darkness of the night.

People sleeping under the bridge tried to protect themselves from the sprays of rain blown in by the wind, screening themselves with worn-out mats and praying that the rain would not turn into a downpour. And the people who slept in the big water pipe that was waiting to be laid underground moved deeper inside, away from the opening where the rain was dripping in.

From time to time the heavy rolling of thunder rumbled above them, and it looked as if the rain was growing heavier. Inside a car, Raden Kaslan sat with his hands folded on his belly, looking out through the windscreen. The wipers swished back and forth, sweeping away the rainwater. At his side, Husin Limbara sat in silence, engrossed in his own thoughts. Husin Limbara's elegant Cadillac turned into the driveway of the Hotel des Indes, and Raden Kaslan and Husin Limbara stepped out.

"Be back by midnight," Raden Kaslan told the driver.

They entered the restaurant.

"Let's sit and have something to drink until the rain lets up," Raden Kaslan suggested.

They ordered coffee and some hors d'oeuvres.

"Is everything set?" said Husin Limbara, continuing a previous conversation. "Are you sure nothing will leak out?"

"Don't worry. When I take care of things, it's always well done."

"But…?"

"There are no buts," Raden Saleh immediately interjected. After taking a sip of coffee, he added, "For us older men who are near or over fifty, it's a very good way. You'll see for yourself. Indonesian women don't seem to like to oral sex, but the young Eurasian ladies seem to like it very much."

"What's the name again of the woman who's making the arrangements?" Husin Limbara asked.

"She's known as Aunty Bep. You'll meet her soon."

As the rain had by now begun to let up, Raden Kaslan summoned a hotel boy and ordered him to call a *becak* for them.

In the *becak*, whose driver was Itam, Raden Kaslan was saying to Husin Limbara, "It's better to go to Aunty Bep's place by *becak*. In my car, someone might recognize us. And if it happened to be an unfriendly reporter, it could get into the newspapers." Raden Kaslan burst out laughing.

The *becak* soon brought them to Petojo, and, following Raden Kaslan's directions, entered a lane, and then stopped before Aunty Bep's house.

"Do you want me to wait, sir?" Itam asked.

Raden Kaslan looked at the sky where clumps of dark clouds were still hanging, felt the thin drizzle in the air and said, "All right, just wait here." Then he hurried into the house, drawing Husin Limbara in after him.

Aunty Bep, who was waiting for them in the front room, rose quickly to shake hands with both Raden Kaslan and Husin Limbara.

"Oh my, my good sirs," Aunty Bep was saying, "I had begun to think you wouldn't come at all because of the rain. We agreed on nine o'clock, it's already close to ten now."

"Have the young ladies arrived?" said Raden Kaslan eagerly.

"Yes, they're inside but they were just about ready to go home," she told the men. "Come with me, please."

Husin Limbara, drawn along by Raden Kaslan, went further inside the house.

Raden Kaslan said jokingly, "This friend of mine's a virgin, and still a bit shy!"

Aunty Bep laughed as she led them to the back verandah where two Eurasian girls were sitting at a table. They remained seated as Husin Limbara and Raden Kaslan approached and then sat down.

"Good evening, Eve," said Raden Kaslan to the one with black hair. She had a lovely figure and wore a gown cut so low that half of her full white breasts were showing.

Raden Kaslan introduced Husin Limbara to Eve. "This is a friend of mine."

Eve extended her hand with a slight smile.

Raden Kaslan glanced at Aunty Bep and then at the other young woman. "I haven't met this young lady, but isn't she lovely, too?"

"That's Eda," said Aunty Bep in introduction.

Eda's hair was of a russet color and she was slightly smaller than Eve. Indifferently she gave her hand, first to Raden Kaslan, then to Husin Limbara.

"So there," said Raden Kaslan to his friend. "Which one do you want? You're the guest of honor tonight, and you may choose. As for me, I want Eda here, she's new!" and he caressed Eda from behind her chair.

Eda slapped the hand grasping her breast. "Not so fast!"

"It's ten o'clock," said Eve. "Come on, it'll be getting late."

Eve drew Husin Limbara into the room adjoining the verandah, and Raden Kaslan led Eda to the middle room.

As soon as they were inside Eve turned the key in the door, and said to Husin Limbara, "If it isn't locked, Aunty Bep is likely to peep."

Husin Limbara sat down on the bed. From the moment they'd entered the room Eve's behavior had changed completely. The nonchalant attitude she'd exhibited on the verandah had vanished, and now she was a young woman greatly taken with him. Her eyes, her smile, and the movements of her body excited the fifty-year-old man.

Earlier, on the back verandah, he'd still felt reluctant and confused, but now, alone with Eve, he was delighted to feel the pulsing of his aroused blood. He was getting on in years and, having stopped doing anything with his own wife long ago, he could hardly remember the pleasure of having sexual relations with a woman. But now he felt the surging joy of his virility once again as he saw Eve taking off her clothing, one item after another, and then coming to him in only her bra and panties. Eve took hold of Husin Limbara's hand. Husin Limbara trembled, his breath tightening. The experienced Eve had seen it all before. She helped Husin Limbara off with his jacket and then he lay back on the bed watching Eve slip off her bra and panties, and, swinging her hips, go towards the door and turn off the light. The room was now in semi-darkness, some light still filtering from the back verandah.

Eve came over to the bed and whispered, "Do you want me to use my mouth?" And she laughed softly.

Outside in the drizzling rain, now falling more heavily again, Itam sat huddled in his *becak*, clasping his shoulders with his chilled hands, waiting.

On that same rainy night, Fatma came to Suryono's room, where he was reading a Western. When Fatma locked the door, he knew at once what his stepmother desired. During the past few weeks all the initiative had been coming from her. Fatma herself had brought up the subject several times, but Suryono had always managed to avoid it up till now. During these last weeks, Suryono's feelings had become more and more mixed up. Fatma, Dahlia, Ies: the three of them were in his blood, each attractive to him in her own way, yet Fatma was gradually being pushed to the background by Dahlia and Ies, and Dahlia in turn was being supplanted by Ies. None of this was clear to him yet, but some subconscious process had already thrown him into a state of great confusion and robbed him of his peace of mind. It was as though his life were threatened every moment by some great disaster and destruction. From just what direction and in what form the calamity would descend upon him he couldn't imagine.

Fatma came to Suryono as he lay on his bed, drew his head into her arms, and kissed his mouth in a long-drawn, deep kiss. She whispered, "I've been longing for you so much. It's been two weeks!"

For a moment Suryono decided to resist Fatma's caresses, but his resolve was dispersed like wind-blown smoke by Fatma's passionate kiss.

Later, when they had calmed down, Fatma got out of the bed and sat in a chair. Suryono lit a cigarette and asked her, "Have you ever stopped to think of the future?"

"I don't understand what you mean."

"This can't go on forever. Sooner or later Father will find out, and then what will happen?"

"Even if he does find out, what can he do to us?" she pouted. "Don't I know he's playing around with other women himself?"

"Yes, but I'm his son and you are my stepmother!"

"So what?" Fatma replied. "We have enough money that there's no need to worry. We could move out of this house any time we like."

"You don't care about my father at all?"

"I'm too young and he's too old for us to be together."

"It's strange that there should be no emotional or spiritual bond between myself and my father at all now," Suryono said, addressing himself mainly. He remembered that when he was a child he and his father had been very close. But then later he had spent many years in his uncle's care while at school, far from home. Having no brothers or sisters, and having lost his mother, the old intimacy with his father had slowly vanished. Moreover, watching his father's activities during recent months had in no way enhanced his respect for him. From time to time he even felt contempt for his own behavior as well. Emotionally he knew that what they were doing was wrong; that even though it was all quite legal, to exploit the party's power to enrich oneself was still improper, somehow.

It was the same with his relationship with Fatma. He felt that it was not proper, yet every time he succumbed again. It was the same, too, with his acceptance of the special licenses. He felt that it wasn't right for him to be getting them, but the hundreds of thousands of rupiah these licenses yielded excited and pleased him, reminded him of Dahlia's caresses, the bright polish of a new car, the pleasure of eating in a fine restaurant, the weight of the wallet in his pocket. Unable to resist this temptation, he even experienced a kind of pleasure in trading his special licenses.

"What did you say?" Suryono said suddenly, coming out of his musings and noticing that Fatma was speaking.

"You weren't even listening," Fatma said in annoyance. "Where on earth have your thoughts been? You've been like this a lot lately.... Is there another woman?" she asked.

Suryono gave a little laugh. "I'm upset for some reason; haven't been feeling too good the past few days. God knows why…"

"You didn't answer my question. Is there another woman?"

Suryono looked at Fatma, and decided to test her.

"And if there were, what then?"

Fatma laughed, and said, "If there is, it's none of my business. I'm not your wife, but your father's. But if another woman is giving you trouble, tell me about it. Maybe I can help you."

Suryono was startled. "Don't you don't have any moral sense?"

Fatma burst into laughter. "Do you? Morality is just a burden that causes people trouble. People should do what gives them pleasure while they're still alive to do so. Don't rack your brains about things you're not responsible for. I care for you, and I'm happy when you're carefree, and that's why I want to help you. Come on, tell me!'

Suryono laughed. "Dear Allah! I've never met a woman like you!"

Fatma laughed again, then took a cigarette from the table and lit it. She puffed the smoke into Suryono's face. "I'm still young, but I've had my lessons in life. Listen to this. I told you once before how I came to marry your father, but you don't know the whole story. Before I married your father I was already a widow. My husband was killed during the revolution. He was a lieutenant. I loved him, and with his death my love died too. Unfortunately his rank was too low for him to be remembered by the government, and he was not included among the 'great heroes to be remembered by the people'. Naturally no one paid any attention to me as his widow, either. I wasn't given a penny of support after his death. But I had to live, so I moved down to Jakarta where my aunt put me up in her house. Believe me, a young and pretty woman has no trouble making money if she's prepared to use her body and beauty. But I was very cautious. I chose the men very carefully. That's the only way to take good care of your body and your reputation and see to it that your price stays high. It's always like this with men: the more difficult it is to get a woman, the more they desire to possess her.

"When I first met your father, I was not attracted to him at all. He was too ostentatious about what he could get with all his money, as though simply having money allowed him do anything he pleased, even buy a person entirely. The more I withdrew from him, the more he longed to dominate me. So I told him that I would submit to him, but only on one condition: that he would marry me. And so he married me. He married me not because he loved me or cared for me, or because he really desired me passionately. No, the first night after our wedding he just slept through it, snoring. He'd drunk too much! After that he didn't come to me very often because I didn't like to do the thing he asked. But it seems that your father is pleased to have a young, good-looking wife, enjoys hearing his friends admire her beauty and seeing other men try to approach her. Your father is satisfied; he knows that he owns something that many others would enjoy having. That is what I mean to him. Why should I try to be moral as far as he's concerned if he's completely immoral himself? Besides, as we sit here talking, he's probably having his way with another woman!

"I've learned from life that you must seize whatever you desire, and whatever makes you happy, quickly and without hesitation.

And that there's no use worrying about what might happen later. Our fate is in the hands of God."

Suryono smiled at the contradiction in Fatma's statement which mentioned God. Inwardly he wished he could be as free of doubt in facing life as Fatma was.

"There are three women in my life now," Suryono told Fatma, answering her story about herself with one about himself. "You, a woman named Dahlia who is also married, and Ies, an unmarried girl. I care for all three of you. I love you all, and each time I am with one of you I feel happy and at peace, satisfied and pleased with life. I'm happy to be alive right now, and feel no need to think about tomorrow or the day after. With Dahlia I experience another kind of joy, though it's somewhat like the feeling when I'm with you. With Ies my feeling of joy is different; it's full of hope and promise for the future and I feel that, if given the opportunity, I would not hesitate to face life with Ies forever."

"Have you slept with both of them yet?" Fatma asked.

Suryono did not notice the jealousy in her face. "With Dahlia, but not with Ies."

"What is Dahlia like?"

"Like you."

Fatma laughed. "To speak as a mother to her son, it would be best for you to forget Dahlia and concentrate on Ies. But apparently the girl does not fully respond to your feelings towards her?"

"Could be," Suryono said. "Sometimes it seems as though my own doubts are mirrored in her."

"Don't worry," Fatma told him. "Everything will come out all right by itself. The fire that now consumes you and Dahlia will stop burning some day, and, when the time comes, between the two of us, too, maybe, but it won't matter. I'm not dreaming of living with you as husband and wife, though it's quite an attractive possibility." Fatma smiled, and quickly added, "But I suppose it's impossible, isn't it? Or maybe if your father dies?" She paused. "I know the way a man must act to overcome a girl's hesitation, but I'm not going to tell you. I'll lose you too soon. So you'll have to find out for yourself."

Fatma stood up, pressed her cigarette butt against the ashtray, bent over, kissed Suryono, and went to the door. "Sleep well!" she said as she closed the door behind her.

Yasrin had just finished informing Pranoto that, starting today, he was leaving the journal Pranoto was promoting to work for a people's cultural periodical which would be launched by a group of his communist friends.

Pranoto had listened in silence while Yasrin talked. "Well, what can I say?" he said finally. "I fully respect your new convictions, but I'm also deeply sorry that you're leaving us. Our struggle is far from over. We still have a long way to go."

"I hope I have explained everything clearly enough," Yasrin said.

"Oh, yes. I don't want to quarrel with your decision. But there's something I can't help telling you. You've said that our group is nothing but a salon whose members talk about the people in a purely academic way without doing anything for them. Lots of talk and no action. In contrast, the communists, you say, work among the people. Don't you see that once we've chosen democracy it can't be otherwise? We're not going to force the people to swallow our ideas. We can only inform them of these ideas and hope that people will gradually understand, accept and make these ideas their own. Therein lies the strength of democracy, but its weakness as well. But once we are determined to follow the democratic way, we must have the courage to accept both its strengths and its weaknesses."

"That's where I disagree with you," said Yasrin. "As I see it, all this is merely a pretense to cover up your incapacity to work among the people."

"Look!" said Pranoto. "What do the cultural activities promoted by the communists amount to? They send our young painters and writers to all sorts of festivals in communist countries, and when they come home they write glowing reports about the cultural activities there. What good does this do our people?"

"That's because, unlike the bourgeois clique, we're not in power yet," Yasrin answered.

Pranoto smiled.

"Well, there's no use in our arguing about it here," said Yasrin.

Yasrin's leaving their club created a little stir among Pranoto's friends. Some denounced him, some approved his action. One comment was, "At least he has the courage to choose sides." Someone else observed rather cynically, "All he wants is the thousand-rupiah salary. It's all the same to Yasrin whether it comes from Indonesia's pocket, from Peking, from the Kremlin, or from Washington. All he sees are ten hundred-rupiah notes."

CITY BEAT

"I suggest, gentlemen, that you settle it amicably between yourselves. Why make a case of it?" said the police commissioner to the two men seated before his desk.

"But I have the proper permit for the house," said Abdul Manap as he took a housing bureau certificate from his briefcase. "This man, Suparto here, occupied the house before I had a chance to move in, though he has no housing permit at all."

"The problem is that you two were disturbing the peace," the police commissioner pointed out. "The best thing for you to do is to settle this between yourselves."

"I am willing to make peace if Suparto, who has no permit, is prepared to move out," Abdul Manap replied.

"I am willing to move out, provided that I am given another place to live," said Suparto.

"There's nothing I can do about that," the police commissioner told him "That's a matter for the housing bureau."

"It's not my responsibility either," said Abdul Manap. "What about the order-to-vacate which the housing bureau has issued to Suparto? Aren't you going to enforce it?"

Suparto raised his voice. "Shoot me dead, if you want, I'm not going to move out unless I have another place in exchange."

"Stop your talk about shooting," the police commissioner warned. "I didn't ask you to come here to start fighting again, but to make peace."

Abdul Manap's frustration was showing: "All I know is that I obtained a legal housing permit and that I'm going to occupy this house legally. And, if it comes to dying, I'm not afraid of dying either!"

"Easy, easy," said the police commissioner. "I see that both of you gentlemen are still agitated. There's no use our continuing this discussion any further as long as you're in this state. I suggest that you go home now, and that neither of you trespass on the place until a final decision has been made."

"Does this mean you're not going to enforce the order-to-vacate issued by the housing bureau?" asked Abdul Manap.

"Have patience, sir. I'll take care of it myself. Everything will come out all right."

The police commissioner stood up, forcing the other two to rise as well, and ushered them out of his room. "Now let's all be friends. We've all got families. Let's be patient."

When the two visitors had left, the commissioner took a handkerchief from his trouser pocket, wiped his forehead, and sighed to the inspector who sat at a desk in one corner of the office, "I'm sorry, but this is the responsibility of the housing bureau. Why don't they just abolish it?"

December

Hasnah sat sewing clothes for her unborn child. According to the doctor, she could expect it by the middle of February. She had asked Sugeng to choose two names for the new baby—one for a girl, and one for a boy. They both wanted Maryam to have a baby brother. But Hasnah's joy at the coming of the new child was now often clouded when she thought about her husband and the great change that had taken place in their family life. Their luck in getting a house of their own had not brought the happiness they had hoped for. On the contrary, doubts kept assailing her. She didn't enjoy the refrigerator, the large radio set, the electric record player Sugeng had bought for them. They stirred up uncomfortable feelings and troubling questions.

She felt more keenly than anything that a kind of estrangement had grown up between her and Sugeng. It had started when Hasnah had asked Sugeng where he had obtained so much money. At first he'd evaded giving her a direct answer, but later, when pressed by Hasnah, he had said that he was now a partner in an import business run by a friend.

Hasnah's uneasiness had been further aggravated in recent months, seeing Sugeng more and more often leaving the house in the evening. When he was still an ordinary official with a meager salary he'd never acted this way. Sugeng had of course gone out sometimes in the evening by himself, but then Hasnah knew precisely where he was going: usually to a friend's house, to chat and gossip while playing chess or bridge. Now Sugeng was gone as early as 7 PM, sometimes even before having his supper and didn't get back till midnight or even one in the morning. Considering the advanced stage of her pregnancy, Hasnah sensed that Sugeng's frequent absences were not necessitated, as he said, by urgent work or the need to attend to some business transactions. She suspected there was probably a woman, but she carefully concealed these suspicions from Sugeng.

Hasnah heaved a long sigh, hearing the big clock in the middle room strike one. So it was already one o'clock. Sugeng would soon be back from the office for his midday break. The clock was a large upright piece which had cost six thousand rupiah. Hasnah didn't really like it. She had been quite satisfied with their old bedside alarm clock. She felt it was just showing off how rich they were to have this useless big clock. But Sugeng had been set on buying it. He had seen one like it in Raden Kaslan's house—and it looked very beautiful there. Hasnah herself had met Raden Kaslan only once; two weeks ago she and Sugeng had been invited to a party at his house. She had seen Raden Kaslan's wife, who was still quite young, as well as his son, Suryono, and intuitively sensed that things were not right in Raden Kaslan's family.

Back home, after the party, Sugeng was speaking animatedly about Raden Kaslan and Suryono, when Hasnah suddenly dampened his enthusiasm by observing, "I don't know why, but I didn't like Raden Kaslan or his family. That tough old guy is a bit too slippery for my taste; his tone of voice and laughter don't ring true. His wife doesn't seem to pay any attention to him. And his son is a womanizer, I think."

Hasnah put her sewing down on the table and went into the kitchen to see to the food. In the old days she used to cook on charcoal braziers and sometimes her eyes smarted from the smoke while she fanned the flame; now she had a modern gas-cooker, costing no less than seven thousand five hundred rupiah, complete with oven. But Hasnah didn't enjoy cooking in her modern kitchen as much as when she had to squat down to fan the fire. Now two servants were working in the kitchen, and all she had to do was to give orders. And of course to light the gas, you didn't need anyone to blow! After making sure the meal would be ready in time for Sugeng when he got in, Hasnah went back to the middle room and then into her bedroom.

All the furniture there was new but Hasnah's sadness at parting with their old familiar furnishings had far outweighed her pleasure in getting this new elegant bedroom set. And now Sugeng kept saying that as soon as he could afford to stop working as a civil servant he'd immediately buy a car.

"If I buy a car now, while I'm still a civil servant, people would say all sorts of nasty things," Sugeng had said.

Hasnah had made no reply then; she didn't want to tell Sugeng that among themselves his friends had been discussing their new prosperity for quite a while now. Even her friend Dahlia, when she'd visited them in their new home, had remarked, "Your husband's got very smart at making money. Not like mine! He keeps telling me that a government official must be honest. And no matter how many examples I show him of honest officials living in misery nowadays, he still wants to stay honest. He says the time will come when righteousness will come to our country and those who stay honest will have their reward. Isn't he stupid, though? If I weren't smart enough to make some money on my own, I'd..."

Hasnah had felt as though Dahlia was beating her, blow after blow, that her heart was almost breaking with mortification. She couldn't say a single word. For quite some time she had felt sure that Sugeng must be doing something wrong to get that much money. But she hadn't found the right opportunity to broach the question to Sugeng again.

The last time she had asked him how he made the money Sugeng had said, "Why do you keep on asking? Isn't it enough for you to be getting so much every month now?"

And when she had insisted further, he'd said, "Hasnah, if you think that I'm making this money in some improper way, you must realize that I'm doing it for you. You yourself begged me to do it. Don't you remember giving me the ultimatum, that before we had another child we first had to have a house of our own?"

So she had been silent, unable to answer. Deep down in her heart she admitted the possibility that it was she who had been at fault pushing Sugeng into doing something that was wrong. Perhaps she had insisted too strongly on having a house of their own. But she'd never expected that Sugeng would get in so deep. And besides, even when she begged for a house, she'd never asked to live in luxury. What she'd imagined was just a house all to themselves, no matter how small, no matter where—even on a small side street. A table and chairs bought from a roadside peddler would have been quite good enough. And she'd have made the little house beautiful just with the radiance of her love as a wife and a mother.

Hasnah decided then to pray to God that He might protect Sugeng and save their family. Forgive me, oh, God, she had prayed in her heart. And then she began blaming herself. What have I done to Sugeng to make him like this? I'm to blame, I am the guilty one. She was startled as she heard the sound of a car horn blowing in front of the house. She stepped outside, and what she had guessed in a flash proved true. Sugeng, with a broad smile on his face, was there, sitting in a car, tapping on the horn and opening the door for Maryam who had come running, dropping her toys. Hasnah forced herself to smile.

Sugeng immediately announced, "You may congratulate me now! I've been given permission to resign from the service starting from the end of the month, but from tomorrow I won't have to go to work anymore. I was expecting this, and picked up this car at once. Now we're importers. I'm a director of Mas Mulia Corporation. Come on, get in, let's try it out!"

Hasnah got into the car and Sugeng drove out of their yard. Maryam was squealing with pleasure.

"Dear God, protect my husband," Hasnah prayed as the car swung into the roadway. "I am the guilty one; it was I who made him become like this!"

Laughing, Sugeng said to Maryam, "Isn't your papa's car beautiful?"

Murhalim was looking out of the window of the Garuda Indonesia Airways plane flying over Sumatra on his return trip from Padang to Jakarta. He had spent a week organizing meetings of the newly established Indonesian Islamic Youth Corps. He felt very satisfied with the whole trip. Especially with his meeting with Achmad, who, as a communist activist, had come from Jakarta to bolster communist influence in central Sumatra. They had spent a night in the same hotel, and Achmad had boasted that the meeting he was organizing on the same day as Murhalim's would draw a far greater crowd. For the fun of it, they made a bet of twenty-five rupiah. Murhalim smiled, remembering Achmad giving him the twenty-five rupiah afterwards and admitting defeat. The communist meeting had been a complete flop. Only about fifty people had turned up. On the other hand, according to a newspaper estimate, the meeting Murhalim had organized had attracted no less than eight thousand. This event had caused such a stir that several newspapers had carried the news, comparing the attendance of the two meetings.

That evening after paying his debt, Achmad said to him at dinner, "This still doesn't prove that the people understand what you're telling them."

Murhalim laughed. "You communists always make the same mistake. You look at people as though they were cattle, or machines you can manipulate any way you want. It's not enough for men to have a full stomach every day. They also have a soul. You don't admit that the human soul has a life of its own. The communist is an incomplete human being, because he's trained and conditioned to live only in a materialistic world. Human life is rich and varied, it's like a woven fabric with multi-colored designs: man can love God, he can love his family, he longs to create eternal values: beauty, justice, truth and so forth."

"What a lot of nonsense," said Achmad. "These are the ideas of your decadent bourgeoisie. You just won't admit that religion is a socio-political factor, and that the history of religion, whether Christian or Muslim, has demonstrated its essentially reactionary and anti-popular nature. All through human history, religion has been inseparably connected with enslavement and exploitation by the feudal and capitalist classes. Look how the Spaniards in spreading the Catholic religion plundered, burnt, and ravished the Indians in Mexico; and how in our own country the Dutch came bringing priests and the cross to help them consolidate their domination."

"If your communist theory is true, how do you explain so many adherents of Christianity and so many Islamic leaders joining the vanguard of our revolution?"

"But what are they doing now for the people?" said Achmad. "Nothing! Don't you see that? And as for Islamic religious leaders, don't you know that Islam is a faith invented by bourgeois Arab traders? You can see for yourself what Islam means in the Arab countries. All through the ages the masses have always been maltreated, while the feudal cliques lived in extravagant luxury, and now look how many of our own Islamic leaders are in the race to get rich."

"There's no use our debating this now," Murhalim answered, smiling. "It will lead us nowhere. You will never accept the fact that God exists, that the evils perpetrated in the name of religion do not mean that the religion itself is either evil or wrong, but that it's men who commit wrongdoings and evil, and that there's no connection between their behavior and the religion they profess to follow. Religious people who perpetrate deeds forbidden by God break the prescriptions of their own religion, and they deceive themselves if they continue to claim to be religious."

"That's an easy way out, to dissociate religion from the corruption we see all round us nowadays," Achmad retorted.

"Many Muslims feel the need to renew and purify the spirit of Islam, to bring it into harmony with the teaching contained in the Holy Quran and the Hadith of the Prophet Mohammed."

Achmad shook his head. "You're still just the same. You don't believe in the progress of human thought."

"Not true," said Murhalim. "The greater the progress in human thought, the stronger is man's conviction that God exists. Look at the history of man's development: at first he had no belief at all; then he began to worship fire, then trees, stones, spirits, gods, and finally the one and only God."

Achmad merely laughed.

Murhalim looked out of the window again. Below him spread tall and steep mountain ranges, valleys in greens and yellows, and from time to time the brilliant light of the sun flashed on the surface of rivers which gleamed in their winding course below. A yellowish-white road stretched through the countryside. From above, it looked like a fine, smooth road. But Murhalim knew how it was in reality: murderous for vehicles, full of pot-holes, deteriorating with every passing year, never repaired and like a thorn in the people's flesh penetrating deeper and getting more painful all the time. Murhalim recalled the typical resentment of an inhabitant of the region, just back from Java, who had told him that he had seen how the excellent paved highway between Bogor, south of Jakarta, and Cipanas, site of one of the president's palaces, was being further widened and improved, while the roads in his region were not being repaired at all. Let alone reconstruction of completely ruined roads, he complained. There's no maintenance to speak of on the passable ones.

He'd experienced it himself as a passenger in a car which took over twenty minutes to cover a distance of five kilometers because the road was full of pot-holes. Murhalim felt strongly that the government leadership of Indonesia had been making terrible mistakes. The source of Indonesia's strength lay with the people of the regions outside Java and yet they were the most neglected and poorly administered of all. Hundreds of millions of rupiah were being divvied up among political big shots in Jakarta to buy or set up large enterprises, but year after year a pitiful few tens of thousands for a small clinic couldn't be spared. He recalled the words of a provincial sub-district head who had said to him, "We people outside Java are treated like beggars. All we can do is beg from the central government. If the center has pity on us we get something; if not, well, tough luck!"

Murhalim had also heard younger people voicing their dissatisfaction with the central government with much greater vehemence. There were some who were plainly threatening rebellion and the founding of their own republic; and because the central government was located in Java, many showed anti-Javanese feelings.

"It's *our* people who earn the foreign exchange, but it's spent by the Javanese," someone had said. Murhalim had answered that it was not the Javanese people who were the enemies of the regional people, but the leaders now in power who were mismanaging the country. And though some of these leaders were Javanese, they also included some local leaders from their own region. The problem was not one of the outer regions versus Java, but of getting a responsible leadership for the state, one capable of furthering the country's development.

As he had seen, however, it was difficult to convince his friends in Sumatra that this was the basic problem. Murhalim had promised to communicate their feelings and opinions to the leaders in Jakarta, even as he knew that he could not persuade them to attend seriously to these regional problems. He thought, it would go in one ear and out the other.

Suddenly Murhalim felt utterly powerless, as though he were no more than an ant. He thought of the divisions among Islamic groups, about how backward they were, and how important it was for the Muslim community in Indonesia to be stirred by the dynamism of true Islam. There was too much to do and too few people capable of doing it. Murhalim remembered that he had often been disturbed by a dream of a solitary man in a boat, straining at the oars until his strength gave out, overcome by weakness, no longer able to fight the rushing current and his boat beginning to drift downstream…. He silently uttered, "*Ashadu allaillah aillallah waashadu ana Muhamad arasullullah!* I witness that there is no God but Allah and Mohammad is his Prophet."

Suryono leaned back on the seat in his car, closed his eyes, and held Ies's hand. She leaned on his shoulder, looking out over the sea, its rolling black waves breaking into whiteness on the dark brown sand. The strong wind felt fresh on Ies's cheek, and the sky above was studded with stars. "Mood music", as Suryono called it, was streaming from the car's radio. For a moment the interior of the car was lit up by the headlights of a car turning around to park nearby. The end of the road leading from the Tanjung Priok Yacht Club was crowded with cars that night. In some of them couples were embracing and kissing, paying no attention to the cars close by, and stopping only when the headlights of a passing car suddenly shone in on them. The satay vendors were doing a brisk business selling their skewers of grilled meat on the beach, and the night wind was heavy with the scent of satay spices.

Ies looked at Suryono's face. He attracted her strongly at that moment. She had an impulse to discard all her doubts and plunge into bliss with Suryono. His face was handsome. The thin moustache accentuated his full lips, though upon closer examination the lines of that well-shaped mouth also showed weakness; it was not the mouth of a strong man, but the sensuous mouth of a man enslaved by his passions. But neither the lines of that weak mouth nor the shape of Suryono's rather pointed chin disturbed Ies at that moment. Unconsciously, her hand slipped out of Suryono's and her fingers sank into his wavy hair, slowly winding and unwinding it. Suryono growled as though he were a satisfied tiger.

"If only you'd do this with my hair every day," he said, without opening his eyes. "I'm very happy tonight."

He put his hand on Ies's neck and drew her head towards his own until their mouths met and Ies, forgetting herself for a moment, let Suryono kiss her mouth, and answered his kisses. But the next moment she pulled herself up, quickly withdrawing her lips from Suryono's kiss.

"Why not, Ies? Please!" Suryono begged.

"There's a car coming," Ies said, as an excuse.

Suryono, giving in, removed his hand from Ies's neck, embraced her shoulder with his left hand and then his hand slipped downwards and his fingers pressed her breast.

Ies pulled his hand away. "Please don't!"

Suryono opened his eyes completely. "Why are you like this tonight? Such a romantic night, with music, and the waves whispering on the beach. And I'm here with you." He sat up straight and looked at Ies. "I don't understand you. Sometimes you seem to want me, but sometimes I feel as though you really dislike my kissing you."

Suryono looked at Ies with a peeved expression, displeased but restraining his annoyance. And suddenly, as though a pitch-dark place had been lit up in a flash by a bright lamp, Ies was able to see deep into the recesses of Suryono's soul, to see through his face, his wavy hair, and his love-filled words. What she saw made her shiver as if she were gripped by a fever, yet at the same time she was overcome by pity for Suryono. Now she knew why she'd been wavering all this time and what her answer would be, were Suryono to speak. Intuitively she had sensed Suryono's state of mind and knew that tonight he would propose to her. She now felt relieved, strong and confident in herself. All her doubts were gone. And for some reason she suddenly thought of Pranoto—but her thoughts were immediately interrupted. Suryono was speaking to her.

"Ies, I want to tell you something."

Knowing what she would have to tell him, Ies felt sorry for Suryono. "What is it?" she said softly.

The softness of Ies' voice conveyed something entirely different to Suryono and, sure of his prize, he held her shoulders. "I love you, Ies. Let's get married."

He tried to draw Ies to himself and kiss her, but Ies freed herself from his embrace and moved away. "I am sorry, but I cannot."

Completely surprised by her refusal, Suryono did not believe what he had heard. He put his hand back on her shoulder, and again tried to pull Ies closer to himself. "You're joking, aren't you? It can't be true. Don't you love me?"

The possibility that Ies did not love him was inconceivable. After all this time, after all the embraces and kisses…. Now she was saying that she did not love him and did not want to marry him?

Ies spoke in a soft but firm voice. "I'm sorry, but I've thought about this a long time and have concluded that you and I are not suitable for each other. We can be friends, but I don't think we should marry. I'm not sure we'd be happy together."

Suryono abruptly pushed a radio button and a voice resounded in the stillness of the car, the voice of a bewildered heart not understanding how it had lost everything it had believed till now to be true.

"I don't understand!"

Deep below his consciousness, Suryono's male pride, hurt by Ies's repudiation, began to smart, and as he became aware of the pain he also understood that he loved Ies now more than ever before; without Ies he could not live and he would gladly do anything if only he could have her. At the same time, because he sensed that Ies would withdraw further if he pressed his suit more strongly, he modified his approach.

"I don't know what to say," Suryono said. "Forgive me if I've hurt you or offended you. I know that I'm nothing, a man without any status, as a merchant a mere beginner. There's nothing I can offer you but my love."

"It's not because of status or wealth…" Ies began to say.

"I love you, Ies, and can't live without you. Give me some clue why won't you have me?"

Ies looked at Suryono. If she weren't as fully aware of Suryono's true character as she was, this was the moment when she'd have surrendered to him. His face gave the impression of absolute honesty, as though he really meant what he said.

"Without you my life will be utter desolation forever," he was saying.

"May I be frank?"

"That's what I want," Suryono replied. "Because of my love for you, I can bear whatever you may say."

"I'm full of doubts about you because you are full of doubts yourself," Ies told him. "One moment I see one kind of Suryono, the next moment another one appears, and later still, yet another. I don't which one of these Suryonos is the real you. I'm also confused by the way you suddenly became so rich."

Suryono was quiet. Inwardly he admitted that what Ies had said was right. Hadn't he recently been increasingly driven by doubts and premonitions, as if a disaster were to overtake him any minute? His sleep was filled with frightful nightmares. In his dreams he would be driving a car, alone or with Ies, or with Fatma, or with Dahlia, and as he reached top speed he'd suddenly feel that the car was out of control. He'd try to step hard on the brakes but they wouldn't function and the car would keep rushing onwards; his heart would be gripped by terror as the car headed either for an abyss, or towards an inevitable collision with another car, or into a crowd. Then he would scream, and wake up bathed in sweat. And when he realized that it had been only a dream, that he was in his bed at home, he would be filled with relief and glad of his safety, only to be plagued the next moment with doubts and questions as to the meaning of the dream.

As he recalled all this, the expression of his face was like that of a child who'd lost his way, a look that filled Ies with pity. Had he said nothing for a few minutes longer Ies might have changed her mind but, instead, Suryono pressed on, trying to strengthen his case by making use of what Ies had said about him.

"What you're saying is true," he told her. "For some time I've been bewildered as to where I belong in the struggle our people are waging. Sometimes I hear calling the bells of independence in 1945, but then I'm filled with disgust at the doings of those who claim to be our fighters and I am seized by indifference. I need you to help me find myself again."

The last phrase struck Ies as empty, and strengthened her resolve to refuse Suryono. "Really, Yono, it's no use."

From the tone of her voice Suryono at last understood that whatever he might say or do would not reverse Ies's decision. Resentment, anger, and spite rose in him and he was gripped by an irresistible desire to hurt her in return. He looked at Ies, and her whole body excited his passion beyond control. He threw his arms around her and pressed his body against hers, his mouth seeking her lips.

Ies shook her head as she fended him off. "Don't, Yono, don't. I don't want to!"

Suryono ignored her pleas and rubbed his hand against her breast. Ies pushed him away and they wrestled silently in the car. Just when she was about to scream, Suryono suddenly released her, sat up behind the wheel, started the motor, backed up a little, and swung the car towards the highway.

"All right, I'll take you home," he said abruptly.

Ies didn't know it, but while they were struggling Suryono had spotted a patrol of three policemen on bicycles who were conducting a check of the vicinity.

They were both silent during the whole trip to Ies's home. In front of her house Suryono cried, "Forgive me, Ies, I didn't know what I was doing!"

Ies made no reply and rapidly walked to the entrance of her house.

Suryono stepped on the accelerator and the car jerked forward with a loud squeal. If Ies wouldn't have him, Suryono decided, then he would see if he could ease his tension at Aunty Bep's.

A short while later, as Suryono approached Aunty Bep's, he noticed a *becak* waiting outside the house. Its driver was sitting on the passenger's seat, smoking. Suryono stopped the car behind the *becak*, got out, and asked the driver, "Who'd you bring here? Was she pretty?"

Itam, the *becak* driver, shook his head. "No, I brought a couple gentlemen visitors."

Suryono went to the front verandah, and just as he was about to open the door he saw through its window a sight that startled him and made him stop: his father being led into a room by the young woman he knew as Eda. Just as surprising, moments later Husin Limbara came in from the back verandah with his arm around the young woman he knew as Eve.

Suryono backed away from the house slowly until he reached the courtyard and then, half amused, half shocked, he hastened outside. At that point, the comical side of what he'd just seen—his father and Husin Limbara—made him laugh inwardly.

On the way to his car, Suryono stopped to speak to the *becak* driver who was standing near his pedicab. "Those two guys you brought here…. Do they come here often?"

"Not too often," Itam answered without a thought. "With me, just three times, counting today."

"From where do they take your *becak*?"

"They arrange for me to pick them up at the Hotel des Indes."

Suryono gave Itam a Lucky Strike cigarette, laughed softly to himself, got into his car, and drove home fast. What sly old fellows, he thought. I hope Fatma is home.

He was in good spirits again, as though having seen what his father and Husin Limbara were doing made his own transgressions less wrong.

"Good God, if the opposition papers only knew this!" He laughed at the thought, but not for long, as the possible consequences occurred to him.

Later, at home, he was much more passionate with Fatma than usual. Fatma was both surprised and pleased.

Towards the end of December the rains became much heavier, pouring down day after day, so that many places in Jakarta stood under water. The smaller streets and alleys were a morass of deep mud. The people's hardships increased with the rains.

Dissatisfaction with the government and the parties in power also grew more evident as it became ever more difficult to fill the needs of the population for rice, salt, and kerosene. Opposition newspapers carried ever harsher criticisms of the government and of pro-government political parties. Several newspapers pointed to one party especially, and singled out the names of those of its leaders engaged in the special operations for building up the party's funds. The rising tide of discontent had become so threatening that Husin Limbara decided at last to invite the editor Halim for a conference on how to counteract it.

When the telephone rang at Halim's house that afternoon he was asleep, and relishing his sleep particularly because of the heavy rain outside. When his wife woke him, saying that Husin Limbara wanted to speak with him, Halim said, without thinking, "To the devil with him. Tell him I'm sleeping."

His wife left, but was back a moment later saying, "He doesn't want to go to the devil; he says he must talk with you, it's very urgent."

Swearing, Halim got up and went to the telephone. He altered the tone of his voice to conceal his annoyance: "Hello, Husin. What can I help you with?"

"Could you come to my house at seven o'clock?" said the voice at the other end of the line. "It's urgent. We need to meet. If we can't fix the situation, we're all in for a lot of trouble."

Halim was shocked. "What's happened?"

"Just come along at seven!"

Halim put down the receiver very slowly. His sleepiness vanished with Husin Limbara's words. His instinct as a newspaper man quickly told him what was probably troubling Husin Limbara: it was surely the precarious situation of the cabinet and the "special operations" of Husin's party.

"What is it?" his wife asked as soon as he returned to their bedroom.

"Husin Limbara is scared," Halim answered. He told his wife about the possibility of a cabinet crisis, or, at the very least, of a possible big scandal involving the financial activities of Husin Limbara's party.

"But if a scandal breaks, that means we'll be involved, too," his wife pointed out.

"Don't worry," Halim told her. "I think we've got it covered. I'm not a party member, and there's no way to prove that the loan we received has any connection with the party. The loan agreement was drawn up in a purely businesslike manner and is based on our newspaper's documented circulation of forty-five thousand..."

"Which is actually only twelve thousand," his wife corrected with a laugh.

Halim laughed too. "But I didn't lie. In the loan application I mentioned that this number was based on the information ministry's allotment of newsprint, which allows us to print forty-five thousand copies daily."

Halim wasn't at all happy to think of his newspaper's steadily declining circulation, which he blamed on its support of the government. In his conversations with Husin Limbara and other party members, he never failed to stress that they had a moral obligation to compensate him properly for his losses.

"We've sustained heavy losses," he'd told them, "with our circulation falling by five or six thousand every month, all as a result of our staunch defense of the government and your party."

Of course, he never mentioned the fact that his newspaper's circulation had actually never gone beyond twenty-five thousand,

and that he'd got the newsprint permit from the ministry of information only by special manipulations.

The party leaders had accepted the newsprint allowance as the basis for the loan extended to him and later had approved another loan for an export enterprise he'd also established. All in all, his decision to help the government and to support the party, far from causing him any personal loss, had left him pretty well off.

Having explained all this to his wife, both of them laughed.

"They're really stupid," Halim told his wife. "They think they can use us as their tools. But we'll use them. I don't care who's in power, so long as we get our proper share."

No sooner had Halim said this than he suddenly saw very clearly how he could dissociate himself from the impending scandal. He slapped himself on the forehead and embraced his wife. "I know a way to keep us clear of this mess."

He pulled her off the bed and made her dance with him, waltzing around the room to the tune of "The Blue Danube" which he was singing at the top of his voice. Thus they whirled about in their bedroom, Halim singing, and his wife laughing.

The rain had grown heavier, and suddenly a thunderbolt shook the air outside. It felt very close, but Halim didn't care; he laughed, picked up his wife, flung her down on the bed, and then embraced her with great gusto.

In the evening, at Husin Limbara's house, when Halim intentionally arrived fifteen minutes late—to let them see that they needed him and not he them—he discovered that all the party's top-level personnel had gathered. All eyes were on him as he entered. In a voice that was far more hospitable than usual, Husin Limbara invited him to sit down.

"Ah, here's our champion," exclaimed Harjo, a lawyer and member of the party's executive council; he was also a member of the party's faction in parliament and president director of a bank established by the party with government funds.

Halim took the empty chair at his side, and looked around the room with a smile on his lips.

Dr Palau was an old party member from pre-war days, very proud of his record, always bragging about his role as chief of the united command of the Sumatran military forces during the revolutionary struggle. Since then he had managed to become the very wealthy owner of a rubber factory in Kalimantan, an import concern in Jakarta, a textile factory in Surabaya and—very soon, if nothing went wrong—a Dutch automobile import business, also in Jakarta. He sat smoking a large cigar, his completely expressionless face giving no clue to his feelings.

Next to Dr Palau sat Kustomo, also an old party member and the party's strong man behind the scenes, with great influence in Central and East Java, the regions where the party's strength was concentrated. A lawyer, he held no official position in the party and wasn't a director or board member of any enterprise; but Halim knew that he was receiving regular honoraria from all sides as legal counselor for various business concerns established by party members. Halim guessed he was making at least fifty thousand a month, and probably tax-free, too.

Next to Kustomo sat Kapolo, yet another lawyer, a youth group leader who could have exercised a strong influence in the party had he wanted to. But, lacking a strong personality, he was inclined to look for the easiest way out of difficulties and so was very quick to compromise. On two occasions at the party's congresses he could have been elected party chairman had he been willing to fight, but both times he'd been defeated and only made vice-chairman. He had no work to do in the party, but because he was well known as a youth group leader and had a reputation for honesty, he was successfully used by the party for propaganda purposes. He was on the boards of three private concerns and acted as chairman of the board to a state enterprise.

At Kapolo's side was Syahrusad, a former communist who had joined Husin Limbara's party. Halim didn't trust him; he was too good a talker. He was also a member of a state bank's board of directors. Next to him sat Rachmad, a government minister.

Looking at the assembled members of the party council, Halim was impressed by the fact that practically all of them had huge incomes from directorships either in their own concerns or in state-owned enterprises.

Husin Limbara opened the meeting. "Good evening, gentlemen. Our meeting tonight is an extremely important one. While it is not an official meeting of the party's executive council, and not all of its members are present—some were unable to come, prevented by other work—it is still of utmost importance.

"As you well know, the opposition parties are using their sensation-mongering press to step up their campaign to smear the reputation of the government and the parties supporting it, our party in particular. They started by raising questions about the party's business transactions: the enterprises, the banks, and so on that the party owns and which, I state here, are run in an officially approved and legal manner. The public, however, is easily influenced, especially now in these times of economic difficulties when, we must frankly admit, the nation is suffering from shortages of rice, salt, and kerosene. These shortages are not the fault of the current cabinet—it's only fourteen months old, after all—but of the preceding cabinet. Even so, it is difficult for the general public to understand the true state of affairs.

"You should also know that cabinet members from other parties have learned of special measures taken on behalf of some of our party's members and have raised questions in the cabinet. In fact, several of them have approached our minister directly…" He paused and turned towards Rachmad. "…and have asked for loans and special licenses for themselves, too. Moreover, three days ago a minister who represents another party officially informed Rachmad that if their demands were not met, they would resign from the cabinet.

"Finally, it appears that the opposition parties have managed to collect enough bits of information to put a story together that is likely to involve the party, the government, and ourselves personally in a big scandal.

"We have assembled here tonight to discuss how to prevent this from happening—which is why I invited Halim to attend. He is, as you know, the leader of the pro-government press association.

"I would like to say at this point that I do think a cabinet crisis is avoidable, but only if we manage to nip the scandal in the bud. For the time being, this possible cabinet crisis has been postponed by the approval of some special licenses for leaders of the other parties. This can't go on, however. In the end, the issuing of loans and licenses in such numbers will completely destroy the government's planning."

Dr Palau was the first to air his opinion. "Scandal? Why be afraid of a scandal? What kind of scandal? And why fear the opposition? We're only doing what goes on elsewhere. The party in power always helps its own members and friends first. The same thing happens in other countries. Suppose the opposition parties were in power. Do you think they would give us anything? I say let them fume. Nothing's happened so far, Husin, so why be frightened? Anytime you do something, you have to be brave enough to take the consequences!"

Dr Palau slapped his chest, inhaled on his cigar and then expelled a dense cloud of smoke. The others laughed. They were accustomed to Dr Palau's cocky talk. He had been made a member of the council only to please the people of his region and several resistance groups who still regarded him as their leader.

Then Kustomo, the youth group leader, spoke up. "Even though there's some truth in Dr Palau's words," he said in a calm but authoritative voice, "we must still consider the problem carefully and thoroughly. Politics is a high art, and good politics means heading off trouble long before it can happen."

"That's true too," Dr Palau agreed, "but when an enemy comes at me, I'm going to go at him!"

The men laughed again.

"Wouldn't it be advisable to discontinue, as soon as possible, the activities in question?" Kapolo asked Husin Limbara.

"Indeed, it would, and we've already decided to stop as soon as we reach the thirty-million-rupiah party fund we're aiming at," Husin Limbara replied. "We're almost there. Another three months of undisturbed work and we could reach that mark."

"If that's the case, attack must be answered by attack, and scandal by scandal, and here's the man to lead the way," Dr Palau said, looking at Halim.

Halim hesitated before speaking. "Something that appears to be simple can turn out to be difficult. But before I make any suggestions, I would like to learn from you how long it will be before the current cabinet is disbanded."

Husin Limbara coughed and looked at Kustomo, party strongman, who gave Husin a nod.

"The party hasn't yet made an official decision," said Husin Limbara, "but, depending on future circumstances, it's quite possible that we'll call for the cabinet's resignation ourselves and return our mandate. Because of ever increasing popular dissatisfaction with the government as a result of the shortages I mentioned, when election time comes around, it's going to be hard for whatever party is in power to win the popular vote. In times of hardship, voters usually turn to the opposition parties in hopes of improvement. So, in short, the idea of returning the mandate before the elections is now being entertained. If the opposition parties take charge of the government for a few months before the general elections, it's pretty certain that their hold on power would be short-lived."

The wheels in Halim's brain were turning rapidly and smoothly as he evaluated the information he just received.

"What would happen if the opposition parties managed to improve the economic conditions while they're in power?" Halim asked. "Might they not win the general elections? Besides, just by being in power they could influence the outcome of the elections in a number of ways."

"According to our calculations, no new government could possibly improve the country's condition within a period of six or eight months. That's approximately the interval we have in mind. And we needn't worry about the opposition parties influencing the elections. Our party has a firm hold on people in very important positions—in the civil service, in the information field and so on. We won't lose them and definitely not all at once. There's no need to worry about that, at least!"

Halim offered his conclusion. "So, from what you've said, it seems safe to assume that within about two months we will know for sure whether or not there will be a crisis and if the current cabinet will continue."

"More or less," Husin Limbara said. "So the most important problem now is how to protect ourselves from attacks by the opposition."

"That's easy," Halim announced. "We fight the opposition groups by stirring up a scandal about them, one that is much bigger than the accusations they are trying to pin on us. We'll have to step up our earlier charges that the opposition leaders are selling out the country to foreign capitalists and imperialists, and implicate some big names, too. I can do this, but it will involve a considerable sum of money, probably about two hundred thousand for a start."

Halim was fishing, watching the faces of Husin Limbara and Kustomo.

"Pay him, then; we're ready!" said Dr Palau.

As soon as Dr Palau had spoken, Halim knew he'd get the sum he'd asked for. He didn't stay on long after this. He excused himself on the pretext of having to finish some writing at his office for tomorrow morning's edition.

Outside the rain was still dripping, but in his car Halim was whistling "The Blue Danube".

The looming scandal Husin Limbara referred to exploded sooner than anticipated. Two days after the meeting at his house, the opposition newspapers carried in large banner-headlines the news of the "special operations" of some of the government parties and that of Husin Limbara in particular. Husin Limbara's name was mentioned as the behind-the-scene "minister" of financial and economic affairs; this was accompanied by a list of the business establishments involved and their presidents, directors, or trustees—all members of government parties. The name of Raden Kaslan appeared in connection with five concerns, Husin Limbara's with three, Suryono's with one. Sugeng, too, was mentioned as involved in an import concern called Mas Mulia. According to the reports, it had been approved by the ministry of justice within two weeks, and had obtained its importing license from the ministry of economic affair within five days. The names of Dr Palau, Harjo, Kapolo, and even of Rachmad, the minister, were also mentioned as trustees of a certain bank, which, according to the opposition press, was contrary to the existing regulations. The newspapers printed pictures of them all, as well as stories about their luxurious cars and houses in the city and in the hills of the Puncak Pass south of Jakarta.

Husin Limbara came to Halim's office in person. In self-defense Halim started to attack, saying that he'd often warned his friends to exercise self-restraint, not to display their wealth in public by buying two or three cars, building large houses, and even taking a second wife (actually he'd never said this to anyone). But now it was too late, and the only way out was to get the counter-campaign going. "And I still haven't received the two hundred thousand you promised me," Halim added.

Husin Limbara immediately picked up the telephone to contact Raden Kaslan. Raden Kaslan wasn't there. Finally he got assurances from Harjo that the two hundred thousand would be sent to Halim by noon.

"Now it's up to you," Husin Limbara said to Halim as he was leaving.

After closing the door of his office, Halim laughed and returned to his desk. He sat down, put a sheet of paper into his typewriter and began writing an editorial attacking the opposition groups.

> Opposition groups and their newspapers are now demonstrating, even more clearly than before, that they have absolutely no sense of responsibility towards our country and our people. With a total lack of scruples, they are flinging unfounded charges and indiscriminate abuse at the government and the parties supporting it. And this opposition clique is shameless enough not even to hesitate in disclosing the private lives of the pro-government parties' foremost leaders, discussing their private connections with enterprises which are in no way involved with government policies.

> Although the cabinet is only fourteen months old, it is being blamed for the nation's shortages of rice, kerosene, and salt. Even the most ignorant person, if he has any common sense

left, can clearly see that it's not the present cabinet that should be blamed for these shortages, but the preceding cabinet, which was led by the opposition parties themselves.

It's clear from the way they're slandering the present cabinet and undermining the prestige of the pro-government party leaders, that the oppositions' tactics and aims are just the same as the foreign capitalists' and imperialists' who don't want our country to advance. As the president himself mentioned in a recent speech, he has received reports about the existence of a Plan A and a Plan B for subversive activities being conducted in our homeland by foreign elements, and one about the leaders of certain political parties who are getting money from foreign powers to betray our country.

This newspaper therefore proposes to publish in the near future the names of party leaders who have received money from foreign powers and to expose their connections with the subversive activities mentioned by the president.

The government has been patient with the opposition parties far too long, with their newspapers continually abusing the freedom of the press and hiding behind their democratic rights to conduct activities which are endangering the state. The attorney general should take speedy action against those who abuse their democratic rights to destroy our beloved republic and make a mockery of our proclamation of independence.

It is also obvious why the attacks of the opposition on the government, and on the personal affairs of several individual cabinet ministers, have reached a peak at precisely the time these leaders are attending the debates on West Irian at the United Nations. Their actions coincide with Dutch efforts to ruin the reputation of the Indonesian Republic abroad in order to defeat Indonesia's international struggle to regain possession of West Irian. As to just how closely the moves of the opposition and its press are geared to these Dutch activities, the reader can easily draw his own conclusions.

It is regrettable that there are Indonesians who, because they are set on overthrowing the present cabinet, are prepared to sell themselves to foreign powers.

People, beware!

Halim chuckled as he re-read the editorial. Two hundred thousand is cheap for such an editorial, he thought. He pushed a button on his desk, and soon the office messenger appeared.

Halim gave him the editorial. "Take this to the editorial office and tell them to set it up. And tell Sidompol to come here right away."

Halim leaned back in his chair, very pleased with himself. Hearing a knock on his door, he called out, "Come in!"

The door opened and Sidompol, the news editor, walked in.

"Sit down," Halim said to him. "There's some work to be done, along your line!"

After telling Sidompol about the editorial he'd just written, Halim said, "Now I'd like to compose a front-page report, one that appears to have been obtained from reliable sources close to the state investigation service. Give it a sensational headline, like 'Opposition Leaders Involved in Subversive Activities?' or 'Authorities Conducting Intensive Investigation'. Make sure there's nothing in it the opposition could sue us for, but make the report suggestive enough for readers to reach the conclusions we want."

"OK, boss!' Sidompol said, then rose and left the room.

Alone in his office again, Halim opened a desk drawer, got out a bottle of whisky and poured himself a glass, adding some ice water from a thermos bottle. He emptied the glass in a single gulp.

He laughed inwardly again, thinking of Sidompol writing the news story he'd just made up. Halim recalled that his was the only newspaper that had been willing to employ Sidompol. The other newspapers had refused, because during the revolution he'd been a traitor. At first he'd been a journalist supporting the Republic; then later he went over to the Netherlands Indies Civil Administration, working first on Van Mook's staff and then with NICA's information service. Finally he'd gone so far as to publish a paper, subsidized by NICA, which attacked the Republic daily.

When Halim was reproached by his fellow journalists for being willing to employ this ex-NICA man, he'd answer them, "He's my loyal dog now. He knows my paper is the only place where he can get work."

Halim smiled to himself. So long as Sidompol worked for his newspaper he could make him write anything he wanted. Then, remembering something, he picked up the inter-office phone and called the editor. "Don't forget to send the report you're writing to the other pro-government papers!" he told him.

It was noon; Saimun walked wearily home from the police office. He'd intended to ask for a form to fill out for getting his driving license. But after half an hour, with a horde of people crowding in front of the window and hearing stories about the difficult tests one had to pass, he suddenly lost heart. He saw people dressed twenty times better than himself—he was in shorts and a worn-out shirt, even torn at the collar, and without shoes or sandals.

Saimun was so frightened by the scene at the police station that he left. He felt very small, very weak, with no hold on anything, hopeless. It's just my fate, he thought. Once a little guy, always a little guy; you can't become anything else until you die. And he suddenly longed for his village; life in the village was better and happier—if only there weren't any bandits. Just to smell the freshly hoed earth again and be sprayed by the falling rain, to walk at dawn on the cool morning grass, the dew wetting his feet, to feel the rays of the morning sun warming his whole body, to bathe in the river, to fish in the river, to snare a turtle dove, to eat an ear of roasted corn freshly picked from the stalk, to sleep on the grass under a mango tree. Tears filled his eyes. Then all at once he was knocked out of his reverie by a heavy shove on the shoulder and a man passing on a bicycle shouting, "Hey, look where you're going! Didn't you hear my bell?"

Saimun was badly shaken. Lost in his thoughts he hadn't noticed that he'd strayed into the middle of the road. Startled, he tried to run to the side of the street, and was almost run over by a passing convertible. The car brushed his thigh, not too hard, but hard enough to make him fall on the pavement. The car stopped, its brakes screeching, and Suryono got out. Several cars behind him stopped, too.

"Wait here a moment," Suryono said to Dahlia, who sat at his side. "There's always something that gets in the way."

Suryono was very annoyed; he had just been taking Dahlia to Aunty Bep's. And, even if he hadn't hurt the man he'd just hit, it would still mean explanations to the police, and who knows what else. The day would be wasted. But as he was approaching the man he'd hit, he was already on his feet and brushing down his shorts. A passing policeman stopped and came over.

Suryono was very glad to see that the man wasn't hurt. As he came close he heard Saimun say to the policeman, "It was my fault, sir!"

The policeman turned to Suryono and saluted him. Suryono said, "It's all right, lucky nothing happened."

"It was my fault!" Saimun repeated.

Suryono took a five-rupiah note out of his pocket, feeling suddenly that the man he'd hit should be given a present.

Since no harm had been done, he could continue with Dahlia straight to Aunty Bep's house.

The policeman could not refrain from giving Saimun a last bit of advice. "Look out, though, when you're crossing. You're going to get yourself killed!"

Back in the car Suryono said to Dahlia, "It's lucky nothing happened to him." And he pinched Dahlia's thigh which was pressed close to his own.

Saimun hastened away from the place where he'd almost been killed. His gloom changed to a kind of joy. Five rupiah in his pocket meant a lot of money to him. What a good heart that man has, Saimun thought, and his appearance shows it, too. It was my fault, but he wasn't angry at me, even gave me a present; not like some other people who'd just finish you off with their scolding. Saimun thought, wouldn't it be wonderful to work for a man like that. Whatever he ordered me to do, I'd do it gladly.

In front of the telephone building, across from the president's palace, Saimun heard Itam calling him. *Becak* drivers usually stopped and gathered there around a food vendor's stall. Several were eating, while others sat in their *becak* waiting for passengers. Some were playing paper dominoes on the ground; and others squatted, gambling for money. Itam sat on the bench in front of the stall; he'd just begun to eat.

"Where are you coming from, Saimun?"

Saimun remembered that he hadn't eaten yet, sat down next to Itam, and ordered a plate of rice and vegetables. Then he told Itam of his morning's experiences. "Looks like I can't become a driver if things are like this. I'm still not so good at reading, and how can you remember all the road signs and traffic rules? Just seeing the police who give the examinations scared me."

"But that man in the car turned out to be OK," Itam consoled. "You don't find many like that. Most people who drive cars act like they own the road. We're like stray dogs for them. I don't know how many times I've almost gotten into fights with drivers of showy cars. If we go slow they get angry and blow on their horns, like we can pedal fast on command. If we don't get to the side of the road fast enough, they scream at us. Nope, it's not easy to be a little guy."

In the last days of December the tensions between the government and the opposition parties, the newspapers supporting the cabinet and the opposition press, had reached a climax. Halim's editorial and the report his paper published provoked a violent reaction. One of the opposition papers exposed the machinations of government ministers belonging to Husin Limbara's party. Sugeng's name was mentioned as one of the ministry officials involved—the same man, opposition papers reported, who had later left the ministry to become director of an import company whose operating license had been approved with lightning speed by the ministries of justice and economic affairs. To this scandal a new scandal was added: one of the cabinet ministers allegedly was selling his signature, granting foreigners admission to Indonesia. This had all the opposition papers asking, "Who is selling Indonesia to the foreigners: the government or the opposition?"

Hasnah could do nothing but cry all day, and would hardly speak to Sugeng anymore. Distracted as he was, Sugeng tried to assuage his wife's fears: "Don't worry, the party will protect us."

"But why did you ever have to join them?" she railed.

"Didn't you insist that we move to another house? If you hadn't insisted on a house, I wouldn't have done all this!"

Hasnah's expression immediately changed to one of distress, as if she were indeed to blame. "It's my fault, it's my fault!" she said through her tears. "Why wasn't I patient? Why did I have to ask for a house? Forgive me, dear God..." She cried and cried and cried.

Halim guessed that the cabinet couldn't last any longer. Opposition party members within the cabinet continued to pressure Husin Limbara's party to surrender the cabinet's mandate. There was a strong probability that the prime minister would resign before Christmas or at the beginning of the new year. Halim had to dissociate himself from the collapse of the cabinet he had thus far supported, and had to do it quickly.

He wrote an editorial for the December 24th—Christmas Eve—edition of his newspaper, which ran as follows:

> Ever since the present cabinet was formed, this newspaper has never tired of warning and urging the cabinet to make a serious effort to secure the public good and to devote special attention to the needs of the regions outside Java. Up to now we've given strong support to the cabinet, because we disliked seeing cabinets change from minute to minute as in the past, and believed that this cabinet should be given proper time to prove its abilities. This cabinet has managed to obtain satisfactory results in a number of fields. This is especially true of international relations, where the government has won unprecedented and brilliant successes. The name of Indonesia has become famous all over the world (which continues to shrink because of technical progress in air communications), and in the United Nations our voice commands the attention of all countries.

> However, there's truth in the old saying, "There's no ivory without a crack", and although we don't agree with all the accusations launched by the opposition newspapers against the cabinet and the parties supporting it, the government's shortcomings in the questions of rice, kerosene and salt supplies, for instance, have to be admitted. Apart from this, the cabinet parties have not been selective and vigilant enough

about their own members. As a result they have succumbed to temptations and abused their positions in order to enrich themselves.

If a cabinet crisis, as we hear, is indeed inevitable, it can't be helped—let the cabinet fall for the sake of our country's and people's welfare. A further heightening of tensions between the government parties and the opposition parties, if permitted to continue, can only endanger our state and close the door to wider inter-party co-operation. Wouldn't it therefore be only right if this cabinet did indeed surrender its mandate? A new cabinet could speedily be formed which would assure firm co-operation between the parties, and harmony and peace for the nation."

Halim was very satisfied with this. He re-read the editorial several times; it had appeared in his newspaper that morning. Husin Limbara couldn't be angry. I haven't said anything that could commit me, and we're opening up the possibility for supporting some new cabinet. Halim laughed, extremely pleased.

Dahlia had not been feeling well for a week and in the last few days had felt nausea. She knew that her monthly period was a week overdue. While she was taking a bath, Dahlia felt her belly and decided to visit a doctor to find out whether or not she was pregnant. The trouble was that she wasn't sure who might have caused her pregnancy—Suryono, Sugeng, or maybe that Chinese man whom she'd accidentally met on the street, who took her to town, paid her five hundred rupiah, and then saw her home, but whom she'd never seen again since.

If it wasn't the Chinese it wouldn't really matter, thought Dahlia; Idris might be pleased to think he had begotten a child—but if the baby were to have slit eyes.... Dahlia laughed, amused by this possibility. She decided to go to a doctor who she knew was prepared to perform a guaranteed abortion for a thousand rupiah flat. She'd be able to get the money from either Suryono or Sugeng, just by telling either of them that he was responsible; maybe she'd even ask both. Dahlia became cheerful again, finished her bath and attended to her body, which had undergone no change as yet.

Raden Kaslan was preparing to go abroad at the beginning of the new year. He told Fatma that, because he had been the author of the plan for raising funds on behalf of the party's election campaign, it was better for him to be out of the country for the time being; he said that Fatma could join him in Europe later.

During these last days of the year Suryono stayed mostly at home. He didn't go to the meetings at Pranoto's house any more, since he was ashamed to meet his old friends. Practically every night he was pursued by the nightmare of the car whose brakes suddenly gave out.

Only Fatma remained calm, as if she didn't care at all about what might happen.

A kind of panic broke out among the leaders of Husin Limbara's party; however, they concealed it from the outside world. The party newspapers were ordered to continue their violent attacks on the opposition and to say that the cabinet would continue to do its duty and that no government party was planning to call for the formation of a new one.

Halim's treachery had badly affected Husin Limbara, the more so because Husin had been bringing Halim's name before the party leadership to help him get a bank loan and other financial support.

Then, on December 30, the prime minister returned his mandate to the president, a move that was precipitated by the decision the day before of two government parties to withdraw their ministers from the cabinet; they no longer wished to be held accountable for the government's policies. With that, the cabinet fell.

CITY BEAT

The rain had been pouring down since noon. But it seemed to Zakaria that instead of letting up it was becoming even heavier. The sky over the city was dark and from time to time there were outbursts of deafening thunder, with flashes of lightning cutting through the heavy, billowing clouds.

Zakaria sought shelter under the roof of an ice depot. Several other people stood there with him. Zakaria's empty stomach churned; hunger had been gnawing at his guts all day.

He was exhausted. He had just got a new job as an office messenger, and had to walk from his home to work and back again. It usually took him about three-quarters of an hour to get home; he usually got back by three o'clock and could then eat and calm the gnawing hunger. But now it was almost five o'clock and the rain wouldn't stop. He didn't dare walk home in the rain for fear of becoming ill; and, more important, if the jacket he was wearing got wet, he wouldn't have another dry one to put on tomorrow for working at the office, unless he wore just a shirt. But his shirt was already worn and had several holes.

One after another, the people who were waiting with him went off, saying, "Ah, this rain won't stop until night. So we'll get wet!"

Finally Zakaria was left all by himself. Near *magrib*, the time for evening prayers, the city was already dark, and the rain was still pouring, but Zakaria felt that it was getting lighter. By six o'clock the rain began to ease off and fifteen minutes later it stopped altogether. Relieved, Zakaria stepped out to go home. Though he felt weak, the hunger didn't bother him anymore. The street was flooded with stagnant water, and Zakaria decided to cross at once.

But no sooner did he start crossing the street than a car was blowing its horn at him. Zakaria saw it approaching at great speed and jumped back to the sidewalk, but the car passed so close to the

curb that the water whirled up by its wheels splashed Zakaria from
head to foot. Zakaria had jumped away hoping to avoid the spray,
but was too late. The front of his jacket and trousers were soaking
wet, his face and his hair were dripping.

Dumbfounded, Zakaria just stood there. Then, realizing that
the calamity he had tried to prevent by waiting out the rain had
overtaken him after all, he burst into tears, which streamed down
his cheeks and mingled with the rainwater. Then a wave of violent
and bitter hatred swept through his whole being. Zakaria looked
at all passing cars with glaring, hate-filled eyes. And he cursed all
people who had cars.

January

In the first days of the new year, Hasnah's baby began stirring restlessly in her womb, and she feared it would be born prematurely. Sugeng was seldom home now, day or night. Sometimes he stayed away all night. Hasnah felt the distance between them growing all the time. All she could do was to cry and cry, always accusing herself: it was she who'd ruined Sugeng, she who had caused the calamity that had befallen them. All the luxurious objects in the house served only to remind her of her troubles and make her even sadder. Her eyes were constantly filled with tears.

The doctor had warned her to control her emotions or she might endanger herself and especially the child she was carrying. When Sugeng was home, she hardly dared to speak to him. She'd seen how it consoled him, even cheered him, to have her admit that she was the one to blame for his wrongdoings.

Meanwhile Sugeng was busy transferring the titles of their possessions to other members of his family. He sold his car and invested the money in a business officially headed by a relative. A new house he'd just built in Kemayoran Baru was likewise registered under the name of another relative after a legal sales agreement had been drawn up, though of course no actual transaction had taken place. "If anything happens," Sugeng said, "we'll at least save what little we have now."

One day he asked Hasnah whether she'd mind if he also sold the refrigerator and changed the big radio in the living room for a smaller set instead.

"We'll do without a refrigerator for the time being," Sugeng said. "We'll just buy ice." Then he added, "We'll get at least forty or fifty thousand for it and we'll put the money away somewhere else."

Hasnah left everything to Sugeng. The refrigerator and the big radio set were sold, and Hasnah was even somewhat relieved not to see them in the house any longer. Even so, she could not stop crying.

"It's my fault!" she swore at herself. "Why did I keep asking for a house? I only wanted it so we'd be happier and love each other better. I didn't ask for a house to make Sugeng do wrong. I wasn't asking for luxury and riches."

It was beyond Hasnah's understanding why their life had become what it now was. The days ahead seemed dark to her as the new year was opening. Something shadowy and frightening seemed to hang over their home, poised to drop down and crush them all at any moment; ready to destroy even the last sparks of their happiness, like Maryam's hearty laughter as she played. And it was only occasionally that Hasnah managed to forget it all and cling to her memories of the warm and intimate life she'd had with Sugeng in the past. But that had all been long ago, in a very different world, she felt. And she'd become even more dejected, bursting into tears again and again, until her eyes were red and swollen. When Maryam stopped laughing and, coming to her, asked, "Why are you crying, Mother?" it seemed as if Maryam's world, too, had become very dark.

On January 5 Raden Kaslan left the country after a farewell party given by Husin Limbara and several members of the party council. Suryono and Fatma took him to Kemayoran Airport.

Returning from the airport in the car, Suryono said to Fatma, "Now with Father gone, we're left here. What are we going to do?

I can't stand to be in Jakarta any longer, especially the next few weeks ahead."

"Where do you want to go?"

"Anywhere, who cares? But I don't want to go alone," said Suryono. Then a thought struck him, and he said, "Why don't the two of us go somewhere together?"

Fatma smiled, a challenge on her lips: "What will people say?"

"Who cares what people say?" Suryono replied. "Why stop half-way? What do we care, whatever happens?"

Fatma smiled. She realized that, were she to go with Suryono, a new bond would grow between them. The showdown with Raden Kaslan they'd managed to avoid so far was sure to come and would have to be faced. To go off together was different from being secretly in bed together at home. If she went off with Suryono she couldn't possibly remain Raden Kaslan's wife. Nor could Suryono very well continue to be his father's son. If I marry Suryono, Fatma thought, I certainly won't lose anything. He's young, handsome, has money. I'm rich enough myself, too. Even if we have to separate somewhere along the line, I won't have lost anything.

"Why don't you say anything?" said Suryono.

Had Suryono ever thought of marrying her? Fatma wondered. She decided that it hadn't entered his mind. She suspected that for him all this was still playing around. By Allah, even stealing his father's wife was still "just fooling around" for Suryono!

"Don't you want to come with me?" Suryono pressed.

In his unnerving state of constant anxiety, Suryono now felt that the only way for him to regain peace of mind and soul was to go off some place with Fatma, hide there from the world, and find release from all the fears and premonitions of disaster which pursued him, by drowning them in an orgy of lust. It was as if he could in this way freely express his real indifference to society, politics, and the parties whom he considered responsible for the disasters he felt threatening him, threatening his welfare, threatening his very life. By defying what people thought, by asserting himself, he'd be free from the standards and judgments of others.

"Fatma, let's go," said Suryono.

Fatma smiled again. She knew she could now do anything she wanted with Suryono.

"Well, anyway," she said, "we still have to consider what people will say."

"Why worry about people?" retorted Suryono. "If we want to, we'll do it."

"Haven't you thought what it may lead to?"

"Who cares what it leads to?"

"Don't you think of your father?"

"What about Father?"

"This is sure to mean our divorce."

"Why worry about him? When trouble came, he just left. He's left us in the lurch now. But he was the one who persuaded us to join him."

"You're his son."

"What kind of father abandons his son when there's trouble?'

Inwardly Suryono now felt relieved, even satisfied. Of course all this was his father's fault. It was because of his father that he'd got involved. He himself had never dreamed of piling up money when he first returned from abroad. It was his father's fault. Compared with what his father had done, his affair with Fatma was nothing.

"If your father divorces me, will you marry me?" said Fatma levelly.

"I'm ready to marry you this very moment," he answered quickly.

Fatma suddenly felt herself very powerful, as though a man's fate were in her hands and she could twist it any way she wanted. The life of Raden Kaslan, her husband, and the life of Suryono, his son, were now completely in her power. It was gratifying to feel this power.

"How about it?" Suryono urged again.

"Let's talk it over a bit more at home," said Fatma. "Why the hurry? We've got lots of time."

Ever since the prime minister had resigned, political activity in Jakarta had reached a new pitch of intensity. Though inter-party conflicts continued to rage, behind the scenes several of the parties which had supported the retiring cabinet were establishing contact with the opposition parties. It looked likely that a new cabinet could be formed quickly, most probably without the participation of Husin Limbara's party.

In Husin Limbara's party the executive council had split in two. Some of the younger leaders at last dared to challenge the policies of the top leadership, and Husin Limbara was singled out for particularly violent attacks. In return, he went so far as to threaten to resign if the party wouldn't give his policies complete and unconditional support. But then, towards the end of a council meeting, Husin Limbara was suddenly seized by a heart ailment. His physician advised him to take a vacation and not to work too hard. Husin Limbara accepted his advice and, greatly relieved, left Jakarta for a rest in his native village in the mountains of East Java.

Editor Halim changed the line of his paper completely and ordered his news editor Sidompol to interview the leaders of the opposition parties whose names were being mentioned as candidates for posts in the new cabinet. His editorials now criticized some of the old cabinet's policies and placed the whole blame for the rice, salt and kerosene shortages at its doorstep. When a number of readers sent in angry letters reminding the editor that he'd previously defended the old cabinet to the hilt and had asserted that it bore none of the responsibility for these shortages, Halim gave orders that none of these letters were to be printed.

The new cabinet was formed on January 12. Husin Limbara's party was not in it. Halim immediately wrote an editorial welcoming the new cabinet and promising to support it as long as it was going to work for the welfare of the people and the state.

January 16. All morning Hasnah had felt that her time was very near. Sugeng had left the house early in the morning, and Hasnah was waiting for him to come back and take her either to the doctor or to the hospital. If this was really the beginning of her labor, the baby would be a month early—the doctor had said it was due in February. But Hasnah had already foreseen the possibility of the baby's premature birth because of her own poor state of health during the last few months. Towards noon Hasnah could no longer bear the pains that now came at regular intervals and decided to go directly to the hospital. She asked a neighbor to telephone her doctor, quickly packed a small suitcase with things needed for the baby, told the servant to tell Sugeng that she'd left for the hospital and, after kissing Maryam while tears streamed down her face, went off to the hospital in a *becak*, accompanied by her friend.

She was taken at once to the delivery room. The hospital doctor made a preliminary examination. Then he telephoned Hasnah's doctor. Half an hour later he arrived. He told Hasnah that it did look as though the baby wanted to be born. His face was gloomy.

She was taken to the operating room of the maternity ward. The neighbor who'd brought her to the hospital pressed her hand and went home.

Sugeng didn't return home until five in the afternoon. Hasnah had left about noon. When he learned about it from the servant he jumped into a *becak* and hurried to the hospital. As he reached the maternity ward he saw the doctor who'd been attending Hasnah, ready to leave.

"How is it, Doctor?" Sugeng asked with a racing heart.

"Your wife is well, but we couldn't save the baby," said the doctor, pressing his hand.

Sugeng was overcome by a feeling of weakness.

"May I see her?" he asked the doctor.

The doctor took him to one of the hospital's second-class wards, which had four beds in it. Only two of the beds were occupied. On one of them a woman who'd just had her child lay reading. Opposite her lay Hasnah.

"Don't try to talk," the doctor advised. "She's too weak."

The doctor left Sugeng. Sugeng stood near the bed, looking at Hasnah. She was very pale. Her lips were white, and low, choking moans escaped from them. Tears welled up in Sugeng's eyes and streamed down his cheeks. Then Sugeng stooped to grasp Hasnah's hand. He sat down on the edge of the bed, and remained there silently, until Hasnah opened her eyes and looked at him. She tried to smile at him with her eyes, didn't quite succeed, and closed them again. Sugeng whispered to her softly, "It was all my fault, not yours. I should have known where to stop."

Remorse overwhelmed Sugeng, crushing his heart. He remembered all his wrongdoings, starting with his yielding to the temptation to make a lot of money, and then still more money, and later playing around with women because he had too much money and didn't really know what to do with himself. Now he saw how cruelly he had treated Hasnah, piling the guilt upon her because she'd been urging him to get a house for themselves. He saw now that Hasnah's plea was only the desire of a devoted wife who longed for a good family life, undisturbed by other people; and that it was he, Sugeng, who was guilty of going far beyond what Hasnah had wished for. He remembered how happy they'd been when they were newly married, and later when Maryam came, and though they'd led a simple life they'd been at peace with no dark clouds threatening them.

I beg you to forgive me, Has, Sugeng was murmuring in his heart. I want to start all over again; I want to start clean again. If you'll forgive me, I can face everything—whatever may happen. I won't run away, I'll be strong, if only you'll go on loving me.

As though she'd heard the whispering in Sugeng's heart, Hasnah opened her eyes and looked at him. Their eyes met, and Sugeng bent down and kissed her forehead. Then Hasnah closed her eyes again. Sugeng sat very still holding her hand, oblivious of everything that was going on around him beyond the bed where Hasnah lay, until a nurse came, tapped him on the shoulder, and said that it was time for him to leave.

January 20 was Pranoto's birthday, and he'd invited his friends over to celebrate. That evening, in his room, he re-read the letter he'd got from Connie the day before, although he'd read it over several times already. Connie never forgot his birthday. After congratulating him, she'd gone on to write that since he'd now reached the age of thirty-five she hoped he'd be able to look at things more sensibly and propose to her at last. "I'm not getting any younger," she wrote. "I'll be twenty-eight in July of this year— an unpopular old maid, pining for a lover who doesn't return her love. How I long to be with you to celebrate your birthday, just the two of us together—only you and I."

Pranoto stopped reading when he heard a knock on the door. The servant announced that the guests had begun to arrive. He went quickly to the front room and saw that the first to arrive was Ies.

"Congratulations on reaching old age!" Ies joked, and Pranoto answered, "I feel greatly honored tonight, because you're my first guest. This promises me happiness."

He seized Ies's hand, and as they looked at each other Pranoto saw something in the radiance of her eyes which completely flustered him. He let her hand go and said, "What'll you have to drink? I'll go get it."

"Anything, so long as it isn't alcoholic," Ies replied.

Pranoto went inside, still disturbed by what he'd seen shining in Ies's eyes. And while he was pouring Coca-Cola into a glass, he suddenly remembered, he'd seen the same radiance before… in Connie's eyes.

"My God!" The English expression escaped involuntarily from his lips. Ies, for me—it's impossible, he said to himself. Isn't she with Suryono? To calm himself down he lit a cigarette before he went out with the drink for Ies.

Later, after they'd eaten, several of the guests suggested that the chairs and tables be moved aside to make room for dancing. The big lamp was turned off so that the room was lit only by a small wall lamp which cast a dim greenish light. Pranoto got the first dance with Ies. Later on, with only a few couples still dancing, Pranoto realized that he'd danced with Ies uninterruptedly through three records, the last in a slow, swinging mood. It brought back the peculiar radiance in Ies's eyes which had so surprised him at the beginning of the evening. The night was now far gone and Pranoto, who'd had quite a few whiskies, felt an impulse communicating to him from Ies's body. It made him lower his head, brush his nose along her cheek. Ies pressed her cheek against his. Pranoto tightened his grip on her body and it came close to his own. And so they danced in close embrace, cheek to cheek and body to body.

Pranoto was startled when the music stopped and the remaining guests said it was time for them to go home; it was already three in the morning.

Ies drew a long breath, looked searchingly at Pranoto for a moment as though hunting for something she'd not yet been able to discover. Then, together with his other friends, she wished him a good night; and they all left.

Pranoto could not fall asleep until dawn, disturbed by what he'd seen in Ies's eyes. If only it wasn't for Connie, he thought. He sighed. He'd never suspected that love and marriage could pose such difficult problems, so complicated that it was impossible to know where one was drifting with each new turn.

On January 23 the doctor told Hasnah that she could go home the next day. Sugeng and Maryam had been visiting her daily while she was in the hospital. She was beginning to reconcile herself to the loss of her baby, particularly since it was evident that Sugeng had changed completely. Every time he saw her he assured her of his love, repeatedly asked her to forgive him—Hasnah was not to blame at all, it was his fault; everything that had happened to them was his own doing. Hasnah felt that they'd be able to start afresh.

Towards noon of the twenty-third, while Hasnah lay reading, a stretcher was wheeled into her room and the nurses lifted a woman into the bed next to hers. With a shock Hasnah recognized Dahlia. She was unconscious.

"My God, this woman is a friend of mine!" Hasnah said to one of the nurses.

"She'll wake up soon," the nurse answered, "and then you'll be able to talk with her."

"What's the matter with her?"

"I can't really say," the nurse said quietly, "only that she lost her baby—but she was only a few weeks pregnant."

A few hours later, when Dahlia had come to, Hasnah said to her, "How terrible for you, Dahlia, to have lost your baby! I lost mine, too!"

"Yes, it is terrible," Dahlia said, though inwardly she was cursing her own carelessness. A few days earlier she had gone to the doctor, and the doctor had confirmed that she was indeed pregnant. But her plan to ask Suryono for money had not worked out. He'd stopped coming to her since the beginning of the new year, and every time she telephoned him at the office she was told that he was out. Similarly, her efforts to reach Sugeng had been fruitless. Like Suryono, he, too, could never be reached at his office.

Finally Dahlia was forced to use her own savings. She had had to pay seven hundred and fifty rupiah plus the costs of hospitalization.

"Lucky I'm only here for a short time. The doctor says I'll be able to go home in three days," said Dahlia.

"I'll be able to go home tomorrow," Hasnah told her. "Where is your husband? I didn't see him."

"He's out of town again," answered Dahlia.

But she didn't tell Hasnah that she'd intentionally gone to the hospital only after her husband had left, having ascertained beforehand that she'd be back home before he returned.

On January 24 Hasnah went home. Because she was still weak and the loss of her baby still weighed on her heart, Sugeng was very loving and solicitous. He looked after her, kept her in bed and didn't let her get up; he fetched water for her to drink and served her meals in bed.

Before going to sleep that first night at home, Hasnah felt sure that they could make a new start together and regain their lost happiness.

Sugeng put Maryam to sleep by telling her a little story. When he came and lay down by Hasnah's side she stretched out her hand, drew his head to herself and kissed him slowly. And then she fell asleep with a smile hovering on her lips.

At nine o'clock the next morning three police agents headed by an inspector came to the house to arrest Sugeng. They searched the whole house and ransacked his desk and bookcase for letters and papers. The police inspector handed Sugeng the warrant for his arrest on the charge of taking bribes while employed in the ministry of economic affairs.

Sugeng told Hasnah that he'd expected this to happen, and said that he was more determined than ever to start afresh. He begged her to be patient.

In the face of the disaster that had befallen her husband and family, Hasnah showed a fortitude which Sugeng had never suspected in her. Strengthened by the old hope and faith which had now returned to her, Hasnah was determined to fight with all her strength to cultivate the seeds of love now sown anew between herself and Sugeng.

"Don't worry!" Hasnah said, as Sugeng was ready to leave with the police. "I will be with you, always."

Sugeng kissed Maryam, who was crying, frightened by the police.

He now felt strong enough to bear anything that could happen to him. Whatever might happen, he was sure Hasnah's love would always sustain him. It would always be a cool, green island where he could take refuge from the bitter and painful ordeal that he now had to face.

Jakarta's morning papers of January 25 carried a report of the arrest of several officials from the ministry of economic affairs, among them a man named "S" no longer employed there now, but heading a business of his own. They also reported that the police had uncovered a series of manipulations in the ministry of economic affairs dealing with import licenses and their certification. As a result, the papers reported, Raden Kaslan, a well-known figure and prominent member of the party, was being recalled from abroad for questioning; the authorities concerned had wired abroad to the Indonesian embassies to make Raden Kaslan return to the country.

On the afternoon of January 25, Suryono and Fatma read the various reports in the newspapers, including the news that Raden Kaslan was being ordered to come home. One of the papers also mentioned the possibility of further disclosures of the operations of certain parties who had collected funds running into the tens of millions for election purposes.

They had not gone away together, because Fatma's cautious attitude made Suryono himself uncertain about the idea. But after reading that his father was being recalled, Suryono again started urging Fatma to leave.

"The day after tomorrow we'll be called as witnesses," Suryono said to her. "It would be better for us to get out of town—anywhere."

Fatma inwardly reviewed her situation. Since Raden Kaslan was now involved in such a big scandal, his social position was ruined and there was no advantage in remaining his wife any longer. They decided to drive across Java to Malang in the eastern part of the island. They would leave the next day.

For more than a week, the queues for rice, kerosene, and salt had been growing with each day. During the first days they were not so long—fifteen to twenty buyers would come to a shop and that would be the end of it. But two or three days later, when it became increasingly clear that the new cabinet was set on fighting corruption, the opposition, to discredit the new cabinet, launched an intensive campaign, blaming it for these shortages. A whispering campaign was spread in the poor areas of the city that the supplies of these goods would be exhausted in a few days, and the people were urged to stock up before it was too late.

Itam told Saimun that some strangers had come to him and other *becak* drivers, saying they should tell all the people in their areas to get out in crowds and quickly buy up as much rice, kerosene, and salt as possible.

On the morning of January 26, when Suryono and Fatma were leaving Jakarta to go to Malang, they could see long lines in front of the shops along the road. They also saw many *becak* with women and children in them, carrying empty bottles and baskets. And when they reached Jatinegara they even saw several trucks filled with women and children in rags, all of them carrying bottles and baskets, too.

"What's all this?" Fatma asked Suryono.

"Who knows? All sorts of things happen in Jakarta nowadays. But whatever happens, we won't be in Jakarta anymore. Who cares!"

By ten o'clock the police stations all over Jakarta were flooded by telephone calls from shopkeepers and district offices asking for police protection, since the crowds waiting to buy rice and kerosene were getting out of hand.

It was reported that two shops in Jatinegara had been invaded by a mob because the owners had announced that their supply of kerosene was exhausted.

Murhalim was in a *becak* going to Senen Market when it was held up near the railway crossing by several dozen other passenger-carrying *becak*.

The passengers called out to Murhalim's driver. "Come and help. That shop over there won't sell us kerosene and rice!"

The *becak* driver told Murhalim to either get out or join in and help the people. Murhalim decided to join; he was curious to see what would happen. He'd already heard during the last few days that the crowding of the rice, kerosene, and salt queues was really being instigated by a political party that wanted to create trouble for the new cabinet. There were many stories about trucks rounding up crowds to be transported from one place to another to fill the queues, and also that *becak* drivers were being given money to swell the crowds. But this was the first time he could get a first-hand impression of this organized movement.

Murhalim asked the driver whether anyone was giving them orders.

"No one's giving orders," the driver said. "But we little guys, if we can't defend ourselves, who's going to defend us? If we don't line up for rice, we go hungry. Those big shots, though, they don't have to stand in lines."

They turned into an alley and all the *becak* stopped. Murhalim got off. In a crowded line, about a hundred yards long, people were shouting,

"Come on, hurry up, where's the rice? Where's the salt? Where's the kerosene? Don't lie! Show your support for the little guy!"

Several young men could be seen wandering up and down the line, as if giving orders. The *becak* drivers, who'd arrived in great numbers, were gathered into a group and moved up to the front, close to the shop. Among them was Itam, cheering and yelling the loudest. He was very happy this morning. He'd fight for the little people, the nobodies. He'd fight for his own fate. They would beat up the oppressors of the people and the exploiters of the common man. The foreign enemies of the people would be destroyed. The common man would come to power, and everybody would be happy forever after, living in a fine house, owning land, with no difference between the overlords and the common people. All this had been conveyed to them the night before by several young men, who had also given them some money, because "tomorrow they'd not be driving their *becak*, but fighting for the interests of the little guy".

The crowd in the queue was becoming more excited. The people's shouts grew ever more threatening. Here and there people shouted, "Break in!" "Burn!" "Kill!"

Murhalim stood under a tree by the roadside, looking on. He felt very worried that the shop would be invaded and its owner beaten to death by the mob. And there were no police in sight.

As he stood there he suddenly heard a voice near him saying, "A beautiful sight, isn't it?"

Startled, Murhalim turned around. It was Achmad.

"Achmad! Don't talk like that. These people are degrading themselves, acting almost like maddened animals, and you say 'beautiful'!"

"As usual, you don't understand what I mean," Achmad said with a smile. "Look at that." He pointed at the crowd, now moving forward relentlessly like a stream of lava blazing with heat, like some wild howling beast pawing the ground and filling the air with frightening noises. "Isn't that a beautiful sight? The little guys who've never known their rights till now are finally daring to close their ranks and shout out their right to rice, salt and kerosene. That's just a beginning, friend. Last week they wouldn't have dreamed of doing this. Listen what they're shouting: 'The Little Guy Must Eat! The Little Guy Must Win! Down with the Capitalists!' If they dare to do this now, they'll dare to do much bigger things later. And this is not the dynamism of Islam, my friend!"

Murhalim looked at Achmad with astonishment, but then, as he grasped the full meaning of his words, he slowly filled with anger.

"This has all been organized. So it's true what I've heard. There's no use my arguing with you here, Achmad. It's clear that for you and your friends these people are merely objects to be manipulated, so you can achieve your political ends. You don't really care whether they get rice, whether the lamp in their hut will be lit or whether there'll be salt in their cooking pot. Human beings have no value for you, you don't respect them at all! May God forgive you!"

Achmad laughed loudly. "If I were to yell out now and tell them that it was you that has caused the shortages of rice and salt and kerosene, do you know what would happen to you? What they'd do to you?"

Murhalim looked at Achmad. He was seeing a man whom, it seemed, he'd not known at all, as though Achmad had never been his friend. Achmad's eyes glittered. His face shone with joy, and his body seemed coiled as though ready to spring—his whole being reflected absolute faith, readiness to do anything to win his battle.

By Allah, Murhalim thought, if he felt it necessary he wouldn't hesitate a moment to tell the crowd to tear me to pieces!

Murhalim felt as though he were seeing something black— something very dark, very evil—as though a fiendish spirit were passing before him. And his conviction grew all the stronger that what Achmad represented was evil, contrary to the dignity of man, contrary to the injunctions of the Lord and the precepts of Islam. Murhalim was calm again.

All at once the group of *becak* drivers shouted together, "Break in! Break in!" and they started forward. But at the entrance to the shop they collided with women and children who filled the door. Seeing the *becak* drivers come on for an assault, the owner of the shop locked the door from the inside, and with his wife and children fled through the back.

A scuffle started at the door, everyone wanting to get in first. The sight of the abandoned shop ignited the people's craving to break in and grab anything they could carry off with them. The mood was growing wild.

Something stirred within Murhalim. No, he said to himself. No, not here! This isn't the place, it's not the time. But this something was urging him again.

Achmad was looking at Murhalim with a smile. Their eyes met. Achmad's eyes were full of mockery—you wouldn't dare to risk your life for something! You petty bourgeois are just a bunch of talkers. Only we, the communists, have the courage to act.

Something in Murhalim's body was crying out, ascending to the tip of his tongue.

Murhalim protested again. No! It's not the place, not the time.

Achmad's eyes were saying to him, you're just looking for something to hide behind, something to cover up your fear. This is the bourgeois way of avoiding responsibility. You're weak, you have no passion!

Murhalim broke into a sweat. Something inside him cried out, its din filling his ears, commanding him. He felt an irresistible power rising within him, forcing him to run toward the crowd, who were now pushing at the shop door.

A strange force seemed to fill his body. Murhalim broke through the crowd at the door, and he turned quickly to face the now half-maddened mob.

For a moment the hot smell from the bodies and mouths of the people he faced overpowered him. Their eyes seemed to shimmer, their faces seemed to dissolve in a haze. But then he pulled himself together and could see clearly again.

Murhalim held up his hands and shouted, "Stop! Be calm! Be patient!"

The crowd seemed to hesitate, not knowing how to react to the man who'd just appeared before them. Hope rose in Murhalim's heart.

"Calm down! Calm down! I'm just a little guy too. I, too, need rice," he shouted. Then suddenly he heard Achmad's voice yelling from behind the crowd: "Come on! Attack! Burn the place! He just wants to confuse you!"

At the sound of these words the tide of passion welled up again in the frenzied crowd. Those in front raised their arms and Itam jumped forward, swinging a heavy club.

"Stop! I'm your friend! I want to help you!" Murhalim cried to Itam.

He turned away, covered his face with his hands to shield it from Itam's blow, but Itam swiftly changed its direction and the club landed heavily on Murhalim's head.

Murhalim collapsed. The crowd closed in. They beat him and trampled on him. Blood streamed from his head, his nose, his ears and mouth.

At that moment a police truck arrived. Policemen jumped off and ran to the shop. The seething crowd ignored the police's order to disperse. Only the tail end of the line, which was not involved in the brawl at the door, retreated. A few policemen reached the shop entrance, and when their order to disband was not obeyed, they fired a few shots into the air.

At the sound of the shots most of the crowd scattered quickly, running; but a hard core of impassioned people didn't budge. A policeman raised his pistol to shoot into the air. Itam leaped towards him, shrieking, "Come on! Attack!"

They grappled together and the barrel of the pistol was jostled; the finger, ready for the shot into the air, pulled the trigger and the bullet pierced Itam's temple. Itam crumpled to the ground. His body jerked for a moment and then his head sank down, bathed in a spreading pool of blood.

The next moment the shop was deserted. All the people had fled and only some neighbors looked on from a distance.

It had all happened very quickly. Achmad was long gone.

Murhalim and Itam lay on the ground close to each other. They lay there in the scorching heat of the sun, a ball of red fire in the sky. Murhalim's hand was stretched out on the ground, almost reaching Itam's hair. Its fingers were slightly extended as though wanting to touch Itam. Thus the two who had wanted to fight for the little guy now lay together. The one who'd been trampled on had fought, and the one who had fought had been trampled on. Murhalim's hand stretched out towards Itam as if inviting him to join in a common struggle.

On the same day, January 26, Yasrin left on a Garuda plane for Singapore, to go on from there to Peking. He had received an invitation to attend the Festival of Asian Artists in Peking and from there he was to go on to Moscow, Prague, and Warsaw. As the plane reached its ceiling and turned towards the sea, Yasrin looked down, remembered his old friends for a moment and thought how lucky it was that he had broken from Pranoto and his group.

He was very pleased and mentally began to compose a poem depicting the heroic struggle of the Chinese people. Later he'd send it as a souvenir of his trip to the magazine he was editing.

It was past one o'clock when Suryono and Fatma crossed Puncak Pass on their way from Jakarta to Bandung, the first leg of their cross-Java trip. They'd stopped for a rest and had a meal and something to drink at the restaurant at the top of the Pass; but when their car reached the beginning of the eastern descent and Suryono saw a sign showing a skull and the warning "Low Gear!" he suddenly became panic-stricken. He remembered his recurrent dream of driving a car whose brakes suddenly gave way. He thought of his father—of what he was doing to him now: stealing his wife—and all at once he couldn't face the future, imagining what would happen when his father, his friends, and everyone else found out…. Abruptly he stepped hard on the brakes, pulled up the hand-brake and clutched his head with both hands.

Fatma was jerked forward. She turned angrily to Suryono. "God! My face almost hit the windshield! Why did you stop so suddenly?"

Suryono rested his head on the steering wheel and held it between his hands.

"Are you ill?"

Suryono began to moan and then suddenly burst out crying. When Fatma tried to massage his head, he slapped her hand away.

For about ten minutes, Fatma let him be, not saying anything at all. Finally, softly she asked again, "Are you ill?"

Suryono merely shook his head, his eyes looking straight ahead. His head, neck, and back then stiffened into a rigid upright line and he said, "We're going back to Jakarta."

"But we're supposed to be going to Malang. What's the matter with you?"

"We're going back to Jakarta," Suryono said again, "and I can't drive. My head is killing me. You'll have to take the wheel."

Something in Suryono's behavior told Fatma that there was no use arguing, so she got out of the car. Suryono moved over, Fatma took his place at the wheel, and she turned the car round in the direction of Jakarta. She drove fast, faster than usual.

Who does he think he is, she thought, as if he were the only one with any feelings.

Suryono slouched, dropped his head, and closed his eyes. Accusing voices beset him: You can't go on. You don't know what to do. You're a failure, a confused young man. You've lost your grip. You've been wrong, you're guilty. Wherever you turn is a dead end. Frightening visions kept flashing before him of his father returning and discovering his affair with Fatma; his friends finding out about his affair with Fatma; the police coming to arrest him; Dahlia denouncing him to the police; Dahlia's husband coming in a rage...

Suryono groaned. Fatma turned to look at him. She saw him now with new eyes, saw now the weakness of his character in the lines of his mouth and in his chin. But she felt no pity toward him; she simply thought that she'd been stupid to give herself to such a weak and worthless man.

Fatma stepped on the accelerator to give vent to her frustrated feelings, swerved too far to the right on a curve and so failed to avoid an oncoming truck which hit the right front side of the car.

Spinning out of control, the car hurtled into a ditch by the roadside and crashed into a large rock.

Fatma was shaken. She'd bruised her shoulder. She was dazed and felt stiff and ill. But apart from the shock she was unharmed. But Suryono, whose head had banged against the door, had fainted and lay white-faced.

In a few minutes a small crowd had gathered. Fatma and Suryono were helped out of the car. Suryono was laid on the ground and Fatma sat near him.

Then the police came and an ambulance arrived. Suryono, with Fatma at his side, was taken to the hospital in Bogor. A doctor examined Suryono and said he had suffered a brain concussion. The doctor advised against moving Suryono to Jakarta, and suggested leaving him in the Bogor hospital.

As to Suryono's car, Fatma left the arrangements to the young and very friendly police inspector who'd come to take care of the accident: he telephoned to Jakarta for a tow truck to come. After agreeing with the doctor that she'd come back the next day to see Suryono, she returned to Jakarta in a taxi.

That evening the Bogor hospital called Fatma in Jakarta to inform her that Suryono had died. She was shocked by the news; yet she felt that for Suryono himself it was perhaps the best way out.

On the evening of January 26 the discussion club met at Pranoto's house for the first time in the new year. Before the meeting started they discussed Murhalim's death. Many said they couldn't understand why Murhalim had helped lead the crowd. But Pranoto told them that he'd heard from a police commissioner he knew that Murhalim had not been shot by the police, but was killed by a mob which ran amok and beat him to death. The first police reports, stating that there had been two victims of the shooting when the police tried to control a looting gang, had been given out hurriedly, and now the police were unraveling the true course of events. Several persons had been arrested. According to their confessions, it appeared that Murhalim had been trying to restrain the mob when the disaster occurred.

Pranoto also told them of Murhalim's experiences during his trip to Sumatra and his conclusion that the central government should be giving the regions more support, since the strength of the Indonesian nation actually depended on the fortunes of the regions outside Java. Murhalim said that these regions were now constantly neglected and perhaps even exploited; it was almost as though the country's center was sucking out the wealth created by the labor of the regions and spending it on luxuries in the capital.

"What is the actual problem now? Speaking plainly, it's to give the masses something to hold on to. Something that would make them work joyfully, make them work hard, make them strain their minds and muscles to build up the country. Nationalistic slogans used to have a magical effect in creating unity in the nation and giving fire to the revolutionary struggle. Too many of our leaders keep throwing around these nationalistic slogans, while in fact nationalism by itself doesn't actually accomplish anything. The goals of independence are for a better life.

"Moreover, this nationalism still being touted by many of our leaders is laced with all sorts of emotional attitudes and irrational ideas—it's all mixed up with myths and hero-worship. The real work of leadership is further impeded by such ambitions as the building of a grandiose national monument, the pursuit of still more myths, the ever-growing distrust of foreign nations, the drummed-up fears of subversive activities allegedly conducted here by foreigners as agents of the capitalists and imperialists, who are kept in the limelight to make the people feel constantly threatened from all sides. All this is symptomatic of the emptiness of the nationalistic slogans and their lack of creative power.

"The result is that the people become listless and don't care anymore. Many become cynical, and the disintegration of society gets worse. It is therefore essential to find a new rallying point for the people. The only thing that could inspire them with the old spirit is if they could see the government working to provide them with a decent standard of living. The steady decline in the value of money could be speedily reversed. All activities must be aimed at raising the level of the people's welfare, and not merely at enriching a few small cliques of leaders.

"The ways of thinking we've used so far must be discarded."

Pranoto added, "Regarding the conditions in the regions as seen by Murhalim, the situation of the new cabinet, and the riots that have occurred... and if we'd analyze the present situation..." Suddenly Pranoto stopped speaking because Ies interrupted him.

"I'm ashamed to hear you speak," she said angrily. "Murhalim was killed for trying to defend the common people. Our country is in a mess; our leaders are like drunkards without any sense of responsibility, stealing and plundering a people unable to defend itself—and here we gather from evening to evening to analyze what's wrong with our country. Isn't there anyone here who realizes that the sickness of our country has already been analyzed and discussed more than enough? Hasn't the moment come for all those who care about their people to take action?"

"That is exactly what Murhalim said to me when he returned from Sumatra," Pranoto told the group. "Murhalim said that we must have the courage to pledge our whole beings, our physical and spiritual selves, to the fight for the common people. If we don't, we're sure to be defeated. According to Murhalim, the communists promise the people everything under the sun, but they also dedicate themselves completely to their cause. They live and work among the people. Although they pass off lies to the people, they also work themselves to death to build up their influence. Even though the people will realize how badly they've been deceived when the communists have won and they're oppressed under a totalitarian communist regime, this awareness will come too late and will be utterly futile.

"Murhalim also said that we who have chosen democracy as the way to improve the welfare of the masses and have chosen a society which guarantees justice, the rule of law, and the rights and dignity of man, must work ten times harder than the communists, because we cannot fight with lies, deceit, and empty promises as weapons. The communists promise: join us, and if we win you'll get land, a house, and good wages; the property of the rich will be confiscated, and so on. We, however, must spur the people to work harder and to sacrifice more. But the masses are easily taken in by the promises of the communists, because that is human nature.

"That's why Murhalim decided to dedicate himself completely, dedicate his whole being, to the struggle he outlined."

"And now he is dead!' said Ies. "And we're still talking and analyzing!" Her voice broke. "None of you are men. You're like a bunch of women gossips." Ies got up, sobbing, and ran out of the room. The rest sat staring at one another.

Finally, Pranoto rose, looked around at his friends, and said, "There is truth in what Ies said. Up to now we've been pretty pleased with ourselves, thinking we were serving our country and our people by analyzing conditions in the peace of this room. Now the time has come for us to get out of the room!"

Pranoto walked out to join Ies who was sitting on the wall of the front verandah, crying to herself. Pranoto came up to her and put his hand on her shoulder. Ies took his hand.

"I was thinking of Murhalim," she said. "He's dead and we're still talking. It felt like we were betraying him."

"I understand," said Pranoto. "Our mistakes are clear to me now. We thought our good intentions would just communicate with the people all by themselves, and they'd follow us automatically. But it seems that actually it isn't so. The good must also have the courage to fight the evil."

"Isn't it too late?"

"No," said Pranoto. "It's never too late to fight in defense of good against evil."

When Ies tightened her grip on Pranoto's hand, he suddenly saw Connie's face in the air before him.

On the night of January 26 security measures were strengthened in Jakarta. Police patrols made the rounds more often. On the same night, the vice squads took special action and rounded up street prostitutes soliciting customers at the roadside or riding around town in *becak*. About fifty women were arrested that night. Neneng was detained while she was standing with a few companions in front of the Catholic cathedral on Banteng Square.

At sundown Saimun learned from Itam's friends that Itam was dead, shot in an incident at a queue for rice and kerosene. He wanted to see Itam's body, but was afraid. All that night he stood in front of the police headquarters, hoping to hear something about Itam. Later, as he sat for hours at the roadside near a vendor of fried bananas, some police trucks came by and turned into the yard. They were full of women picked up in the raids. That night the police station was very busy. Not long afterwards a number of men appeared, as though on orders, claiming that their wives were among the women arrested by the police and that their wives had not been soliciting but turning down offers when they were picked up by the police.

Saimun joined the men claiming to be the husbands of the arrested women when they went inside, into the room where the police were conducting their investigations. Suddenly Saimun saw Neneng. He plucked up his courage and approached the group of women. As no one interfered, Saimun went up close to Neneng and said, "Neneng, what happened?"

It was the first time that Neneng had been arrested by the police, and she was frightened, though her companions, who were quite used to it, had already told her, "There's nothing to be afraid of; you'll be released tomorrow."

But that night Neneng was badly frightened, and she was happy to see Saimun.

"Oh, Mun, please help me. They say if someone says he's my husband I can go home now."

"I do want to marry you, Neng," said Saimun. "We'll get married and go live in my village. What's the good of living like this in this crazy city? Do you want to?"

Neneng thought of how peaceful village life was, free of the kind of work she was doing now. Her life in Jakarta was full of fear: of the police; of rough men who wanted you to do indecent things; fear of the day and fear of the night, a fear that never stopped. Neneng nodded to Saimun.

A great surge of pride welled up in Saimun. A policeman shouted at him, telling him to get out: "Hey, what are you doing getting so close. Is that woman your wife?"

Saimun answered bravely, "Yes, sir, she is my wife," and as he took Neneng by the hand, his fear of the police vanished. He was now ready to fight for a life with Neneng.

CITY BEAT

The night held the city in tight embrace. The streets were deserted. Later a great storm descended on Jakarta, blown in from the sea by a torrential downpour. But all through the night, dark shapes crept stealthily about, feeling their way, slipping into the houses of people who were fast asleep, thieves of the night doing their work…

The Author

Mochtar Lubis was born on March 7, 1922 in Padang, West Sumatra. After graduating from high school, he worked as a teacher on the island of Nias, but after a year he left for Batavia (Jakarta). When World War II broke out and the Japanese occupied Indonesia in 1942, Lubis began working for the Japanese authorities, translating international news. After Indonesian independence in 1945, Lubis joined the Indonesian news agency Antara as a reporter.

In 1949, Lubis co-founded the daily newspaper *Indonesia Raya*, later serving as chief editor. His work with *Indonesia Raya* led to him being imprisoned numerous times for his criticism of the government. In 1958, Lubis shared the Ramon Magsaysay Award for Journalism, Literature, and the Creative Communication Arts with Robert Dick.

From February 4 to April 14, 1975, Lubis was imprisoned on charges related to the riots that had broken out in Jakarta the previous year when Japanese prime minister Kakuei Tanaka visited. *Indonesia Raya* was shut down not long after the riots, due to its reporting on corruption.

Lubis founded and co-founded numerous magazines and foundations, including the Obor Indonesia Foundation in 1970, *Horison* magazine, and the Indonesian Green Foundation. Lubis had a reputation as an honest, no-nonsense reporter, and was the author of six novels and two short story collections,

In 2004, after a long struggle against Alzheimer's disease, Lubis was admitted to Medistra Hospital. He died on July 2, 2004 at the age of eighty-two, and was buried next to his wife in Jeruk Perut Cemetery.

The Translators

Claire Holt (1901–1970) was a pioneer of dance ethnography before it had a name (she described herself as a "choreologist") and a Javanese dance practitioner. Born in Riga, Latvia, she became part of a dedicated network of Euro-American scholars and arts practitioners who sought to understand East Indies culture from the inside. Colleagues included dance scholars Curt Sachs and Beryl De Zoete; anthropologists Franziska Boas, Ray Birdwhistell, Jane Belo, Margaret Mead, and Gregory Bateson; ethnomusicologists Alan Lomax and Colin McPhee; and painters Miguel Covarrubias and Walter Spies. Holt went on to hold many important yet eclectic posts, including worker at the American Museum of Natural History; founder of the East Indies Institute (later renamed the Southeast Asia Institute); scholar at Columbia University's Navy School for Military Government (1942); and policy analyst at the US Office of Strategic Services (later renamed Central Intelligence Agency) from 1944 to 1953, before resigning in protest over McCarthyism. She finally located her intellectual and spiritual home at the Cornell Modern Indonesia Project (CMIP) in Ithaca, New York, where her landmark book on Indonesian art, *Art in Indonesia: Continuities and Change*, was published in 1967, three years before her death.

John H McGlynn, originally from Wisconsin, USA, is a long-term resident of Indonesia, having lived in Jakarta almost continually since 1976. Through the Lontar Foundation, which he established in 1987 with four Indonesian authors, he has edited, overseen the translation of, and published more than 100 titles containing literary work by more than 275 Indonesian authors. McGlynn is the Indonesian country editor for *Manoa*, a literary journal published by the University of Hawaii; the senior editor for *I-Lit*, an on-line journal focusing on Indonesian literature in translation; a contributing editor to *Words Without Borders* and *Warscapes*, two US-based literary journals; and an editorial advisor for *Jurnal Sastra*, an Indonesian-language literary journal. He is a member of the International Commission of the Indonesian Publishers Association (IKAPI), PEN International-New York, and the Association of Asian Studies. He is also a trustee of AMINEF, the American Indonesian Exchange Foundation, which oversees the Fulbright and Humphrey scholarship programs in Indonesia.